THEY'RE HERE YOU KNOW

STEVE PRICONE

DIVERTIR
PUBLISHING
Salem, NH

THEY'RE HERE YOU KNOW

Steve Pricone

Copyright © 2018 Steve Pricone

Cover design by Kenneth Tupper

Published by Divertir Publishing LLC
PO Box 232
North Salem, NH 03073
http://www.divertirpublishing.com/

ISBN-13: 978-1-938888-25-0
ISBN-10: 1-938888-25-1

Library of Congress Control Number: 2018967636

Printed in the United States of America

Dedication

For my beautiful mother, forever young.

FAITH

IN OUR LAST conversation, while my mind was still functioning, before this horrible disease destroyed it, my granddaughter, my budding scientist, told me about dark matter. Annie said that it makes up seventy four percent of the universe. Almost three quarters of it is invisible and a mystery to scientists, but all that black emptiness out there is really a form of matter and energy. She said that no one can measure it or analyze it, and the only reason we know it's there is that its gravity seems to affect the motion of stars and galaxies. I asked her, "Is that enough evidence to make you believe in dark matter?"

Annie said, "Sometimes you have to have faith."

THEY'RE HERE YOU KNOW

1

I WAS TOTALLY IN the dark.

Night can be so absolutely black. There was a new moon, meaning there was *no* moon in the sky. I've always hated the name *new moon*—it was so deceiving. We haven't gotten our night vision yet. It was the last night of my Marie Curie Science and Technology Summer Camp, and we were doing the famous "One Hour Alone in Woods at Night" activity. Most kids do swimming and play volleyball at their summer camps. Here we raised mutant strains of bacteria and extracted DNA from strawberries. We shot off rockets and built bridges, but no volleyball.

Actually, I was not *alone.* There were twenty of us senior group fourteen-year-olds, scattered around the forest, sitting alone about twenty feet away from each other. We were told to stay perfectly quiet for an hour and just soak in all the sights and night forest sounds. Eight others backed out of this final rite of passage here at Camp Curie. They're scared of the dark. Fraidy cats. The only danger here was the possibility of immense boredom. But for me, there was no such peril; my mind was full tonight, even if the moon wasn't. A letter had come from my mom today, informing me that she had something to discuss with me about my Nonna. I thought I knew what it was, and the thought of it made me happy.

Nonna had been getting forgetful and confused, and I bet she was coming to live with us so we could take care of her; that was such great news! She was very special to me, and I hadn't had as much contact with her since she moved to South Carolina.

"Jay, stop that humming," a counselor hissed at one of the campers.

"Sorry, Ms. Bastian."

"Quiet!" she implored.

It did get very quiet; sounds of a distant screech owl could be heard way off beyond the big pine trees that surrounded us, and a second one even further off answered it back. Not a mating call…it was a warning. *This is my hunting range. Get out.*

I made out the sound of terrified rodents, probably field mice and voles, signaling distress to each other; not only were the humans hanging out here, but there were two screech owls on the prowl. Not a good night to be a rodent. A mental note was made of those sounds. The counselors were sure to quiz us tomorrow. With no moon, I could easily make out the constellations and beautiful, bright Saturn. It never ceased to amaze me how far away those stars are, how alone we are. Those stars are light years away. They seem like insignificant points of light. In reality, they are massive balls of fusing gases, with worlds of their own spinning around them. There are countless quadrillions of stars out there, yellows and blues and reds and oranges. It took my breath away just thinking about them.

Off to the north was old Cassiopeia sitting upside down on her throne. Over towards the east was her beautiful daughter Andromeda, with Perseus right there to protect her from the Cetus, the monster. My Nonna had told me the whole story of how the gods punished Cassiopeia by putting her upside down in the sky because she was so impressed with herself and her daughter's beauty. Andromeda was to be devoured by Cetus as punishment for her mother's vanity, until Perseus came, saved her from the beast, and as a reward married her. In my youth, we'd sit on Nonna's porch on summer and autumn nights, and she would point out the constellations and teach me the stories about each. There wasn't a Greek god or animal or planet that I couldn't identify. We even made up our own constellations and stories, playing "meet the dots" with the stars. There was Jenni the Lady Bug, Mairin the Dolphin, and Molly the Lacrosse Stick.

A shooting star! Such a quick flash of red. I knew the others had seen it too by the sound of hushed gasps. Nonna told me to always make a wish when I saw a "shooting star," because they were good luck. I don't wish on shooting stars and don't believe in luck. Science is to thank for my not believing in such things. Shooting stars are hunks of nickel or iron that have broken off an asteroid somewhere in our solar system. Its red flash told me that it was probably a small one made of iron that burned up streaking through our atmosphere about eighty miles up.

It was all about science. There was no such thing as luck or magic. By far the calmest camper out here in the darkness was me, because I could explain every sound and every shadow. There was nothing "unknown" to frighten me. Science explained it all! And that was my greatest joy, how perfect science was, and my greatest sorrow, how limiting science was. There was no *otherworldliness* in the universe, nothing to be scared of. No, wait… sometimes my dreams frightened me. I'd been dreaming a lot lately about flying. Usually I was flying through complete darkness. It was weird. There was no sense of my body. I was just a mind, a spirit flying through the unknown.

The forest silence out here was so soothing; it was like floating on a warm peaceful, tropical sea.

Then, on cue…Lyndon Antonelli farted. The sound cut through the silent night like thunder. Laughter and giggling broke out among the isolated campers…mainly the boys. Why do boys find flatulence so funny? The expulsion of nitrogen and carbon dioxide from air entering our stomachs and methane and hydrogen produced by *Methanobrevi smithii* bacteria breaking down food is just chemistry, not slapstick comedy. It never ceases to entertain boys or annoy me. With the male subspecies, the more they tried not to giggle, the more they did.

Ms. Bastian knew exactly who had done it, as did the rest of us. "Lyndon!" she cried out. That was Lyndon's sense of humor. Lyndon probably had planned this out all day, waiting for just the right moment, perhaps enjoying an extra helping of beans at dinner. Lyndon was actually quite brilliant—just very immature and crude.

"Well, I believe we're done out here. The mood has been broken." Ms. Bastian fired up her flashlight and shone it directly at the grinning Lyndon. "Everyone back to the cabins. Lyndon, I'll see you in my office."

Starting back with the others, I made sure to be the very last in line. After about two hundred yards on the trail I stopped. Once the others were out of sight, I took a small trail that cut into the woods to my left. I'd taken this trail many times before in the dark of night and knew that I wouldn't get in trouble. Hannah, my partner in crime and our cabin captain, had been clued in that I'd be late tonight, and I knew that she would cover for me. Even if I did get caught, I didn't mind. Camp was over in two days, and this would be my last year at camp, so what could they do to me?

My night vision kicked in, making maneuvering down the dark trail simple. A coyote howled off in the distance in the opposite direction of camp. It didn't frighten me though; coyotes are generally afraid of people. Tonight's goal was to find something to frighten me. A coyote howl would not make the grade.

After ten minutes of walking I whipped out my flashlight, snapping on the narrow beam of light toward the old shack. I called it "Slabsides" after the cabin that John Burroughs built in the Catskill Mountains in the 1800's. It looked really old, with worn and fragile stairs. I needed a flashlight to step gingerly around the cracks and holes.

"Hello, Slabsides," I whispered in a hush, my eyes caressing the soft darkness as if seeing an old friend. Slabsides had just one room. There was a paneless window in the front and one in the back. It had been stripped of all furnishings save the remains of an old rusted bed frame against the back wall and a corroded lantern leaning in a corner. Maybe there never was anything to strip away from this place. Maybe that was it—just a bed and a lantern. I sat here sometimes trying to imagine who would have lived here, so far and so isolated from the world. Maybe it was a scientist, poet, or a philosopher who would come out here to be one with nature, to just think and write. Perhaps it was just an old hunter's cabin. Anyway, Slabsides was mine now. There was a big oak tree stump that served as a table, with two wooden tomato box crates for seats. Those were my additions, along with a carton of stick matches and several candles that I had hidden under one of the crates.

Originally, I came out here to see *them*, the ghosts that were rumored to inhabit these woods. I had read that in 1783 some Lenni Lenape Indians were killed on this spot by some settlers, and I came here to meet them because…that's what was most important to me…to see ghosts.

I didn't always sneak out here alone. Last year Jared Aberson took me out here, or should I say, I took him. Jared was what we called a Z-boson at camp. A Z-boson is a tiny nuclear particle that exists for about one octillionth of a second. When a camper signed up for just two weeks, he was a Z-boson. Z-bosons wouldn't be here long and they wouldn't be coming back, so we knew it was not worth trying to form a relationship with them. If we did get to like them…poof! They were gone. In a moment of weakness, I told him about Slabsides and the ghosts. Jared pretended he wanted to see them.

When I came out here with someone else, I didn't plan on seeing ghosts. It was the times I was alone here that were ghost business. If there was company, there was usually another agenda. Jared wasn't interested in ghosts—he wanted to make out. He was kind of cute, harmless, and a Z-boson, so there would be no time for drama afterwards. Jared was a good kisser, but not very knowledgeable when it came to astronomy. Whoever I fall in love with someday must be a good kisser and very good at astronomy. How could anyone with a soul not be infatuated with the cosmos?

In my first year, I came out with two girls who unfortunately were not Z-bosons. They had smuggled cigarettes into camp and wanted to puff away in some place "safe." Curious about what the big deal was about smoking, I took a couple of puffs. *Oh, gross!* I coughed like I had double pneumonia and almost threw up. No, actually I *did* throw up. A person smokes, stinks, and then dies from all that smoking. What's the attraction? They weren't invited back. In fact, I've nailed up a "No Smoking" sign on the wall.

Tonight, I was here on business. Forget about the Lenni Lenape ghosts. So many attempts had been made to contact them. If they were here, we'd have been close friends by now. I was here tonight to say goodbye to my little cabin. I leaned on the crate, pulled out a last quarter remnant of a candle, and lit it. A warm glow filled the cabin. My long black shadow danced on the wall and floor as the flame quivered in the night's breeze. I sat down on the other box, my hands on the oak trunk, and sighed.

"Last chance, ghosts! This is my last night here."

It felt silly calling out to the dark, that *nothingness* that lay around me. But the feeling was worse than silly; there was loneliness. Nothing supernatural was out there, and I had become resigned to that. It was all protons and neutrons and packets of quantum energy. It both fascinated me and saddened me.

A universe filled with huge gaps of mystery with thousands of unexplainable dimensions was my hope, my dream. Why couldn't the life force that is our soul never end? Unexplained possibilities should be the norm. So, science be damned. There must be proof out there that the supernatural exists. But hoping doesn't make it exist. As a good scientist, I needed observation and data. I had visited so many "haunted" houses and found nothing—not a vapor or a knock. My mind was open, but I feared the "other side" did not exist. Just science existed. It was all just protons and neutrons.

In kindergarten, I was the only one who didn't believe in Santa Claus. Santa just didn't seem logical to me. An older person like himself and Mrs. Claus working in arctic conditions all those years had to take a toll. There were flying squirrels and flying fish, but the mass to aerodynamic ratio of a reindeer just did not allow for them to achieve flight. And a twenty-four hour period to visit each home of every child on the planet to deliver presents just didn't jive with Einstein's Space-Time Continuum. I tried to win the rest of the class over to my side by explaining these ideas, but that didn't make me very popular, and I got shouted down. Actually, I got cried and screamed down. One girl threw up on me she was crying so hard. Another girl hit me with a soft, overripe banana. Nothing wins an argument like screaming and crying and soft mushy bananas.

I was suspended for a day for inciting a riot. When I returned, the kindergarten teacher pulled me aside and called me a very bright girl, but she said I shouldn't make the other kids cry. Santa was real, and all those

theories I had put to the class could be overturned by one single detail…
MAGIC. After I laughed at her, they suspended me for another day. My
Nonna believed in miracles…and she tried to make me believe in them too.

Ms. Farley, my chemistry teacher, told me that I took things much too
seriously and that I should lighten up. She told me once that inside of me
lived an "Old Soul," whatever that meant.

"It's all protons and neutrons, Ms. Farley," I would tell her. "After
the Big Bang, it's all one grand party of nuclear and chemical reactions."
She told me that there was so much more going on in the universe that
we didn't have a clue about.

"Atoms and molecules. There are no miracles," I'd repeat.

Patting me on the head, she would say to me, "Annie, it's *all* a miracle."
She added that someday I'd get *younger* and realize that. That confused
me. How would I get *younger*?

Ghosts were my holy grail. What would the existence of ghosts do
to all the hard science we believed in? It would open doors to new dimensions, but proof was lacking. There was no data.

"Ghosts, please!" I shouted.

Maybe since they were Native Americans they didn't understand
English. Perhaps they were afraid of *me*. But it always came down to…
maybe ghosts didn't exist.

Then I heard it. It was a deep guttural sound coming from the darkness outside. I left the candle on the stump and stepped softly and slowly
to the window pane. My heart raced. My eyes swept over the dark thick-
ness around the cabin.

"Hea!" I called out. That's "hi" in Lenni Lenape. Candle light ham-
pered my night vision. It was hard to distinguish the shape among the
trees. Then I saw it clearly enough. A dark form emerged from behind
the trees and seemed to float. It was big and moved purposefully towards
me, without fear or hesitation.

"Heeeaaa!" I repeated, shakily leaning back from the window a bit.
A grunt or a growl was returned to me from the dark form that was now
just twenty feet in front of me.

2

HEY YOURSELF. Who the hell's in there? You one of those spoiled genius kids from that camp?"

It was another dead end. A flashlight exploded into my face, stinging my eyes and blinding me for a moment. Turning away, I protested. "Stop that!" I should have been afraid. This was a real person. People scare me, not ghosts. Who knows what he was up to wandering in the woods this time of night.

"I told those damn camp directors to keep you brats out of these woods. You have your own property over yonder. You don't need to be burning up my woods with your candles, your cigarettes, and who knows what else you're smoking up here."

"No one's smoking, and no one's going to burn down your woods," I replied.

A thin old man stuck his head into the window and looked around, darting a bouncing beam of light around the cabin. "Well, your party's over, girlie. Where are the others? Run off?"

"There are no others. Just me," I snapped.

He wore loose-fitting overalls held up with suspenders and a red hunter's cap pulled almost comically over most of his head. He looked about a hundred years old. He came up around the side and walked through the door.

"What are you doing here all alone in the middle of these woods? Are you crazy, girl?" he barked, still shining the light around the room looking for party goers.

I nodded, feeling a little more comfortable as his tone almost had a hint of concern in it...almost.

"Yeah, there are a lot of people who would say that I'm crazy." I had no problem explaining myself to adults. It seemed like I always had to explain myself to teachers or administrators or parents of friends. They always found my thinking weird and in need of footnotes.

"This is no place for a little girl like you this time of night. You got to be up to no good. You must be looking for trouble here," he said, as he returned his beam of light to my face.

"Actually sir, I'm looking for ghosts," I responded with a professorial demeanor.

"Ghosts?" he asked bemused. "You're smoking something, aren't you? Some of that crazy weed."

I pointed to my "No Smoking" sign. "No sir. I've been here on a scientific expedition looking to meet ghosts, ghosts of the Lenni Lenape who were killed long ago."

The man looked at me oddly and turned his head as if he were looking at an alien that had just landed in front of him. "What's…your…name?" he asked as he drew the sentence out much too slowly.

"Annie. What's yours?" I chirped, shining my light into his face.

He squinted at the light and tried to wave it off like an annoying bug flitting in front of him. I moved the beam a little to his right. "Ben. Ben Greeb. How do you know about those Indians? Nobody knows about that story, except for a few of us who are so old we're close to being ghosts ourselves."

"I told you, I'm on a scientific expedition. I'm a scientist. We scientists know stuff." Pausing, I waited for his response. When it did not come, I inquired, "Have you seen them, the ghosts?"

"Shoot, anybody who spends time in these woods has seen those Indians," he said, moving his light off my face.

"I haven't," I said forlornly, gazing out into the darkness.

"Maybe you scare them, Annie." He cackled and spit a brown gob of tobacco juice on my cabin's floor.

I laughed. That had been my contention for years. Mr. Greeb seeing ghosts didn't count. Anyone who told me they've seen a ghost didn't count. That was tainted data. It was *my* quest. For it to be real I had to see them…at least twice.

"What did they look like?" I asked earnestly.

"They looked like Indians…none too happy Indians."

"What makes them 'none too happy'?" I returned, mimicking his voice.

Greeb looked at me long and hard. "Here's the thing. I could make up a story about what happened to them, but the black truth is it's not a story a young lady should hear…ain't a story nobody should hear."

I clasped my hands together as if in prayer. "Please. I've heard a lot of gruesome stories in my day."

"Your day?" he muttered to himself with a slight smile. "Can't be a bit more than twelve years old. You ain't old enough to have a *day*. Tell you what, I'll give you the story if you promise to leave this old claptrap and never come back, cause next time I call the police…or worse, my wife."

10

This was to be my last night here anyway. I smiled to myself. "Ah shucks...okay," I said as I pretended to pout.

Sitting his long fragile body down, he grimaced as if his rickety bones would snap with each movement down. He let out a sigh of relief once he sat and looked at me again. "Can't understand what a little girl like you is doing in these dark woods late at night not scared out of your mind. You remind me of my great-granddaughter."

"Indians?" I reminded him impatiently. "You were going to tell me about Indians."

Looking at me, he cleared his throat and stroked his chin. His eyes closed as if he was trying to visualize the story in his mind. "It was 1750 or thereabouts. A small tribe of those Indians lived here in their long houses. Right about...here, where we're sitting. They farmed the land, corn and beans, with enough deer, squirrels, and rabbits to keep them in meat. They had this spiritual leader like a...a...medicine man."

"A shaman," I interceded.

"Whatever! He was a man connected to the Great Spirit. His name was Lynawana...or something like that. There was a legend that he created, telling the tribe that if only they would drink water from this one creek that flowed out of that mountain yonder," he pointed to a hill that we campers had climbed many times, "they would become invincible and could never die, a gift from the Great Spirit. So, Lynawana instructed his Indians to ignore the threat from the whites and stand their ground. Well, after they had refused the junk glass beads and threats to move, the whites came in one night and slaughtered them, each and every one. This spot right here," he said, as he thumped his finger hard upon the stump three times. "Here was where it happened."

He cleared his throat with a couple of coughs. "They say the body of Lynawana was never found among the dead. White folks said he probably ran off; the Indians...now they said different. They said that he, and only he, got the power, and that he lives forever roaming around these woods. Now there are some strange stories over the years about people getting lost and never being found again. They say Lynawana is always looking to get his revenge on the white man..." Ben cleared his throat again. "Or white woman."

He tapped the stump twice more. "And that's the story. Now you stay away from here. Go back to your camp, and tell all your little friends to stay the hell out of these woods."

I looked at him with skepticism. "Is that really the story?"

11

"No, it ain't. I made that one up. I told you. I don't want to tell you the real story. And trust me, you don't want to hear it. Now I really think you should leave. RIGHT NOW!" he snapped.

I jumped back a bit from his surprisingly thunderous voice. "Okay, Mr. Greeb, I will be leaving, and since camp is over this week and I won't be coming back next year, I will not be back here."

"Well," he responded, shaking his head, "that's a good thing."

I offered him a handshake goodbye, which he ignored. "Thank you for your story, even though it was made up."

"Yeah, well you're welcome. And, well, some of it was true, like those Indians thinking that Lynawana still exists in these woods. Good luck with you seeing a ghost, if that's what you really want. Damnedest thing I ever heard of—a kid *wanting* to see a ghost." With the slow, careful creaking of old knees, he stood up from the crate and looked down at me with a confused and concerned expression.

He took his hand and gently rubbed the top of my head, brushing my hair around—an annoying and patronizing gesture that I hated with a passion. "You're a good kid," he said in a grandfatherly way.

And with that he walked out the cabin door and faded back into the darkness from which he had come. I stuck around a while, hoping to be visited by Lynawana. But after fifteen minutes I stood up, looked around, blew out my candle, and wished my cabin goodbye.

§ § §

Tap! Tap! Tap! After a long moment, I finally got my response.

"Who is it?" Hannah whispered from the other side of the door.

"Enrico Fermi," I responded. That was our secret code.

Hannah slowly creaked open our camp cabin door. "Enter," she whispered. She knew of my nocturnal visits in the woods, and I knew that she sometimes snuck out to meet Luke Harper for walks by the lake, so we had a deal to keep each other's transgressions secret as gatekeepers of the cabin.

"Late night," she commented like a wary parent as she turned to get back into her upper bunk.

Hannah was my best buddy at camp, a year older and a year wiser. Because of that seniority she was my mentor when it came to math, physics, and boys. I was so envious of her auburn red hair, that I would trade a Nobel Prize for, and piercing green eyes. She had a very commanding look.

12

"Yeah," I responded like a guilty daughter as I followed her to my lower bunk and quickly changed into my sweats. In what seemed like seconds I plopped down onto my mattress.

"I hope he was cute," she sighed with sarcasm...or hope, knowing why I spent time out there. I heard her rip open a bag of Oreos, snap one in half with her teeth, and chew each half like a hungry chipmunk. She waved one at me from her perch, enticing me to join her feast.

"No," I begged off politely, "and, no, he was too old for me. Actually, he was too old for my grandmother."

"What!" she gasped, choking on her Oreo. She glared at me with disbelief. "What?" she repeated.

"Yeah. This guy must have been close to eighty." I sighed, knowing that I was making her brain explode.

Hannah slid down and almost fell from her top bunk. "*What* are you talking about? Eighty?"

I giggled and looked at her with a reassuring smile. I reached into the bag and pulled out a cookie. "Here," I offered, waving the Oreo teasingly across her face.

Her hand just slapped it aside. "Annie...eighty?"

"Easy, girl." I popped the cookie into my mouth and chewed up half and swallowed before I continued. "This old farmer, Mr. Greeb, stopped by for a visit and yelled at me for trespassing."

"Oh," she sighed with a big exhale of relief as she smacked my foot. "You should have said that right at the beginning."

"He ended up telling me a story. I think he ended up liking me," I said with a hint of melancholy.

"That's nice. In the movies, he would have chopped your head off and fed your eyes to the chipmunks," she snapped while pointing that wary parental finger at me.

There was a sudden knock on the wall from the girls who bunked next to Hannah. "You girls planning on getting to sleep and shutting up any time soon?" a tired and cranky Julia barked through the wall.

We looked at each other and grinned. I knew Hannah would not sit still for that sort of rudeness. "If you'd stop snoring, you cow!" Hannah shot back. "That's why we're up, you know...all that snoring coming from your side!"

My eyes widened and I covered my mouth to hold back a laugh. Julia never snored, and I knew Hannah was just messing with her head.

"I don't snore!" Julia exploded.

13

Suddenly we heard a knocking on Julia's wall. "Hey! Quiet down in there!" a faint but angry voice directed at Julia.

"But..." Julia stammered.

Hannah raced over to the wall and placed her mouth up to the knotty pine boards. "That's right, Julia. You get to bed right now and stop bothering everyone with your shouting and snoring."

There was a long, harsh silence. I could just see the smoke coming out of Julia's angry red ears. Finally, a restrained bark was returned. "I'll get you for this, Hannah."

There was another knock on Julia's wall.

"Okay. I'm going back to bed," she shouted, addressing the knock.

As Hannah returned triumphantly to the bunk, she fluttered her fingers demanding another cookie as a reward for her mischief. I grabbed the bag and gave her two.

"Didn't your Mr. Greeb scare you?"

"No, Mr. Greeb was nice; he was worried about me." I glanced at the wall again imagining Julia steaming in her bunk.

"I worry about you, too. You know, you're a nut with your ghost quest," she mumbled with her mouth full of Oreo, turning her back on me as she climbed to the upper bunk.

I didn't reply.

"You see any ghosts tonight?" she inquired with genuine interest.

She knew I hadn't. If I had seen a ghost, I'd have come home as if I had just won the Nobel Prize for Chemistry, whooping and hollering and carrying on like a giddy school girl. "No, no ghosts. Just Mr. Greeb's ghost story about the Lenapes."

"I guess you're tired of just stories, huh?" she asked.

"You know it," I said with a heavy sigh. A long silence ensued. I thought she had gone to sleep. Then I heard the creaking of the bunk steps as she stepped down onto the floor.

"Move over, girl," she ordered, sitting on the edge of my bunk. I moved over. Our beds weren't too big to begin with. She squeezed in beside me.

"Have you put a time limit on this folly for hunting ghosts...dead people, Dr. Annie? When will you realize that all you are doing is just a waste of time and that this is a finite universe? Science rules. When will you come back to the dark side?" she added with a creepy voice. I liked it when she called me "Dr. Annie."

"I *am* exploring the dark side. You, Ms. Hannah, are on the light side."

Smiling, she just looked at me for a long moment. "What's the strangest thing you've done on your quest?" she asked earnestly, flipping an Oreo against the wall adjacent to Julia's bunk.

I thought a moment. "I've done some very strange things. I guess the strangest was hiring myself out as a shomer."

"Excuse me? A what?"

"A shomer. In the Hebrew religion, the body of the deceased must be buried within twenty-four hours. During that time, while the family makes preparations for the burial, the body must have someone there watching over it, a guardian."

"I didn't know you were Jewish," she said, giving me a perplexed look since my last name was Barone.

"I'm not. I thought it might be an opportunity to see a spirit rise up or talk or roll its eyes or something. So, I hired myself out as a shomer, or a watcher."

"But you're not Jewish," she repeated, poking me in the forehead, a gesture that she knew annoyed me to no end. I pushed her hand away.

"Yeah, that and being a girl didn't put me high up on the list. But, finally there was a family that was desperate. Their grandfather, a guy named Saul, had died. They explained to me that some of the family had to help out at the deli he owned, while some had to make funeral arrangements. I guess shomer pickings were slow that week and…bingo, I became the first Italian, agnostic, female shomer. I was hired to watch a dead guy."

"Creepy," she uttered.

"Saul looked like a nice guy. He had a very peaceful face. I had to read King David's psalms to him for six hours till the family returned."

"Six hours?"

"Yeah. Couldn't leave old Saul alone. I would pause between psalms and chat with him."

She pulled away from me in mock disgust. "Eww."

"I'd ask him some questions and try to get him to respond, like 'Can you hear me, Saul? Where are you now, Saul? Is there anything that you'd like me to tell your family, Saul?' I tried to raise the dead, but he just laid there…Dead Saul."

Hannah nodded her head. "Yes, I get that. Kind of like trying to strike up a conversation with Steve Mitchell at the last dance…Dead Steve."

At the memory of that frustrating day, I shook my head. "I just wanted a whisper from Saul…a wink, a smirk, a twitch, something! I got nothing."

15

"That's creepy, Annie. You are one desperate ghost hunter. Listen, from one scientist to another, dead is dead. Brain function stops, and you can read the Bible, the Koran, Harry Potter, The Hunger Games, Archie comics…you're not going to get a wink or a smirk from me."

I had no answer for that. That was the problem. She was probably right. Dead is dead. I continued in a flat monotone as if being interrogated.

"One night I went out by myself to an old cemetery in our town with a beanbag seat, a flashlight, and Twizzlers. I sat there in the still darkness and tried to contact spirits. I shined the light on various headstones and called them out by name. I'd pick topics that fit into their time line to discuss. If they had died in the thirties, I talked about the Depression. If they had died in the fifties, I would ask them about Elvis and rock and roll."

"Wow! You're real serious about this stuff, huh? Why the Twizzlers?"

"Because I like the way they taste."

"Oh." She nodded at my logic.

Here's one of the many reasons why I loved this girl so much. She was totally invested in science. Two years ago, she finished fourth in the National Westinghouse Science Fair Competition. She was the youngest person ever to place in the top ten. She showed how a vaccine that cured polio might also be manipulated to cure malaria. Her belief in science was absolute, so for her to entertain my ideas about ghosts and spirits took so much empathy and patience on her part. Inside, I knew she was laughing at me, but outside, she tolerated me. She would listen, smile, and just giggle a bit.

"I'm serious about this because everything hinges on it," I sighed as I shot her a deep urgent look.

"Maybe…just maybe, you shouldn't *want* to believe in it, Annie. Things that you feel you *need* to believe in could break your heart when you find out they aren't worth believing in. Maybe you should believe in the believable. Believe in what is real," she whispered as she rubbed my arm like a consoling sister.

"It can't be so fixed and cold. Hey, light, heat, sound, and gravitational waves never get destroyed; they just go on changing from one form to another. Why not our energy, our essence? There's got to be more of a purpose, a deeper system beyond the physical. It can't be all there is. Where do our souls go?" My eyes grew heavy with those words. I had rerun those thoughts in my head so many times and spoken them out loud so many times. Tonight, I was weary with thinking and hoping.

16

"Can't…but it could…and is." She gave me a hug to ease the pain of reality. Our hug and a silence lasted a long moment. "Well, Doctor Annie, I thought you were with some cute guy out there and had some juicy details to share with me, so you won't be too insulted if I go back up to my bunk now and get some sleep."

"Oh, please do. I'm exhausted," I said, tapping her forehead gently.

There was another hug from her, and she climbed back to her perch. Once there, she craned her head down at me. "You know, Doc, when I was four years old I once put bluebell petals all around a cherry tree in my backyard. That was to attract fairies. Hoping beyond hope to see fairies, I ached. I would have given anything to see a fairy. Well, I stayed up most of the night looking out my window waiting to see them."

"What did you see?"

She paused for dramatic affect and then announced, "A skunk. It ate the petals and sprayed my dog."

I pulled the blanket up tightly to my chin and prepared to sleep, perchance to dream.

Dreams.

THEY'RE HERE YOU KNOW

3

THERE I WAS, *sitting on a tree branch in a park. It was really foggy out. There was a group of boys playing chess. They wouldn't look at me. Nobody in the park would look at me. Had I done something wrong? The feeling of isolation flowed over me like an icy shower. I finally went over to someone and turned them around so they would face me. A shock ran through me. There was no face! I could recognize all the people there by their hair and their clothes; the only thing different about them was that they had no faces. I continued to turn people around. Not one of them had a face. I ran to one of the park benches. A feeling of guilt swept over me; I couldn't understand why. I felt upset and lonely. There was no one to talk to. I cupped my head in my hands and began to cry. Then, I felt a gentle tap on my shoulder. There was a faceless woman standing next to me. Gradually her features began to reappear. It was my Nonna.*

She softly brushed her hand across my cheek and said gently, "You're a good girl. I will ease your pain. Just follow me. I know what you seek."

I followed her as she started to walk away. After only a few steps she turned around, and stared at me with a helpless, pleading look. Her face contorted into a grotesque silent scream, her eyes went empty, and she slowly melted down like a wax candle upon the sidewalk.

"NONNA!" I screamed and jolted up in my bunk, nearly hitting my head on the upper board.

"What! What!" Hannah shouted, having suddenly been awakened by my scream.

I gulped down a couple of deep breaths. "Sorry. I had a nightmare."

"Listen, Doc. I love you, but you're starting to weird me out," she said, trying to recapture her breath from the shock of being awakened by a scream in the night.

"I'm sorry," was all I could offer.

"Scary dream?" she asked sympathetically.

"Kind of."

She yawned and wiped the sleep from her eyes, then leaned over her bunk, looked down at me, and smiled empathetically. "Well, it's almost morning now. It was just a dream. It can't hurt you now."

Just a dream. I had always thought dreams were proof of the supernatural, my proof of immortality. I always thought of these little movies going on in my head as little miracles, voices and pictures from the beyond, clues to the unexplainable—sometimes funny, sometimes horrifying, but always mysterious. Let me see science explain that one away. Well, they did. I read up on dreams, finding out that dreams are the brain's way of making sense of our experiences during the week and moving them through the visual and audio neurons to their target area, the memory neurons for storage, from short term to long term memory. As weird as my dream might be, it was just neuron activity trying to make sense of my crazy ideas. You did it again, science. You explained it away. Science was awesome! Science sucked!

This was to be our last full day at camp. After breakfast, Hannah, two boys, Adam Jones and Kevin Envers, and I were selected to clean out the chemistry lab, wrap up all the glassware and chemicals, and pack them away in boxes. Lucky us. When we were done, they expected us to go over to the biology lab and help clean that up too. Fat chance.

Our chemistry lab was hot and musty from all the chemical residue of the summer reactions. My favorite was vaporizing a gummy bear. After melting down the white crystals of potassium chlorate over a Bunsen burner, I popped the gummy bear into the test tube. Immediately that gummy bear was buffeted around in a fury of purple and pink florescence that lasted a good twenty seconds. In the end, he was gone, but that of course could be explained. Mr. Gummy was changed into carbon, carbon dioxide, and water vapor. Gone, but not forgotten by science. After about an hour, the stuffy lab got the better of us. To escape the heat and the smell of chemicals that were stuck in our noses, the four of us headed out to the far end of the lake for one last swim. Let the frogs and fetal pigs clean up the biology lab.

Both boys stripped down naked on the huge boulder we called Baldy Rock and jumped in, taunting us to join them in a skinny dip. "What, are you girls chicken? Afraid to show what you got?"

I looked at Hannah wide eyed and shook my head. My confident mentor smiled back at me, winked, and then climbed up onto Baldy Rock, cupped her hands around her mouth, and called back at them. "Okay boys! Here we come!"

Hannah grabbed Adam's clothes and dove in fully clothed, much to my relief. I followed her, taking Kevin's jeans and camp shirt. Hannah yelled back while doing the backstroke, "What we got are your clothes! That's what we got!"

We were both pretty good swimmers and kept going all the way across the lake, as the boys screamed and cursed at us. They weren't quick enough to catch us, nor strong enough to follow us. When we got to the other shore, we waved at the boys and threw their clothes up into a tree. They'd have to take a bit of a hike naked through the woods to retrieve them.

"I hate being called chicken," Hannah growled as we started back to the camp for lunch...our last lunch there together.

You think you'll always stay in touch with the people you love, that somehow, they will stay a part of your life. As I watched Hannah nibble at her pizza, I felt like I'd never see her again, even though we vowed to stay close.

§ § §

"I think that's my dad over there," she called out to me as she jumped up and down pointing at a black Mercedes Benz.

We were all assembled in the parking area on that last afternoon, waiting to be picked up and brought home. It was one of those bittersweet moments for most of the campers. For me it was just sweet, except for leaving Hannah.

"You coming back next summer?" she asked as she returned a wave and a blown kiss from her dad.

I just shrugged.

"Well," she sighed, trying to remain cool. "You got me on Facebook. Stay in touch. You certainly are an interesting girlfriend, girlfriend!"

"You're pretty cool yourself," I said, putting my hand on her shoulder.

"Oh, I didn't say you were cool. I said 'interesting.'" She laughed and gave me a genuine hug. "Good luck with your ghosts. I hope you find what you're looking for. Me, I'm looking for a boy with a brain that's bigger than his grabby hands."

"A boy with a brain or a ghost?" I asked with a smirk.

"Coming, Dad!" she shouted and started to wheel her suitcase towards her dad's car. Halfway there she turned back to me and shouted, "Have a good school year! Break some hearts!"

"You too!" I shouted back, blowing her a kiss. I waved goodbye to her as her Dad's car pulled away in a cloud of parking area dust. I liked her.

§ § §

It wasn't too much later when my mother drove up in her Chevy. Mom opened her door, ran over to me, and gave me a hug, a very uncharacteristically hard hug. I thought she'd break a rib. Finally, she let go and pulled back a bit. She looked into my face and kissed me hard on the cheek—uncharacteristically hard.

"I missed you so much, sweetie!"

"I missed you too, Mom," I said with sincerity, returning her hug ever so gently, ever so carefully.

"Kevin!" she yelled, turning towards the car. "Help Annie put her bags into the trunk."

"Ah, Mom, do I have too?" he whined, not raising his eyes from the game on his iPad.

"Yes! You haven't seen your sister in four weeks. Act like you missed her," she demanded.

Putting down his game, he walked over to us. "Okay. I'll *act*." His head cocked to the right a bit, he fluttered his eye lashes, looked at me in mock emotion, and sighed a deep fake sigh. "Oh, Annie Lyn, I missed you soooo much. It's so good to have you home again." Then, he stuck his tongue out at me. "I'll put your stupid bags in the trunk."

I jumped into the front seat next to mom. After Kevin got in and we pulled away from the camp, I turned around, reached out, and pulled Kevin towards me. "I know you hate to get mushy, but I did miss *you*, you little monkey." I kissed him on the cheek.

My kiss was wiped off as if I had smeared the Ebola virus on his cheek. He fell back onto the seat, arms crossed in annoyance at a sister's kiss, and returned to the solitude of his favorite game, killing hundreds, if not thousands, of mutant space zombies.

"I know it was only four weeks but I *did* miss you," I insisted as I tried to make this a memorable moment, a turning point in our sister/brother relationship.

"Phooey!" was all he said in return.

"Hope you missed me too, honey," Mom asked.

"You know I did, Mom," I returned, placing my hand warmly on her shoulder, "and I missed Potter too."

Kevin had been in charge of caring for Potter, my hamster, while I was away. He was in charge of changing the litter once a week, feeding him, and giving him water. How hard could that have been?

"Potter's dead," Kevin announced casually, as if he were telling me the temperature outside.

"What?" I shrieked, turning to see if he was joking. I turned to Mom anxiously. "Kevin's kidding, right?"

"No, sweetie, Potter's gone. I didn't want to email you the news at camp. I thought that it would ruin your fun," she said.

This time when I turned around to face Kevin again, I was much less mushy. He was no longer 'my little monkey.' I eyed him like he was a mutant space zombie. "Did *you* kill him?" I screamed.

"Annie!" Mom scolded.

"No!" Kevin screamed back angrily, curling himself into a ball.

"Annie! How could you think Kevin could hurt Potter? I know for a fact he did a very good job caring for him. Potter was just old and had lived a long, comfortable life for a hamster. You knew that he was on the edge of death all year. The poor creature just died on Kevin's watch."

"Yeah!" Kevin shot back, sticking an angry tongue out at me.

Mom was right. Potter was five, quite up there in years. That's about ninety in human years. *It was a good hamster life. He was just protons and neutrons anyway*, I thought.

"Sorry," I semi-apologized to Kevin, arms crossed without turning to look at him.

"I flushed Potter down the toilet," he casually added.

"You what?" I cried out, spinning back around like a top. "Mom!"

"Yes, honey, your brother flushed Potter. It happened before I had a chance to stop him."

"You idiot! You flush goldfish down the toilet, not hamsters! Hamsters get buried in the backyard in a little box with a small bunch of flowers. It's supposed to be a sweet and tearful ceremony, not flushed down a toilet. How'd *you* like to be flushed down a toilet?"

"Annie!" Mom scolded again.

"Well, it would save on funeral expenses."

"Annie, stop that right now!" she demanded.

"You're right, Mom, what we save on the funeral, we'd lose on the plumber's bill."

The next fifteen minutes of our trip home were total silence, except for Kevin humming *Row, Row, Row Your Boat*. I didn't give him the satisfaction of telling him that he was annoying me, and he knew that without me telling him—that's why he was doing it. I finally broke the silence.

"I missed Nonna, too," I blurted out in anticipation of her news about her coming to stay with us.

Kevin stopped humming, looked up, and glanced up nervously at Mom.

"You know, I'm going to start to help out grandma more. I've neglected her and I feel so guilty, so stupid. Poor Nonna was getting so forgetful the last time I saw her. Wow, that was almost four months ago, and she never called me or wrote to me at camp. I started thinking that maybe she was mad at me. I want to spend more time with her. That lady's not getting any younger you know."

My mom did not respond, just looking out at the road ahead. Then she whispered ominously, "Annie, Potter wasn't the only news that I withheld from you. It's about your grandmother."

I knew by her manner and voice the news was not going to be good. "No! She didn't..." I choked, thinking the worst.

Mom answered in slow, measured words. "No, honey, she didn't die." Tears welled up in her eyes. "Grandma's...grandma's in a *home*. We had to place her in a *home*."

"A home? You mean like a *nursing* home? Nonna hates nursing homes. Remember how she couldn't visit Aunt Millie when she was in one. Is she hurt or sick? She would never allow you to put her there." I was angry and confused. How could she put my Nonna in a home, like a prisoner?

"Honey, all that forgetting, remember? It got worse. It got really bad, very quickly. The stove was being left on, and we were told she was walking into neighbor's houses without a reason. Local police called me twice when they found her in her car, lost and confused. Finally, she drove into the city and had no idea where she was. Grandma got out of the car and was just wandering. Luckily some nice people stopped her and questioned her. When they saw how disoriented she was, they called the police. I was called to the station to pick her up. She knew what was happening and was scared and upset. It scared her so much."

"*What* was happening?" I demanded, thrusting my face close to hers.

"Grandma was forgetting my name, Annie...me...her daughter-in-law..." Mom could not fight back the tears any longer and sobbed.

"Mom?" I asked with growing concern and urgency.

My mother paused. "I'll be okay, sweetie," she reassured me, sniffing back some tears. "Your grandma got so mad at me when I took her car keys from her. I never saw her so angry. She screamed at me and told me that she hated me. 'Let me die!' was what she screamed at me…that I might as well kill her rather than take her car keys. But it was getting too dangerous to leave her alone, and especially to let her drive."

"Why can't she live here with us? We can take care of her," I pleaded, grabbing tightly onto her shoulder, tears now puddling in my eyes.

"Annie, she needs a lot more help than we can give her—the care of people who can deal with…people like her."

"What do you mean *people like her*?" I returned angrily. "That's my Nonna."

My mother gulped back more tears. "Not anymore, honey. Not anymore."

§ § §

That night, I Googled *Alzheimer's disease*.

A prehensile form of dementia whose symptoms begin with impaired memory leading to impaired thought and speech, followed by total helplessness.

My father died four years ago. He was killed in a car accident. According to science, my dad doesn't exist anymore. Chemical reactions in his brain and body had stopped. Neurons stopped sparking, the exchange of energy and electrons ceased.

This loving, vital man who tried to teach me to hit a softball and joked with me about being a science geek. He told me bedtime stories that he made up on the spot. This man who laughed often and easily, who kissed and hugged me like I was the most precious thing he had ever seen, was gone forever, like a burnt match…ash…elemental carbon…nothing. It didn't make sense, all his amazing energy gone. I didn't want him to be nothing. I didn't want Mom or Kevin, and especially Nonna, who was getting so old, so forgetful, to someday be nothing…and me, I didn't want to be nothing. It terrified me sometimes to think I would not exist someday. Then why shave my legs?

Helplessness?

That was the last word that should be used to describe my Nonna. But helplessness was what I felt right now. Sleep would not come to me. My mind swam into dark, ugly depths thinking of my poor grandma in a nursing home. How could this happen to her? It was all so dark, so unfair.

My grandparents had come to America from Italy. They had lived in a little village in central Italy called Sala Consilina. I didn't remember my grandpa; he died before I had any real interaction with people. Nonna said he was a good man, a farmer in the "old country." Grandma showed me pictures of him and of the little village she missed dearly. When I graduate from high school, she promised to take me to Rome, Florence, and Sala Consilina as a graduation gift, just the two of us. Italy sounded lovely. She told me Sala Consilina was surrounded by green rolling hills and quaint little stone buildings.

When she retired, she had gardens, vegetable gardens with tomatoes, beans, peppers, zucchini, basil, and oregano. That garden was a tribute to her husband, Salvatore, the farmer. Her real love was her flower garden. In the spring, flowers like tulips, daffodils, pansies, and crepe myrtles were planted. Behind them was a crescent of summer flowers—black-eyed Susans, dragon flowers, zinnias, impatiens, daisies, and so many more. At the sides of the crescent she had her autumn flowers.

"Each moment has its joy," she told me. "Each season has its colors to rejoice in. There should be flowers until the end, when the winter comes. Flowers should greet the last breath of autumn, the first snowflake."

Till the end.

Painting and writing poetry were her passions. That talented lady painted a portrait of me as a five-year-old. It wasn't bad, but the fingers were too fat and short, and my ears were much too small. However, landscapes, like beaches with lighthouses and forests with streams and trees and flowers, she was wonderful at those. My favorite was a painting she did from memory of a little church on a hill in her little village, San Michele Church, St. Michael's.

"No more people. Stick to trees and sand and lighthouses," I recommended to her.

She laughed. She always laughed. The sound of her laughter made me feel safe. It was like, *nothing could harm us or break our hearts; it was just life…and life was good, life was full.* My grandmother tried to teach me to paint and garden and to believe in the beauty of the world. The coolest thing was that she rarely *told* me the answers and how to do things, leading me to the answer and having me discover the truth for myself. Most importantly, she knew how important my ghost hunt was for me and told me that, when the time was right, she'd help me find the truth. We just ran out of time.

26

4

WHY NOT?"
Rarely did I yell at my mom, but I must have been frustrated and scared. I just wanted to visit my Nonna at that stupid home, and she didn't want me to. How could I not visit her there? What would she think if I didn't show up?

"Because it's strange and scary at the nursing home. Your grandmother wouldn't want you to see her like that," Mom explained as she nervously pulled clean dishes out of the dishwasher. A plate fell to the floor and broke into shards.

"You know that I have to see her. What you're saying doesn't make any sense," I said, softening my harsh tone a bit.

"She probably won't even recognize you. You'll be a stranger to her, and that will break your heart," my mom answered in a fragile, quivering voice as she picked the pieces of broken plate off the floor.

Now I knew the gulf between the thought process of adults and teenagers was almost as wide as the gulf between how girls and boys looked at the world, but this idea that my grandmother would not, could not recognize me was incomprehensible. There were just things that I thought were absolute.

"Nonna won't forget *me*, Mom! How can you think such a thing?" I pleaded. I knew my mom was upset, and I was really trying to appreciate that, but there weren't a whole lot of reasons for me *not* to see my grandmother; actually, there were no reasons.

"I'm trying to protect you," she explained tearfully, as she placed the broken pieces into the trash, still not making eye contact with me.

"You don't have to protect me, Mom. I've got to be there for her," I said, bending over and picking up some stray pieces of the broken plate that she had missed. I thought to myself, *Easy now, Annie, watch your tone and what you say to Mom.* I hadn't seen her quite this upset since…dad died.

"She has all the care she needs there. People there are very good, very kind," she reassured me, holding out her hand to accept the pieces of plate.

"*You've* been there?"

"No, you know that I hate those places. I just know they take good care

27

of the patients. I checked it out before I allowed her to go there." A long pause followed. "I...I...can't see her like that. Annie, it's been four months since you've seen her. I didn't have the heart to tell you her condition," she confessed.

"That's why she didn't respond to my letters or answer her phone? So she wasn't away in Florida for two months?" I asked.

"I just said that to get your mind off her, Annie. She doesn't remember things and gets confused and angry." Mom put both of her hands gently upon my shoulders and kissed my forehead, just like she had right before she told me that my father had died.

"How could I *not* visit her? That's insane, Mom," I pleaded, starting to shake.

There was a pause as my Mom just stared at me, moving her hand up to cup my cheeks. I loved when she did that; her hands were so warm and reassuring. They made me feel safe, made me feel loved.

"You know, you have your Dad's shiny brown hair," she murmured, her eyes exploring my face.

"That's the Italian genes," I pointed out with a smile.

"And, there are a few little freckles..."

"Nonna said that my freckles were like my own constellation on my face. 'Annie the Angel' she called it."

"Got those from me," she sighed, gently touching each with her finger tip. "And those blue green eyes," she added, looking proudly into them as if taking credit for my features, which I guess she should, at least for fifty percent of them. I could feel her softening and coming around to accepting that I had the strength to deal with the changes in Nonna.

"Those are the Irish genes," I added.

Her mouth cracked into a subtle grin, eyes raised up and looking beyond me now. "Annie the Angel," she mused. "Your grandma was always right about things." Her eyes shot back to my face. "And your stubbornness, that's from me too. So, Annie the Angel, go on and visit her. Just know, sweetie, she's different now...very different. I don't want you to get hurt."

"Don't worry. I won't."

"You're stronger than me—always were—and more stubborn. I...I...just can't bring myself to see her like this." Her head turned away from me, and she walked out of the room.

It was hard to explain. My dad, my beautiful dad, had been killed while driving to pick me up from my Microscope Club meeting. A guy was texting while driving and ran a red light, ending my dad's essence. After my father was killed in that accident, Mom kind of drifted away from Nonna a bit. I think it was hard to visit and be with her because it reminded Mom of dad. My mom was always a very sensitive woman, adored my father, and depended on him for so much.

I know she doesn't approve of me going to visit the nursing home, but I must, and deep down she knows that. I guess in the "Mom Playbook" there are things you feel obligated to say to your child. Then, there must be things you just know and understand and have to let go. My obsession with ghosts is something she doesn't approve of, and like everyone else, thought it was crazy—like I was tampering with something dark and evil. But she didn't forbid me. We just never talked about it.

I'm sure she will visit once in a while, much as it may pain her. Mom's a kind lady but hates the atmosphere in nursing homes, seeing all that suffering. It scared her. Me? I had never been. But I was about to find out.

§ § §

Wolfing down my breakfast, I tried to sneak out of the house before Mom came down. I knocked over my glass of grapefruit juice, however, and woke her up.

"So, I guess you're going," she said, wiping the sleep from her eyes with the palms of her hands. "Grandma may not recognize you and may act strangely toward you, getting terribly mad at you. And there are other patients there too who may make you feel uncomfortable."

"Yep," I returned coolly, girding for some resistance as I mopped up the grapefruit juice that puddled on the counter. The idea of her not recognizing me was unfathomable. I felt that I shared a soul with this woman. One quarter of my genetic code was given to me by my Nonna, but I felt that most of my soul, if not all of it, came from her. "She'll recognize me, Mom…she has to. I'm her *Annie*. She loves me…*More than to the moon and back again,* as she always told me."

My mom hugged me and kissed me warmly on the forehead. "Well, if she does remember anyone, it will be *her Annie*. Which glasses are you wearing today?"

I have this thing about glasses, especially round black ones. I always thought that they would make me look more scholarly. Probably part of my inspiration was Harry Potter. The problem was my eyes were perfect.

29

When I was eight years old, I complained to my mom and dad about my eyes. When my dad took me to the eye doctor for a checkup, I would lie about what letters I was seeing on the eye chart and would say numbers when he showed me letters. Even when they showed me the gigantic single letters, I would squint and say, "I think it's a bunny," because I wanted a pair of glasses so desperately.

My father and the doctor were astonished by how bad my vision seemed to be. Dad told me later that failing that test made me legally blind. I gave myself away when I noticed, on the doctor's desk, a 5x7 photo of his daughter wearing a tiny gold name necklace which most mortals would have needed a telescope to see.

"Hey! Her name is Annie too!" I chirped out with momentary pride and glee, pointing to the picture on the desk that was ten feet away.

My dad and the eye doctor both examined the photo, looked quizzically at each other and then sternly at me. Being grounded for a week was my punishment—no telescope, no microscope, for a dark, seven-day period. However, once my incarceration was over and I had learned the error of lying, my dad and I came to an agreement. I could wear glasses that had plain glass in them if I promised to always be honest with doctors, police officers, and teachers. The agreement left wiggle room for a few white lies with other people, because he knew that sometimes little fibs were just necessary in life.

"I've got the black frames today," I responded to my mom's query as I reached over across the stack of bagels to pick up the glasses and put them on. I had three pairs. I almost always wear the black ones, but I had a blue pair for when I was feeling depressed—although my friends say I look prettiest when I wear them—and a red pair for when I celebrate something amazing.

I rode my bike as fast as I could to the Sunshine Home. The place was actually a huge, old mansion. I had been afraid it would be like a hospital, but this place seemed special and comfy from afar. It was grand looking, with one of those witch's hat roofs on an upstairs room and a white picket fence surrounding the property. There was a flower garden. I knew Nonna would like that. When I looked over the fence, I saw two gray haired ladies sitting on the porch with a nurse seated between them. There was silence among the three of them as the nurse read to herself from a paperback book. I pulled hard on the gate, but it wouldn't budge.

"Can I help you, darling?" the nurse sweetly called out.

"Yes, I'm here to see my grandmother," I called over the gate.

"Your grandma's name?" she asked as she slowly stood up with one eye on me and the other on the two women on the porch.

"It's Antoinette Barone, but everybody calls her Toni."

"Ah, Toni. You just wait a second, sweetie. I'll open the gate for you." The nurse stepped inside the house, and in the next second there was a buzzing sound and a big bar magnet released the gate, letting it swing open. "Make sure you close it tightly after you come in, dear. Some of our patients like to wander. They always think they're going home."

One of the ladies on the porch was in a wheelchair fast asleep, while the other eyed me suspiciously. "Are you my sister?" she asked sharply.

"No, Angelica, this little girl is Toni's granddaughter, not your sister."

"Is she here to bring me home?" the little lady asked with desperation.

"No, Angelica, she's here to visit Toni. You may go right in, dear. Your grandma's probably watching the television with the others."

Angelica must have been eighty years old. How could I have been her sister? That saddened me. I shyly stepped through the open door and gazed around nervously. It looked more like a boarding house than a hospital, which made me feel more at ease.

As I entered the house I stopped, drawn in by the beauty of the interior. To my left was a wide oak staircase that spiraled to a second and third floor; it brought to my mind a DNA molecule. An old, unused fireplace stood to my far right. It was made of granite stones and had a medieval feel to it. There was a sense that this had been a very ornate house for someone of great wealth and importance. The ceiling was painted like a blue sky with clouds and cherubs flitting about. Hanging from the walls in the living room were some large portraits of people I assumed were the original owners of this house, faces darkened by age.

"May I help you, dear?" a voice from behind me inquired.

When I turned, I saw another nurse waiting on me. "I...was just looking around. I'm here to visit with my grandmother, Toni. The lady on the porch said that I could come in, and I was immediately stuck by the beauty of this old house."

She beamed with pride and nodded. "It is beautiful, isn't it? It was owned by Sigmund Lupescu, a very rich coal baron in the 1800's. Edwina Lupescu, his very last direct ancestor, died in Paris twenty years ago after a long bout with dementia. The family donated it to the town for the care of dementia and Alzheimer's patients."

31

"Wow," I uttered, still gazing about with wonder. The woodwork, hardwood floors, and fireplace all seemed to be original. I would not have minded living here, if it weren't a place for old people.

"Yes, *wow* is what I said when I first saw it. They altered the room sizes and made some other changes for the good of the patients, but it still retains that old rich flavor."

"Rich," I responded, nodding, still in awe.

"Well, I'll let you get on with your visit. I always like to give new visitors a quick history of the house."

I walked into the living room where the patients were. As opulent as the first room was, the décor of the living room was simple, matching the fragility and confused state of the patients. They were mostly female patients with just a few males. Most were sitting on couches and chairs staring absently at a television that was much too loud. A few scurried around looking quite busy. Most looked old and feeble.

One of the women looked much too young to be there, about my mom's age…that was scary. I had once read about the elephant's burial ground, a place where elephants that were old or injured would journey miles and wait to die. That was just a myth, of course, but this house reminded me of that, these old people who had lost their way, collected here in a silent sadness, waiting.

There was a tug on my sleeve from behind. "Do you know where my pocketbook is?" a little gray-haired woman dressed in a purple robe asked.

"No, I don't believe I do," I said shakily, looking around for a nurse to come to my aid.

"Do you know where they hid my cars keys? You know they took my car away, and…I want it back!"

"I…I…" I stammered.

"Now, Emily, you leave that nice young lady alone." A third nurse quickly walked up to us and came to my rescue. "This girl doesn't know anything about your car. You were told not to worry about that car of yours."

"But I need it to go home. I'm going home tomorrow. How can I go home without my car?" she asked, her hands clutched together, as if begging.

"Well, you go to your room and pack, Emily, but leave this child alone."

Emily gave me a confused look. "You look like a nice girl. If you find my pocketbook, please give it to me."

"I…I will," I said nervously. Turning, she proceeded to go to her room to pack, I guess.

"That pocketbook's right there on her bed where she left it," the nurse said. "Always is. And they all think they're going home. They pack up what things they have, and we just unpack it for them minutes later after they've forgotten all about it. Poor souls, keeps them occupied. First time visiting here, honey?"

I nodded.

"Who are you here you see?"

"My grandma, Antoinette Barone."

"Antoinette? Oh! Toni. Sure. Your grandma's in her room. Just saw her a minute ago. Toni's...well..." She smiled. "She's in her room looking through her pocketbook. Room 6, honey."

"Thank you."

Walking down the hall, I peered curiously into the rooms on either side of me. They were very plain—just a bed, a bed stand, and a dresser. There were photos of grandchildren and children, faded black and white photos of the patients when they were young and healthy, photos of loved ones on the mirrors and walls, old black and white wedding photos, with cards and stuffed animals sitting on the dressers...reminders of who they once were. It was both very sweet and very sad. Then, a heavy hand fell upon my shoulder. I jumped away and turned to face the person who owned it. It was attached to a tiny bald man who seemed to be in his 70's.

"They're here you know. Don't let them fool you," he said, looking around suspiciously. He smiled and looked up at the ceiling and pointed. "They're here. They're not lost. Just look for them." Then he looked back at me, his smile turning flat. "Are you Benny, my brother? You're late, you know. I've been waiting for you for three weeks. You're going to take me home."

"No...no...no, I'm not Benny, I'm...I'm Annie," I said, turning my head away and peering down the hall, pointing towards room 6. "I'm Toni's granddaughter. I'm here to see Toni," I said as if that would stop him in his tracks and make him leave me alone.

"Now, now, Albert, there you go flirting with the pretty girls." Again, a caretaker came to the rescue. They were so diligent and omnipresent.

"Didn't you promise to help set the lunch tables?" she asked as if she were a teacher speaking to a little first grade scamp. A flick of her hand towards me was my signal to just walk on, which I happily did.

"They *are* here," Albert reassured me with a wink as he pointed all around us. Smiling, he obediently went off to help set the tables.

My original image was that the residents would just be cute and forgetful, but they were...acting odd, crazy, and immature. It was scary. Do I look like a Benny? It would be such a relief to see Nonna, after dealing with these people and their bizarre behavior. Sweet, dear Nonna. There she was sitting on her bed searching through her pocketbook.

"Hi, Nonna!" There was no recognition of me from her. Moving closer, I put my hand on her shoulder. "Hi, Nonna, it's me, Annie," I reassured her.

Her pocketbook fell to the floor, and she looked at me for a long moment trying to make sense of my face. Her eyes, still and probing, suddenly turned cold, and changed into two peering points of anger. Her face transformed before me into a hateful stranger.

"You! You and your sister! *You* put me here," she said with an icy, angry voice that I had never ever heard from her, even when she had been mad at me. "Where's my car! Where's my money!" she demanded, pounding her fist into her palm. Her face was contorted, and her voice was venomous. It frightened me.

"Nonna. It's me, Annie. Your Annie."

"Oh sure! I know. I'm not stupid. You did this to me. Look at this place! How would you like to be here?" Her hand slapped down onto her bed, and she stamped her foot hard onto the floor.

Who was this woman? Her anger was out of control. I had never seen her like this before, and it terrified me.

"You could have stayed with us, Nonna, that's what I hoped, but mom said that you need special...that you needed to stay here," I explained, inching away. I looked around the room and feigned enjoyment.

"It's a pretty room." It *was* actually kind of nice. There were a couple of her paintings and a few plants. There were photos of Kevin and me.

"Oh, shut up, you. It's a place for *old* people! Not me. I have my own place. I'm going home tomorrow. Where are my cars keys? You took all my money! You took my life. I've worked hard all of my life and now... *this* is what I get?"

"Nonna," I choked out tearfully. "I didn't do anything to you. I love you. I'm Annie." I kept mentioning my name as if the sound of it would instantly heal her mind.

"You're like all the rest, spying and planning to take my money. I hear you at night and all the rest of them sneaking around! And now look at me!" Tears trickled down her cheeks, and she held her face in her hands. "I have *nothing* now," she said in hushed tones.

I wept too. "Oh, Nonna, please don't be sad," I implored. I moved forward and hugged her. This poor confused woman just continued to cry.

A voice once again came to my rescue. "Sweetie, it's time for your grandma's medication." It was a nurse with a cup of apple sauce. "Don't let her anger upset you. This poor lady's confused. It's the disease. It does terrible things to their minds. Deep inside, this woman has a heart of love for you."

"Oh, shut up!" Grandma shot back, sniffing back the last of her tears.

"Come on, Toni. After your applesauce, you're going to help me set the table." You could tell that this nurse was used to the anger and confusion of these poor people, and no matter how venomous my grandmother got, she just remained calm and patient.

"Go away!" Nonna screamed as she attempted to push me away. I put up my hands in self-defense and stepped back again. This woman was unrecognizable, looking so old, so angry, and so crazy. This couldn't be my Nonna. But it was. I knew it was; it was a nightmare.

The nurse stood by me and put her hand reassuringly on my shoulder. "Happens a couple of times a day, sweetie. Then she can be as sweet as peach pie. In fact, *most* of the residents get a little anxious, especially in the evening. 'Sundown Syndrome' they call it. They feel they've lost everything. Well, I guess they have. Let your grandma be. Maybe she'll be better after lunch. Come back again another time to see her. You'll see. It'll be much better for the both of you."

Silently I nodded and backed out of the room. "Goodbye, Nonna," I mouthed. *Or whoever you are.*

At first, I was shocked and taken aback when Mom said that she hadn't visited Nonna, that she wanted to remember her the way she used to be and not the way she was now. I was warned, and now I got it. Now I understood.

5

THE LAW OF Conservation of Energy states that energy can neither be created nor destroyed.

This is a fact…and it is a fact that keeps me going. It links the best of scientific observations with the possibility of a soul.

Energy cannot be created.

But there *is* energy in the universe. In fact, according to String Theory, it's *all* energy.

How did it get here then? I'm holding out for the supernatural.

And when we die, where does the energy of our spirit, the energy of love go, if indeed it can't be destroyed? I think about the Law of Conservation of Energy a lot. I hope it goes on. I want to see my dad and mom and Nonna again someday, and I guess Kevin too. I always want to *be*…to exist.

My dad was so patient with my questions, my doubts. It was just a couple of years after the kindergarten Santa Claus incident, when I attended church with my friends. I didn't understand any of it. Suddenly I just had this urge of "needing to know." I stood up right in the middle of the service and shouted out, "Why are you so shy, God? Why is all of this so mysterious? Please! Please! Please, respectfully show me a miracle right now! I need to know! Why are you hiding from me?"

I waited, as did the whole shocked congregation, my eyes fixed on the ceiling, their eyes fixed on me. Our moment of silence together was terrifying. Then…nothing.

Afterwards they asked me to never return. They called my dad on the phone, and he said that he would have a "strong talk" with me.

When dad hung up, I just knew that I had gone too far and that I'd be punished. He looked at me with such a deep and loving stare. Then he laughed. I will never forget the energy of his laughter.

"You're a pip. You know that?"

"What's a pip?"

He gave me a big, warm hug, a hug that I still felt, that I'll always feel. "A pip is *YOU*. I've got the only daughter banned from Church. There goes your chance of ever becoming the first female Pope. They're probably passing around your photo to all the other churches, temples, and mosques like you're a card counter."

"What's a card counter?" I asked with a smile of relief, my eyes drinking in his smile, knowing I wasn't going to be punished, but more, knowing he understood me. "Am I in trouble, Daddy?" I asked, just to be sure.

"Trouble? No, the world has trouble. I hope you always are creating trouble like that. You just keep asking those questions, Annie. Always question the world."

§ § §

"A cockroach?" Anthony asked incredulously after I explained my plan to him in the Biology lab.

"Yes. I've decided that I don't have the heart to kill a mouse," I confessed, not raising my head as I leafed through my book of insects. I had looked for the insect with the least personality. It had come down to a bedbug or a cockroach. The roach won. I awarded the bedbug *Least Congenial.*

"It's science, Annie. You have to disregard emotions," he pointed out.

From seventh grade until this year, Anthony had always been my science fair partner, even though he was a year ahead of me in school. This year, we decided to go it solo, or at least I did. I had always paired up with him because he was brilliant at science, a year older than me, about a foot taller than me, and much more socially adjusted. I always wondered what he saw in me, because he's in his junior year and brilliant. I was sure he was going to be one of those people we would hear about years from now inventing something really amazing like nano-robotic surgery or a rocket engine that could propel us to light speed. I knew that he chose me because he had a crush on me, not because he admired my scientific knowledge. I'm smart, but he was on a different level than me. I guess he thought I was cute. I figured it out right away because the truth was he never really needed a partner.

There was a time in seventh grade I thought I might like him, too. Picturing us getting married and being like Marie and Pierre Curie, winning Nobel Prizes, and making cameo appearances on TV comedy shows were daydreams that I dabbled with. We even kissed once...it was at the movies. It was a documentary on global warming and climate change, very romantic stuff. That kiss felt awkward. It was like kissing a lab partner. I told him that he was like a brother to me. So that's the way it's been since then, lab partners, platonic lab partners. I think that he still has a crush on me, but he's smart enough to hide it and not be a jerk about it like other boys would be.

"Mice are mammals. They have a fairly well-developed frontal cerebrum and feelings. Plus, I love Mickey Mouse," I confessed, popping my head up out of the book.

"And I love Minnie, but how do you know cockroaches don't have feelings?" he asked, wiggling little finger antennae over his head.

"I don't know, but I don't care. There are no cute cockroach cartoon characters." I got up and returned the book on insects to the bookcase and then looked for another book that might deal more with cockroaches and their care and feeding. Anthony followed behind me.

"So, review this again for me, Dr. Annie," he implored, removing his antennae.

That was his pet name for me, *Dr. Annie* or *Doc*. I liked it. It was nice and platonic, much better than *Honey Bun* or *Sweetie Pie* or *Funny Face*.

"You're trying to measure and observe the release of a soul at the moment of the death of a creature? Are you sure Ms. O'Meghan okayed this topic for your project?"

I knew Anthony outlined my experimental purpose with mocking disbelief, but when he said it and I heard it out loud for the first time, it sounded cool. I was excited. If I could measure the loss of matter at the moment of death, might that be its energy source...its soul?

"Yep. I'm sure that Ms. O'Meghan thinks that I'm crazy...crazy, like you do, but she likes to humor me, like you do. She said that she's tired of talking sense to me and trying to change my mind when I'm set to do something...like you try most of the time."

"You're assuming cockroaches *have* a soul, not to mention mice and people," he said poking my nose.

"Look, my contention is that there is a *life force* in the Universe. It's either in all living things or not. Cockroaches are as good as humans in this experiment—even better. They're easier to kill, I won't feel guilty killing a cockroach, and I won't go to prison for doing it," I said, poking his nose harder in return.

"What if God is a cockroach?" he asked, gently pushing my hand away from his nose.

"Then we're all doomed, especially Monsanto," I explained, dancing my little finger antennae over his head. My search for the supernatural

39

annoyed him, but he tolerated it. The boy was the poster boy for *it's all atoms and molecules.*

"Now for my independent variables," I said. "That's going to be the difficult part, the measuring and observing. I'm looking for the minutest change in mass in the cockroach at the moment of death." I motioned with my open palm, mimicking a rising soul.

He watched my hand rise up. "Loss of the roach's soul, rising to heaven. What a majestic image. I think I remember seeing a painting on that subject by Michelangelo." He looked up at the ceiling, spreading out his arms as if taking in a magnificent fresco up there among the hanging pencils and broken acoustical tiles.

"Skeptic!" I shouted good-naturedly, giggling at the image of such a painting.

"What's your setup going to be, Doc?" he asked in earnest.

Visualizing what I planned, I mapped it out for him. "My roach will be in an airtight chamber to eliminate any air flow changes, resting on a scale that will give mass measurements up to one ten thousandths of a gram."

"What if his soul has a mass less than that?" He squinted his eyes at the thought of such a tiny number.

"Shush! Then I'll use a hippopotamus next time. Okay? Now listen. I will insert a premeasured amount of insecticide into the chamber and watch to see if, at the moment of the cockroach's death, there is a loss of mass."

"And that will prove to you that there is a soul?" he asked skeptically.

"What else could account for the loss in mass? That's why you're here to help me. What variables am I not seeing? Come on, help me see them."

There was a look of annoyance as he scratched his head. "You know, I think all this ghost, vampire, unicorn, and soul searching you waste your time on is pretty silly. Our universe is about science, and you're too good of a scientist to be playing ghost hunter. Think about it…a cockroach's soul? What will you do next year, clone Barbie? You just get obsessed with stuff, Annie, and you let it overwhelm you. Remember in sixth grade when you wanted to see a UFO? We sat out on Federal Hill on too many cold autumn nights trying to see one. You even tried luring them in by playing the chords from *Close Encounters* and spreading Reese's pieces all over the ground up there. All we saw were ants."

I knew never to lose my cool with him because he was too good of a debater, always having facts and logic to back up his points.

"But *if* there is loss of mass at the moment of the…organism's death, what chemistry might account for that?" I asked with the serious inquiry of a professor.

He shook his head and let out a long thoughtful sigh. "Ah…the insecticide could react with the bug's tissue. At death some of the tissue, not getting brain signals, could break down."

I wrote his ideas down. "By the way, those things wouldn't cause a change in the mass. They're just chemical changes," I corrected him.

"Uh, I don't know. Charon the Ferryman might have taken the pennies off the roach's eyes?" he returned with an impatient bite.

"Now, now, Anthony you're being silly…this *is* science. I have controlled my variables—I hope. I will make observations and produce a valid conclusion. Aren't you curious?"

"I am curious about things I can measure, things I can account for."

"Don't you hold out the possibility that there is so much out there and in here," I said, as I pointed to my brain, "that we can't measure, that we as fairly intelligent creatures cannot grasp, amazing things that await a more evolved brain to comprehend?"

He just shook his head.

"Your dog, Fermi, he's pretty smart. Remember how you taught him to bring me his little cushy red toy heart every time I showed up at your door and drop it at my feet."

He turned and blushed with embarrassment over his corny but very romantic gesture.

I continued, looking into his reddened face to prove my point. "You said that it took your dog three weeks to get that trick right…a very sweet trick, I may add. You told me that your pup brought you a dirty sock for a week before he learned the trick. Luckily for him it was your sister's and not yours. Such a smart dog…for a *dog*. But if you tried to explain to him Avogadro's number or Einstein's Theory of Relativity, he'd just run off and bring you back a dirty sock. His ability to understand complex concepts is limited. Maybe in the scheme of the universe, *our* brains are limited. Maybe we are capable of measuring and understanding just so much. Maybe our brains need to evolve more. Hey, we still burn fossil fuels for our vehicles and pollute the water we need to drink. We kill elephants for ivory trinkets and rhinos so we can grind down their horns to make love potions. How smart can we really be? I love and trust science as much as you…you know that, but what if…what if there is more? Six hundred years ago they thought that the Earth was the center of a tiny universe.

41

One hundred years ago they thought that the universe was the Milky Way. Now we know of ten billion galaxies in an *infinite* universe. Infinite! That sounds magical to me."

There was a sigh, and then he put his hand on my shoulder. "You just want to live forever, Annie. That's where all the myths and stories come from. You're afraid that it's all finite. Well, it is. When the chemical reactions are over, it's done…dark, cold, quiet, and final, like when a blazing piece of firewood goes out after the oxidation reaction is over. It's done. That's the truth that you don't want to face. You don't want anyone you know and love to really leave. You, Dr. Annie, are Peter Pan, and you want to take everyone you love to Neverland."

A pause stood between us like an unwelcome guest. We'd had this debate on many levels before. We couldn't win the other over to our side. I wasn't even sure about what my side was. I hated his metaphor that we become burnt out firewood in the end. I knew his protests came from concern for me, but I wished so much that a little crack would open in his imagination about existence, and we could explore the supernatural as partners.

"I will try to get you a more sensitive scale from the university. I don't think yours is sensitive enough to weigh…*a cockroach's soul*…and I'll try to think of more variables that you might be missing," he said in an attempt to break the tension between us and win me back.

It worked.

"Thanks! And don't forget you promised to come with me next time I go the Sunshine Nursing Home. It really freaked me out last time." I gave him a hug. I knew he'd like that.

"Okay, but I don't think that your Nonna will remember me," he said, as if trying to back out of visiting already.

"Doesn't matter," I said sadly. "She doesn't even remember me. I just want a backup with me. *You* can be Benny this time."

"Huh?"

"You'll see, Benny, you'll see."

After a long quizzical look, he asked, "It's four thirty. You want to go to Starbucks?"

"No. I'm going to stay in the lab. Ms. O'Meghan said I can stay till five thirty before the custodians kick me out. I have to work on controlling the quantity of my insecticide variable."

"Okay. I'll see you tomorrow," he said, heading for the door while wiggling finger antennae on the back of his head.

"I'm still a scientist!" I called out to him as he was leaving. "I'm just curious about...this stuff." I wanted him to be proud of me. That was important. I hated it when I disappointed him.

"Obsessed is more like it," he called back from the hall.

"Aren't all great scientists obsessed with their work before their great discoveries?" I yelled back, so he and probably most of the custodial staff could hear.

He came back, stuck his head into the lab room door, and said, "It depends on *what* they're obsessed about. See you tomorrow, Doc."

I walked over to the lab window and pushed aside Ms. O'Meghan's collection of animal skulls, which sat on the window sill. Leaning forward, I had to make sure I could see Anthony leaving the school. When he crossed the street, I knew it was safe to continue. Taking out my phone, I texted *"Ok. In bio lab."* I hated being dishonest with Anthony, but he was weirded out enough with all my spirit hunting. If he knew that I didn't have to measure insecticide but had set up a meeting with the "Goth Twins," he would freak. They weren't his favorites.

Caden Morgan and Christine Grint weren't really twins, not even sisters, and they certainly were not "undead" like in vampires, but they were inseparable and seemed to love the eerie, macabre reputation they had nurtured by dress and deed.

Rachel Carson Science and Math High School is a very elite school. We're intense with the science and the math, but we do have sports as well. There's golf, swimming, volleyball, tennis, and lacrosse. We don't win very often in sports, though we do have our share of victories at science fairs, chess tournaments, and engineering competitions.

Students here are pretty smart and therefore pretty tolerant of other's eccentricities, even, well almost even, of these two girls, who were kind of weird. They said they had traced both their family lineages back to Elizabeth Bathory. Elizabeth Bathory was a horrible countess who lived in Hungary in the sixteenth century. This spoiled ghoul baroness was under the illusion that bathing in human blood kept the skin young and beautiful forever. The fiend was infamous for scores of bloodletting murders. Not quite a role model in my book, but today she might be cast as a star in a reality show.

"Hey!" Caden said as she entered the lab with Christine in tow.

Both of them were dressed in the obligatory black shirts with long sleeves and a matching skirt. Caden had black lipstick and dark purple eye shadow with "fangs" tattooed down from where her canine teeth were;

her eyebrows were cut into the form of two little bats. Skull earrings dangled from her lobes. Christine had purple lipstick and black eye shadow. A pentagram was tattooed on her forehead, as well as two tattooed "tears" dripping from her left eye. When I first met them in sixth grade they were pretty "normal," but I guess they saw a movie or read something, because in seventh grade they went to the "dark side." They really scared me at first. All the kids, along with some teachers, thought they had some dark power. When teamed up with them on the debate team, however, they came across okay, a little strange, but definitely not dark. I came to realize that theirs was just another mode of expression. What they will do with the tattoos when they go for their interviews for medical school…or a job, I don't know. Unless their career goal is to work behind the counter at Zorko's Magic Shop, their style will be a handicap. I guess they'll change. Everyone changes. They're actually sweet girls.

"Hey!" I shot back, still a little shaken by their appearance.

"That note you passed to me in class said you wanted to see ghosts," Caden pointed out, getting right to business.

"Yes," I said with conviction.

Out of the corner of my eye, I saw Christine take some small white crystals out of her pocket and start sprinkling them on the doorway and around the window sills. Caden noticed my eyes as I watched Christine with curiosity.

"The girl's laying down salt—keeps demons away."

"Oh, of course," I said, pretending that this was as normal as rubbing one's hands with sanitizer.

"You can never be too careful," Christine responded, dropping extra salt by those animal skulls on the window sill. After she had looked round the lab suspiciously, she pointed out, "Lots of animals have been dissected in this place…pigs, frogs, and cats. Their spirits may be looking for revenge."

They both gazed at me for a moment. "What's your motivation," they asked in harmony, giving me a suspicious glare.

"For dissecting?" I asked, a bit confused by the question.

"No. What do you want with these ghosts?" Caden asked, as if needing to protect the privacy of her "clients."

"I…I just want to see one. I've never seen one, and I'd like to know if they exist." I felt I didn't have to explain my metaphysical dilemma to the Goth Twins.

"*If* they exist?" Christine cackled.

They looked at each other with knowing smiles. "There is a place we can take you where you can finally know that spirits do exist. What's in it for us?" Caden asked, holding her hand out symbolically.

"How about you do our Astronomy term papers?" Christine offered.

"I...ah...don't do that kind of thing. Call me a prude, but there's this integrity thing about science. Can't do that. Hey, how about if I carried your books for a week?"

They exchanged looks of annoyed disbelief.

"Only kidding," I said quickly before they walked out on me. I forced my hand down into my pocket then lifted it out and towards them. My closed fist opened to reveal two black objects. It was good to see that they were duly impressed. I didn't know how far fetishes would go as currency.

"Fetishes" they said in harmony. They said a lot of stuff in harmony. That was fascinating...and creepy.

"An owl fetish is the controller of the night, the dark side of nature," I instructed. We had vacationed in Arizona one summer, and I had bought these two animal fetishes from a Zuni Native American, an owl and a snake carved from black obsidian.

"And the snake is a powerful fetish controlling life, death, and rebirth," Caden announced.

"We know our fetishes," added Christine, annoyed at being spoken down to.

They each took a fetish from me and rolled it around on their finger tips and rubbed it on their cheeks. They even bit into them. I just hoped that their teeth were strong; obsidian is pretty tough. They told me later they were testing the spiritual integrity of each.

"Is it a deal?" I asked. "Will you show me ghosts?"

They looked at me, then the fetishes, back to me, and finally at each other. Christine bit hers one more time and put it up to her ear.

"Yeah. We're good," they said, again in tandem.

"Great! Then it's a deal," I said, smiling. Putting my hand out, we shook. "When?" I asked anxiously.

"When?" Christine asked with a laugh and an odd look like I should know the answer to that question.

"October thirty-first, of course," Caden responded.

"That's Halloween," I reminded them. I always looked forward to dressing up and going trick or treating. It was a tradition. I knew one day that I would have to stop, but until that day came, I loved getting those

Snickers and Hersey bars. I loved the Mardi Gras feel of the streets filled with costumed kids competing for treats and frights.

Caden frowned at me. "All Hallows Eve, best night. Look, you want to see a ghost, or do you want candy corn?"

I relented with a sigh. Childhood's end. "Ghosts," I returned without much thought.

"Good answer," they said together.

"Where?" I asked a bit sheepishly.

"We'll let you know," Christine said with a hint of espionage in her voice.

Caden took the owl, and Christine, the snake. They nodded at each other. "Cool," they responded.

"We'll talk to you soon," Caden said as she placed the owl into her pocket. Christine gave one more look around the lab, I assumed looking out for demons or frog zombies. With that, they left. It was rumored they had really seen and talked to ghosts. That made me very excited.

6

I DEBATED LONG AND hard if I should ever go to the nursing home again. It was her, but it was not her. Perhaps mom was right; maybe I should just remember her the way she was...but I couldn't *not* see her. Two weeks had gone by before I mustered up the courage to try again. Anthony tried to make an excuse not to come. He said that there was a chemistry test that he had to prepare for.

"You can *teach* that chemistry class. You promised me!" I said, trying to guilt him and flatter him in the same breath.

This time I planned a Saturday visit, early on a sunny afternoon. It was perhaps the bravest thing I had ever done, well, pretty brave. When we walked through the gate, I saw her immediately. There she was sitting out on the porch with two other residents and a nurse. Each of the other residents had visitors also. That little old man who thought I was Benny had his son and grandson with him. They were listening to a baseball game on the radio. The other resident was a tiny, gray-haired woman whose visitor was someone who looked as if she was an old friend or relative sitting next to her. She was holding and rubbing the resident's hand, trying to coax memories from her.

"Do you remember when you met John, your husband, at the beach? We were both sitting under that umbrella, and he walked by and commented on how pretty your bathing suit was." There was a bright, but ever so slight, smile of recognition.

"There were seashells on my bathing suit," the woman offered softly.

"That's right, Cecelia. But I think he really wanted to say how pretty *you* looked."

Her smile broadened.

"Anyway, you and John married right on that very same beach two years later."

Cecelia nodded, pushed her head against the back of the chair, and closed her eyes, seeming to drift back to that very place and time, hoping beyond hope to transport herself to a better, richer time.

"Well, look who it is, Toni. It's your pretty granddaughter accompanied by a very handsome young man," the aide pointed out in her lilting Jamaican accent, awakening Nonna sleeping in her lounge chair.

Anthony's face turned crimson as the nurse gave me a wink.

"You bring your pretty, pony-tailed self here with that tall, good-looking boy—why you look like that Johnny Depp fellow. Toni, I bet you're glad to see your granddaughter today. You haven't had visitors in a while."

Many of the others looked at us for a moment and then went back to what they were doing.

"Hi, Nonna," I said sheepishly, expecting the worst. My hand waved meekly as I fearfully awaited her response. But when her eyes opened, she looked at me with a hint of recognition and studied my face with a hard look of someone searching through her memories for something valuable. Finally, there was a faint smile that broadened as I returned a smile of relief in her direction.

"I know you," she offered happily, pointing a crooked finger in my direction. "You're that girl." Turning to the nurse, she giggled, "She's my mother...no, my friend."

Anthony's eyes widened in shock at my grandmother's reaction to me. He turned to me with concern. I just waved him off. I had read that the ability to translate thoughts into the correct words got altered with this disease. Nerve endings got mixed up. It had to be so frustrating for them and so confusing for people who listened to them, but after the reception I had received on my maiden visit, she could call me her great grandmother for all I cared. Her voice was so pleasant, even cheery.

"No...no, Toni. This beautiful girl is your granddaughter. Don't you remember? She was here a few days ago."

"Oh?" she returned to looking at me. Her gaze was genuine, staring and squinting and trying so very hard to have my face make sense to her. It was like something was speaking to her: *think, this is someone important, someone you love.*

The aide was full figured and had a lovely face that just glowed with positive energy and love. She turned to me and patted my cheek. "You sit right here and take Daisy's seat. That's me, Daisy."

"Hi. I'm Annie, and this is Anthony. Please don't get up," I offered politely.

"Oh, no dear, I've got to go in and start up lunch for all my lovely ladies and gentlemen." She gave me a wink. "Three good meals a day keep them healthy and give them something to look forward to. There isn't a lot for them to look ahead to.

I hesitated to sit. Daisy whispered in my ear. "Don't fret today, sweetie, grandma's having a *good* day. Sit now and take advantage of this good day."

"Thank you," I said, smiling with relief and easing down into the chair.

"And I'll bring out a chair for your young man, that Johnny Depp boy."

Turning a shade of crimson, he shyly looked down. "Oh no, that's okay. I like to stand," he nervously responded.

"If that's how you want it, handsome fella," she returned with a smile. She gave me a wink and called over to Albert and his visitors. "Who's winning the game?"

She ambled over to them, giving me a little behind-the-back wave. The caretakers and nurses had to juggle their attention among all the patients. They always made each patient feel like the most important person there, the epicenter of their world.

"The Yankees are winning, as usual. Mickey Mantle's got two homers!" Albert proudly announced to Daisy.

"Grandpa!" His little grandson was about to correct him when the dad interrupted, giving the boy a knowing look.

"Mickey Mantle was grandpa's favorite player back when he was young," he explained patiently.

"But this is the Mets playing the Giants, Daddy. Mickey Mantle's…"

"Mickey makes grandpa happy, Damien." I could tell that this dad was a veteran at visiting Albert; his words and tone with his son and with his dad were measured and patient, like the caretakers'. He knew what was needed.

Damien just shook his head, confused. "I don't understand."

I was at the same place where little Damien was—*I don't understand.*

"I know you. You're that girl," Nonna pointed out tapping me on my hand intently.

"I'm Annie," I answered, almost pleading, hoping she'd know me, hoping she would be normal again. I knew she would always be far from normal. It was such a moment of heartbreak for me to feel that she didn't know me. I gripped hard onto Anthony's hand. To go from the most important thing in her life, to *that girl* was hard to take. I tried my best not to show my hurt.

"Oh, that's good," was her response.

I drew my chair closer to her. "I'm so sorry that this is happening to you. You're still my Nonna, no matter what."

"Oh sure," she said matter-of-factly, like she really didn't get my words, but I went on anyway.

"I'm going to visit you as much as possible and will take care of you."

"Oh, that'll be nice," she said matter-of-factly again, looking over at Anthony very quizzically.

"We'll do things together," I promised.

"I'm moving out of here, you know. Some friends have a little house for me," she said excitedly.

"What?" I replied.

"Some people are taking me to a new place, a place of my own. I'm not going to be here much longer." Wiggling her finger slowly she beckoned me to lean towards her. She looked around to be sure that no one could hear. "They're too old here," she whispered, "and crazy too!" Putting her hand over her mouth, she giggled.

I found it hard, but I smiled back at her and nodded, "Okay, whatever you say."

There was a silence as I thought sadly about how diminished she was. I was disappointed that she was so much like the other residents, getting ready to leave, confused about the people around her. She had always been so unique. Her reality was different now. *Just make conversation*, I thought. *It doesn't matter what you say. Just say things.*

"This is Anthony. Do you remember him? He visited you at your old house a few times. We had Thanksgiving dinner together once."

"Hi, Mrs. Barone," he offered meekly. This had to be hard for him, too. All he got was a blank look of non-recognition and a nod.

"Are you here to take me home?" she asked anxiously grabbing his arm.

"Ah…no. No, not me," he stammered, recoiling from her touch and looking at me for help.

I quickly grabbed his other arm and changed the subject, pointing to the sparse row of zinnias near the white picket fence. "The zinnias look pretty, don't they? The red ones are so vibrant. Red was…is, your favorite color."

There was no response from her; she just stared off in another direction. I imagined *red* didn't matter anymore.

"Next spring we'll plant our own garden. We'll make it look much prettier. You're the best at gardens. It'll be a sight, a sight to behold," I explained, moving Anthony closer to me and away from her.

"That's nice," she sighed absent-mindedly.

Where is she? I thought. *Where is that sharp, brilliant grandmother's mind?* "Are you painting here? A brochure that mom showed me said that they do art here," I asked.

"Oh no!" she said sharply.

When I saw that brochure, I was so excited for her, thinking that there would be classes with easels and paints and expert teachers that would re-harness the talent of the artists. She could spend her days making beautiful scenes. Instead, what I had seen on the bulletin boards were rudimentary third grade-level art projects—watercolor stick figures, popsicle stick crafts, coloring book pages, and crayon rainbows. I was angered by this at first. My mind seethed, until I realized that level of work was all these poor people could now do.

"What kind of things do you do here during the day?" I asked. All my questions were pretty much ignored. She was focused on her own agenda.

"I'm going home soon, you know. Those people who visit me during the night told me they'd take me to a house, my own house, where I can take care of myself. It has a kitchen and my own bedroom. I won't be here anymore. Do you know them? They're very nice."

"No, I don't think I know them," I said with sadness at the frustration of having to deal with this strange fantasy world that the dementia was creating for her.

She looked directly at me and insisted, "Oh they're nice, the nicest people. They're going to take care of everything."

Sighing deeply, I just shook my head. Our conversation went on like this for an hour. Anthony didn't contribute much. I couldn't blame him because I felt the same way. He was being a real trooper, staying there with me.

It was so hard to see her this way. Each time I would bring up something, the conversation would drift to meaningless fantasies. At least she was in a good mood. It was nice seeing her happy and not acting mad at me. I thought it would be enough that she would be in a happy mood, but what bothered me more than her anger was the thought that I would never have a real conversation with her again. I wouldn't be able to unload my feelings on her, ask for her sage advice, brag about an "A" on a test, or tell her something funny that happened in school or something ridiculous that Kevin did. This disease took so much from so many people.

A nurse came from behind her and lovingly put her arms around Nonna's neck. For a moment she looked startled, but when she looked up and saw the nurse's face, a smile spread over her face.

"Oh, you!" she laughed.

"Toni, you're not going to make me set the lunch table all by myself, are you?" she asked in her nursery-school voice. "Your guests can help."

51

She looked at us with big inviting eyes, nodding her head as if to invite us to come help her.

"This is my sister," she said, introducing me to the nurse.

"I'm her granddaughter," I said, correcting her with an embarrassed grin.

The nurse laughed. "I kind of figured that out on my own. I'm Nurse Natalie."

She was tall. With straight brown hair and a cherubic face, she possessed, like so many of the workers here, such a soothing, patient voice. It was a sage-like voice, understanding the chaotic minds of these poor people and the confused minds and broken hearts of their visitors.

"I'm Annie."

"And I'm Anthony, Annie's...friend."

I grinned momentarily at Anthony. He so very much wanted to say *boyfriend*. I knew the word *friend* just got stuck in his throat.

"Well, Annie and Anthony, your grandma is a big help to me at lunchtime setting the tables. It keeps her busy."

"Let's set tables, Nonna, sounds like fun," I offered, taking Natalie's lead.

Natalie helped her up from the chair and propped her up as she wobbled, unsteady on her feet, another result of the disease. Natalie didn't let go of her until she felt that Nonna had regained her balance, and then she slowly, patiently guided her into the dining room. This woman who just a few years ago was kicking my butt in soccer, tennis, and wiffle ball could now barely walk.

"Grilled cheese today, Toni, your favorite. You two are welcome to stay," she cheerfully explained as we re-entered the home and headed for the lunch tables.

Anthony looked at me and rolled his eyes as if to say *can we go now?*

"Oh, thank you," I responded. "We'll be happy to help," I announced, elbowing Anthony in the ribs.

I helped Nonna put out place mats, plates, napkins, forks, spoons, and a cup at each place. It took a long time, as she struggled a bit with this seemingly simple task. The forks and spoons were the same to her, as were the plates and napkins.

"No, not two forks, one of each," I explained patiently, guiding her hand for the task. "No, you need a plate there, Nonna, not another napkin."

Suddenly, Anthony got a tap on his shoulder from behind and turned with a start.

52

"Are you Benny?" Albert inquired. That old man stared with great hope and need into Anthony's face.

"Ah...ah...no," Anthony stuttered, stepping backwards, confused and a little afraid.

Laughing, I reminded Anthony, "I told you that you were going to be Benny! You're Benny now!"

"Albert!" Natalie called over in a semi-scolding voice. "If you want some lunch, you're going to have to leave those nice people alone." Her busy hands were occupied with making platters of tuna and egg salad sandwiches.

"But isn't he Benny?" Albert asked her with a hint of sadness; the memory of his son and grandson and the baseball game they had shared minutes ago had evaporated into that black hole of memory loss. It was back to Benny again.

"No, dear, Benny's coming later this afternoon," Natalie reassured him with a smile.

"You sure about that?" he asked with desperation.

She came over to guide the old man back to the sofa to stare at the television where most of the others sat watching whatever the workers put on. They just stared, waiting for lunch, killing time.

"Is Benny really coming to see him?" I asked, now fascinated by this Benny character.

"No, sweetie. Benny was his younger brother who died of pneumonia sixty years ago. Tomorrow he'll ask me again if Benny's coming, and again I'll reassure him that he's on his way. That'll be enough for him. Just the *hope* is enough. Each new day's memories are brand new. All these sweet people have lost everything—it's such a curse. At least we can give them lies sugared over with hope. They deserve something to dream about, something to hope about."

That nurse Natalie spoke about them with such respect and reverence, made me feel so guilty. I was feeling annoyance with Nonna and the whole group for what I saw as insanity and childishness. I was feeling sorry for *myself* for having to put up with this disappointment, instead of seeing them as warriors—parents, grandparents, and spouses, whose full lives and memories had been robbed, ripped from them—brave and wonderful just by the desperate fantasies they'd created to somehow go on. Leaning over, I gave Nonna a heartfelt kiss on her cheek and whispered into her ear, "I love you."

"Oh, that's good," she returned, matter-of-factly, as if I had just said that it was a nice day.

Carefully Nonna went through her task, taking pride in her responsibility here, in this place where she really didn't have much to do because the terrible truth was, she wasn't capable of doing much.

"Ah! Beautiful, Toni! Thank you! What a wonderful job you did!" Natalie announced.

Natalie and the other nurses went around collecting all the residents from the rooms where they were sleeping, watching television, looking though pocketbooks, or just staring at the walls. They turned off the television and coaxed those who had been staring with fixed eyes at an old rerun of *Gilligan's Island* to come to the tables.

"Are you joining us today?" another nurse asked us.

"Oh yes!" one chubby little gray-haired woman said, holding her plate up with glee. "You can have mine!"

I thought a moment. I looked around for Anthony, but he was gone. I craned my neck looking for him, but he was nowhere to be seen. Had he left? He wouldn't leave me here alone. Maybe he just had to go to the bathroom. I went back to helping Nonna for a while more. She took her role of helper very seriously. This place was both so sad and so beautiful. All these helpless people, their minds going or already gone, waiting out their lives doing nothing, just waiting. They probably had full lives, ran families, ran companies, loved and were loved deeply, and were vibrant and alive...like my Nonna. It was so unfair. Where did their minds go?

"Going to stay?" the nurse asked again.

You could tell that they liked visitors to be around. It kept some of the patients occupied with conversation. It also gave the aides a chance to have a meaningful dialogue with someone.

"No, I think we have to be going," I sighed, still searching around the room for Anthony. "Another time, perhaps." I turned and looked for Anthony, who was nowhere to be found. I went back to help Nonna back into her seat. It was tricky, as she was getting stiff.

"What a pretty friend you have there," a little lady with white hair tied in a bun said to Nonna.

"This is my cousin," she responded proudly, touching my cheek.

So far, I'd covered a wide range of relationships that she thought she had with me. I guess only *parole officer* and *backup singer* were left. Once, just once, I'd like her to refer to me as her *granddaughter*.

I leaned close to her and kissed her softly on the cheek. "I had fun talking to you today. I'll be back again soon. I love you," I said, holding her face in my little hands. *I love you too* was the response I would have given a year's allowance for.

"That's my brother," she repeated to those at her table.

Better than parole officer.

"Bye," I said moving away from the table slowly and sadly like a mom dropping her child off at kindergarten for the first time. Not bothering to look up, she just fumbled with her salad, picking out the onions and carrots.

"Goodbye, Annie," nurse Natalie piped up. "Let me show you out."

Her hand rested on my shoulder as we walked to the front door. "It must be hard for you to see your grandmother like this. We don't get a lot of children visiting because they usually find it very uncomfortable here. You're a good girl and very brave. You seem like a bright girl as well, so I have to tell you that this disease will only get worse with time. But through all of this, know that on some level she appreciates you being here." She tapped the side of her head, pointing to her mind and whispering, "She's still there, you know."

"I hope so," I sighed, looking back at her.

"You're a good granddaughter, Annie, and a good girl," she repeated.

"Thank you," I modestly whispered. That was nice to hear. I was feeling as if I were letting Nonna down by not connecting to her. I felt like a loser. Like I said, the workers here knew just what to say.

"Please come again. They love visitors, especially children."

"Hey! We going?" It was Anthony. He had come up out of breath and anxious.

"Yeah, we are. Where have you been?" I asked with mixed concern and anger.

"This place is huge and old. I'm sorry, Annie...some of these people were creeping me out," he confessed, still trying to catch his breath. "I had to get away."

I looked at him with a scowl of disappointment. "Oh, how sensitive," I snapped.

"Oh, you know what I mean. They made me feel uncomfortable. I didn't know what to say to them. Anyway, I looked around. This place is incredible!" he said, ignoring the disappointed tone of my voice. He took my hand and led us to two chairs out in the entry room, and he proceeded to tell me the story of his little adventure.

With the residents headed for lunch, he said that he decided to explore this very old house. That was the curious scientist in him, combined with being the uncomfortable visitor.

"I crept down one of the hallways, on the mansion's north side. I went past the patients' rooms. At the hall's end, I came across a wide stairway that spiraled up to the second floor. It was grand—something from *Gone with the Wind*. Each of the aged oaken wood steps sagged in the middle from decades of footsteps."

I knew that residents were not allowed to live up on the second floor. Alzheimer's took away one's ability to walk with proper balance. If you start to fall here, they put you in a wheelchair. Even the best walkers here kind of teetered and swayed. Stairs were their enemy.

Anthony continued to tell me what he had seen. He explained how he carefully made his way up the stairs. The second floor was just one round, grand room with a very high ceiling. A threadbare red carpet covered the floor. Around the periphery, there were rooms that seemed like storage areas and offices, but many were vacant.

He described the two immense stained-glass windows draped by thick purple curtains. The window in the front was a set of twelve stained panels of a glorious rising sun, its many rays cutting across a scene of green rolling hills. The back window was a bleak contrast. Any gold and green were faded. The setting sun was more reddish than gold, and the hills had lost their green, replaced by the browns of deforestation. A vast "celebration" of coal mining was depicted, showing mounds of the black lumps of fossil fuel and vines of railways and tunnels with black smoke billowing up into the gray air to cover most of the setting sun.

Anthony said there were also tapestries, again with coal and industrial themes adorning the massive room. There were a handful of statues and a couple of darkened oil portraits hanging on the walls, perhaps depicting the original owners and their ancestors.

"Then I thought I heard a sound coming from higher up to my right," Anthony said. "It was a whining, groaning sound. When we had first entered the home, Annie, I had seen the huge turret that adorned the top of the mansion, the witch's hat. There was an old door that probably led to a stairway up to the turret, but it had a huge lock dangling from it that cried out *Keep out!* I wanted a closer look and a closer listen. I edged forward towards the door and tried the lock."

He paused a moment to catch his breath; the last time I had seen him this excited was when he went to the University of Cambridge and actually met Stephen Hawking.

"A voice from behind me made me jump," he continued.

"'What do you think that you're doing here?' the voice growled at me. I was so startled that I slipped and fell to the floor."

I giggled just a smidge at the image of Anthony slipping.

"The voice was from a balding man dressed entirely in black, except for a red bow tie. I guess that he had to come from one of the offices," he explained.

"I told the guy that I was here visiting a friend's grandmother and that I guess that I had gotten lost. 'Well you won't find any friends or grandmothers up here. This is the attic, a *restricted* attic,' he shot back at me. I edged my way slowly towards the stairs as I apologized."

"'I'll help you get *unlost*, young man. Turn around, go back down the stairway, and there you are. Will you be needing a compass?' He was pretty mad and sarcastic."

I grinned again knowing how Anthony hates sarcasm directed at him.

"I told him that I was okay, that I would just follow the setting sun west, pointing to the stained glass, adding some sarcasm of my own."

"The upstairs sounds cool, and I'm sorry that the guy scared you, but I was too busy helping my grandmother," I returned sharply.

"Look, I know you're annoyed at me for leaving, but…this place is a real curiosity. It's strange—kind of cool, but strange. Boy, that guy up there scared the crap out of me."

I gazed at my watch. It was time to go. I stood up grabbing his arm for him to follow me out.

"I know it's a very odd place. It was donated by a rich family. You're going to get us kicked out of here if you keep straying around," I scolded.

"I'm sorry, but it just drew me in. Are you mad because I left you alone? You're mad, aren't you?" he asked with a voice begging for forgiveness. He gave me that sad, puppy dog face, finally bridging the chasm, picking up on my thought process. It takes boys a while, but the good ones do eventually come around.

"I should be mad," I sighed, leaning against the front door. "But, I guess not. You *did* come with me even if you didn't want to. I appreciate that…I appreciate that a lot. And to be honest, I got creeped out the first time I came here. I couldn't wait to run"

"And now?" he asked.

We both turned with a start when there was a sudden cry from the lunch table by a woman who demanded a vegetable. Her nurse calmed her down by telling her that there would be carrots at dinner.

"Now, I see them more as poor little kids who have lost their way. I've lowered my expectations," I said, looking beyond him at the table full of 'elderly children,' some enjoying their meal, some being given help with their utensils, and some just staring.

"I heard what the nurse said to you. You *are* a good girl."

Turning my face back to his, I gave him a little hug. "Thank you. I know it was not fun for you in there."

"It's okay. It's fun being with you. It's got to be so hard for you to see her like that."

I gave him a peck on his cheek. "And you're a good boy."

As we walked towards the gate, my eye caught the cutest image. There at a picnic table, a cute brown-haired girl talked non-stop to a patient, probably her grandma, who just looked through her with a vacant stare. She couldn't have been more than nine years old. I loved the parasol she held in her hand to block the sun from their heads. She just chatted away to the woman, seeming well aware that it was a one-way discussion, but it was just being with her that really mattered. Such a wise little girl.

"So cute, Anthony, isn't she?" I said, pausing and nudging his shoulder towards the little girl and her grandma.

Turning to where I pointed, he gave a bit of a nod.

Now that's *a good girl*, I thought.

As I left, the magnetic gate slammed shut behind us. It sounded so solid, so final. It was like we had just left another world.

7

I CRIED IN MY room for the good part of an hour when I got home. My poor Nonna. I took out an old photo album from under my bed. I leafed through it, examining my embarrassing baby pictures. I looked like a peach with eyes. One was of my dad holding me, looking down at his little peach with such love and pride.

In my toddling age, he tried to teach me to catch a softball and dribble a basketball, but he soon saw that my heart was into science…my endless questions, my choice of television shows and books, and my inability to prevent a softball from hitting me in the face when it was thrown in my direction.

"You are my little scientist," he would say proudly, not disappointed that I would not be a star athlete. Instead of softball gloves and soccer balls, he bought me a microscope and a telescope. I loved him for that and for many other reasons. A man so full of love and life, I looked at his picture and thought, *how could he be gone? How could that energy of love just be gone?*

Here was the one and only picture of me sitting on Santa's lap at six years old. I was frowning and shaking my head at the camera in protest of the obvious fraud. Here was a photo of my first bicycle and my first skinned knee. Here, I was baking cookies with Mom, little Halloween pumpkins. And then there was Nonna. It was amazing in just five years how life had changed. I looked at the photo of us sitting on the beach where Nonna was holding a starfish in her hand. On that day she had explained to me how it could pry open an oyster's shells with its system of siphons. This wonderful woman looked so alive and beautiful and happy. That was gone now. Below that was a photo of my first dog, Bojangles, gone as well. All that energy and friskiness gone. Where did it go? I could well recall the day he had to be put to "sleep."

That's such a gentle way of saying it, *put to sleep*. Go now and dream, Bo. Where are you going? Where is the vet sending you with that injection? Bo was kind of old. Mom had him pre-Annie, and he was breaking down physically and suffering. "We have to ease his burden," my mom consoled me as I cried on the way to the veterinarian's office. We didn't want him to suffer. Go to *sleep*, Bo. And then a terrible thought came to me, one that filled me with guilt, but the thought was there and it wouldn't leave me. I envisioned those poor people in the nursing home suffering mentally with an illness that couldn't get better and would only get worse. They were sad, confused, and waiting for someone to come and take them home, a home that they would never see again. Why weren't they allowed to *go to sleep*? Their reality was that they were waiting to die. Why couldn't, why shouldn't we ease their burden? Why couldn't we say, *go to sleep now. You've lived a full life. We'll let you skip this senseless suffering.*

Terrible thought. Horrible thought! Nonna? I mustn't think that way about people. I grabbed another photo quickly. Here was a good one. We were in her kitchen, and she was teaching me to make meatballs. Chopped meat, egg yolks, bread crumbs, and some spices. Roll them up, then fry them in some olive oil and garlic, and then cook in the tomato sauce. There was a gleam of pride in her eyes as I lifted my first meatball from the sauce. There were grade school class photos and science fair photos. I kept going back to the photos of Nonna and me. There were so many photos of us, planting a garden, learning to dance, and playing the piano. And then... the photo...the ghost hunt in Savannah, Georgia.

We were on a trip with the Girls Scouts to visit the home of Juliette Gordon Low, the founder of the Scouts. While the other girls wanted to go shopping, I persuaded Nonna to take me on a ghost hunt, for obvious reasons. That photo showed us in an old basement that was part of the tour. I was being lectured to by the ghost hunt tour guide when a red glowing mist appeared floating in the room. That was what the photo showed. It freaked everybody out on the tour, even the guides.

I figured it out in about 30 seconds. In my quest for real paranormal, I had learned early on to be very suspicious and look for explanations. Everything probably had an explanation. Outside on the street a traffic light was stuck on red. I had noticed it before we entered the basement. It was hard to miss with the drivers beeping and cursing, trying to figure out who had the right of way. Anyway, the light passing through the window bounced off a mirror, which happened to go through a glass flower vase filled with water, finally bouncing off a steel plate that was on the far wall. We all saw the final red misty reflection, which was quite eerie... for only 30 seconds.

I pointed this out to Nonna, but didn't tell the others. I didn't want to ruin their fun. They'd have a cool ghost story to tell their friends about. The other Girl Scouts got so worked up about the green and blue orbs in another photo I took in that basement. I was so tired of people getting fired up over orbs in photos. Photons of light from the flash have a good chance of hitting a dust particle and spreading out in a circular pattern. If you're in a place with dust, expect orbs. That was the truth. Sorry, but I took all this very seriously. I needed to flesh out a real ghost, not dust orbs and stuck traffic lights.

Anyway, back to the photo. It was taken after I had explained the phenomenon to Nonna, and she could sense my disappointment. For about ten seconds I thought I had reached my epiphany, my proof of a "beyond." What the photo showed was her consoling me and telling me that she would, one way or another, help me prove the existence of the paranormal...a world beyond the knowable...a possibility of an afterlife. I felt consoled knowing if anyone could, it would be her. That woman always had the answers to everything.

Why is the sky blue? *Because the oxygen molecules reflect and scatter the color blue around.* Why does helium make my voice squeaky? *Because, it's less dense than air allowing our vocal chords to move faster.* Why did the dinosaurs die out? *They didn't all die out from that asteroid that hit the earth seventy million years ago. The small ones survived, and they're still here...they're the birds.* Where do babies come from? That one I had to wait a few years for, and it was the abridged version. Why did daddy have to die? I'm still waiting for that one. But ghosts, she said we'd get to the bottom of that. That was my most important question. It still is, as she never got around to convincing me. We ran out of time, and now there wouldn't be any more answers. No more solving my problems. Now, she couldn't even help herself.

"You want to meet a dead person, Annie?" She surprised me by saying that once while we were weeding her tomato garden.

I laughed and pulled out a big dandelion with a long, thick white root. *You've got to get the whole root otherwise they come right back.* It felt so unfair. Dandelions can grow right back, but people can't.

"No, really, do you want to meet a dead person. Perhaps he can give you some insights on death and what might follow it."

I needed *facts*. Faith was so unscientific. "Nonna, stop teasing me. How can I meet a dead person?"

"Well, honey, he stopped being dead. Bob was pronounced dead at the scene of a car accident and then came back to life, and he saw some things that might be of interest to you. I met him playing golf a few months ago."

"Sure!" I said. In my search, even back then, I had done a lot of reading on life and death stuff, and this idea of coming back after a near death

61

was not unfamiliar to me. Maybe he had some proof. His name was Mr. Bob DeVita, a retired chemical engineer who lived in one of the retirement communities.

§ § §

"Hi, Toni! And who's this little beauty," he said as he opened the door, sounding so peppy, like a lonely soul anxious to interact with someone new.

"This is Annie, Bob. As I told you, she's very interested in hearing your story."

"Well, you two come right in," he cheerily invited, pointing to his breakfast table.

His home was smallish with a very simple décor. Not a lot of knick-knacks or gimcracks around, no window treatments or vases with flowers. This was certainly a man's home.

"Here, ladies, have a seat. Your grandma tells me that you have a great mind for science," he said, smiling at her.

Blushing modestly, I just nodded.

"Well that's great. We need great scientific minds to get us out of these environmental messes that we've created," he added with a dour tone. Bob sat down and presented us with a plate of warm, freshly baked brownies. "Hope you like these," he said, placing the plate right in front of me.

Chocolate was my favorite food, especially brownies. The rising smell of fresh baked brownies brought such joy to my senses. Forget about cologne, boys. If you wear brownie scent, you'll have me hooked.

"Thanks," I piped up, grabbing one before the plate hit the table.

"Coffee?" he asked Nonna, very politely. I suspected that he had a thing for my grandmother, since he acted so attentive to her, like Anthony acted towards me sometimes.

"Sure, I'll have a cup," she answered very happily.

"Just oter fo mer," I mumbled with my mouth full of chewy brownie.

"Annie, don't talk with your mouth full," she reminded me.

"Orry," I returned, still with a mouthful.

"One coffee and one glass of spring 'orter' coming up," Bob said, teasing my brownie accent. I liked him; he seemed nice.

"What kind of science are you thinking of getting into?" he asked, placing the water in front of me. I took a long gulp to wash down the brownie.

62

"Ah…I really like genetics. When I grow up I'm thinking about getting into cloning. I'd love to clone a mastodon. I think it would be so great to actually see one, to touch a live mastodon. I'd really love to clone a triceratops or a T. Rex but we can't get DNA from fossilized bone. In Russia and Japan, they have plenty of mastodon muscle tissue. No problem with the DNA there."

"That would be amazing," he agreed, nodding his head.

"That would be stupid!" a voice popped out from what I supposed was a spare bedroom in the back. A freckle-faced girl, about my age, popped out of the bedroom into the kitchen.

"This is Carol, my granddaughter, who's staying with me for a couple of days," Mr. DeVita pointed out with a hint of embarrassment.

"Bringing back those big hairy elephants is stupid. They'd be walking around stepping on people and eating them. You can't bring back something that died trillions of years ago!"

"Hi! I'm Annie. Nice to meet you," I fibbed. "They lived about ten thousand years ago, not far from here, and they were herbivores, so you don't need to worry about them eating people—or any animal for that matter."

"I don't care what religion they were. They were dangerous!"

"Carol, 'herbivore' means they only ate plants," Bob explained to her.

"I don't care. It's a stupid, stupid idea," she repeated with venom.

"Now, Carol, you know you don't use that word," Bob reminded her with a soft patient voice.

"I think the word she doesn't use is *idea*," I whispered to Nonna out of the corner of my mouth.

"Then it's a *bad* idea, okay? Once something is dead…it's dead! Can't bring it back! Shouldn't bring it back! You shouldn't mess with nature and make the mastodons suffer even more."

"They wouldn't be suffering. Why would they suffer? They'd be alive. To come back, to be alive again. Wouldn't that be great? Wouldn't that be amazing? It would be like…like…living forever," I explained with an enthusiasm that made Bob smile at Nonna.

"Then what's the point of dying? Leave me alone when I die. Don't try to bring me back. It's just creepy…and scary. Anyway, this is a stu…" Sheepishly peeking at her grandfather, she started over. "Anyway, this is a *bad* discussion."

Finally, we had agreed on something. My Nonna had told me never argue with crazy people, not that Carol was crazy. She quoted Mark Twain to me. "Never try to teach a pig to sing….it wastes your time and irritates the pig" —not that Carol was a pig.

"Well, I'm going back in my room," she announced to my glee. Skulking out of the kitchen back to her room, she punctuated her exit with a door slam.

"You'll have to excuse my granddaughter. That girl's into her cell phone and iPad far more than she should be. I want to take her out for a little miniature golf, some tennis, but she just likes to veg with her technology."

I just nodded, knowing that kind of kid.

"Shall we?" he invited, pointing to the kitchen table.

"How about I make lunch for all of us? I just have to run to the store to pick up some groceries. I'll let you two talk, and I'll be back in about forty minutes," Nonna explained. "Be open-minded, Annie."

She knew how skeptical I was, how much I needed tangible data and not just hearsay. She didn't want me to be rude to her friend. "I will, Nonna. Could you pick me up some blueberries?"

She smiled, nodded at me, and shot a wink at Bob as she left. That creeped me out a bit. I knew old people were people too, but to see them flirting…creepy. I guess I was a bit jealous, too.

"So, you're searching for evidence of God I understand."

Hmm, I thought, a little taken aback. I'm sure that was Nonna's interpretation. That sounded so…so…religious. "There's got to be more than what we can measure and see out there. I feel that the energy inside of us, our soul, should be eternal. The Law of the Conservation of energy pretty much states that."

"Same thing. Your grandma tells me that you're very skeptical, which makes for a good scientist."

"I investigate unexplainable things—spirits, ghosts—that's what I'd love to find…to prove that ghosts exist. That would prove to me life energy, the soul, goes on and never ends, like all the other states of energy."

"You believe in UFO's, Annie? They're pretty *unexplainable*," he said pointedly.

"Mr. DeVita, there are an estimated 15 billion galaxies that we've observed, each one containing about 100 billion stars. This idea that we are all alone in this humungous universe is stu…" I caught myself before uttering the "s" word that obviously annoyed him when his granddaughter used it. "It's unthinkable. There have got to be billions and billions of creatures out there, most of them probably much smarter than us."

"Well, Annie, you haven't seen a UFO but you believe they exist. This is the same. I haven't seen any ghosts, but I do believe that I've seen God, and the idea of a universe without Him is unthinkable."

"What happened to you when you had your 'experience'?" I remained anxious, but skeptical. Like I said, I had read about these near-death events and had found them fascinating.

"Well, about nine years ago, I was driving home from work. I had stayed a little later to complete a project, and I guess I was a little tired. I went driving through a green traffic light when suddenly, *Wham!* A driver, whom I found out later had too much alcohol to drink, slammed into the side of my car. He totally ignored or didn't see his red light, hitting me on the driver's side. Horrible, Annie, just horrible, like an explosion. The moment was so sudden and terrible, the sound of metal and glass tearing apart. Time seemed to go in slow motion. Later on, they told me that my car rolled four times before coming to a stop, upside down."

"Sounds scary," I choked out, holding back my emotion. My eyes began to tear up, and I put my hands together to stop them from shaking, as images of my dad's accident flashed into my head, images that I was hoping to forget.

"It was very scary. I blacked out and allegedly *died*. And then, like awakening from a dream, I felt myself very alive. All around me I could see flashing lights and people, police officers, EMT workers, and a doctor who had seen the accident and stopped to assist. They were all around me, with serious and urgent faces. I saw two women near the curb, crying. The medical people were trying to revive me, with no luck. I tried to reassure them that I was okay, that I was just asleep, but they couldn't hear me. My mouth wasn't moving, but I could hear the words in my head. I still can hear the words that I *spoke* then, *Hey, I'm okay. Don't be so sad. I'm fine.*"

I just leaned forward, blinked and nodded, signaling for him to go on. Biting down on his lower lip, his face contorted pensively.

"Then the strangest thing happened. I could see my own body as they worked on me. Being apart from *me* was the craziest thing, Annie. I floated five feet off the ground, hovering like a feather above all the chaos and desperate activity. I kept trying to call out to them, but I finally sensed that they couldn't hear me. It was so frustrating. I wanted to call out, *I'm here! Don't you know?*"

"Did you freak out?"

"No, that was the odd thing. I saw all this chaos and horror yet felt like

I had just had a really good night's sleep. I felt so much calm and peace around me. All the craziness five feet below me seemed so foreign, so unreal."

Pausing a moment, he continued. "I just kept rising, higher and higher, never once feeling afraid or concerned. That frantic scene below me seemed like a tiny movie that was getting smaller and smaller as I rose higher."

"Didn't you feel like you were going to fall?" I asked, trying to visualize that moment.

"No. I couldn't even feel myself. I sensed that I was just a spirit, like only my mind existed."

I had always wondered what it would be like to be without human senses, just a mind. We would just have our thoughts with no other point of reference to our universe. We would not feel, hear, or see anything. *We would be our whole universe.*

"That sounds pretty cool, floating like a spirit," I perked up.

"Felt pretty cool, Annie. And then, when the accident scene began to fade out, I experienced this intense, but not uncomfortable, pink light all around me. It was as if I were floating under a sea of pink air, like I was approaching a giant pink sun.

"I can recall a big goofy grin on my face, well, my spirit face. I really felt a feeling of peace and calm all throughout. Then off in the distance, to my right, the pink air began to spin in a vortex, slowly turning, forming a dark pink tunnel that seemed redder at its inner area. I felt myself being drawn into it, like a feather, drawn slowly in."

"Come on now, Mr. DeVita, that didn't freak you out, being swallowed up by a pink tornado?" I asked skeptically.

"Nope, not a bit, Annie. I didn't feel threatened or like I was being 'swallowed.' It felt like I was getting an…an…invitation. As I floated deeper into the tunnel, the red turned pink again, getting brighter and brighter, but never irritating. *Amazing* was what it was…and then, I found myself surrounded by an intense, bright, white light."

This was the part that I had heard some things about. This was the tricky part of the experience, the interpretation of that light. I reminded myself to be respectful of Mr. DeVita's experience.

"It spoke to me, Annie. The Light spoke to me, not with words, but ideas, powerful ideas, asking me about my life and the things I'd done and the things that I'd planned to do. It never seemed to threaten or accuse me, never judged me, just allowed me to review my life. I've never experienced such an elevated sense of peace in my life. Now, I was never a very religious man, but I do believe that I met...God. There was no form, no beard or robes, none of those traditional images, but whatever was talking to me really seemed to know his...or..." he smiled at me, "...her stuff."

Pausing again, obviously moved by reliving the experience, he cleared his throat. "Then, I saw a figure of a person, a dark shadow revealing her beautiful glowing face. It was my sister Emma, who died of the flu when she was eight years old, three years younger than me." His voice choked a bit and he paused again.

Bowing my head, I just stared at the table, not wanting Bob to see me stare while he mourned.

"Emma held out a delicate, white hand to me. I wanted so much to run and hold her and never let her go, but it was not to be. As if she could read my thoughts and the thoughts of the Light, she smiled and waved at me, waving goodbye...for now. And with that, she was gone...again."

He cupped his hand over his mouth as he lowered his eyes. I knew he was seeing Emma's face again in his mind. A single tear streaked down his cheek.

"There was a sense that, if I had continued down that tunnel, I'd be on my way to whatever was to be the next thing...death, heaven, reincarnation, whatever...who knows. I have to tell you, Annie, that it was tempting, this feeling of expanded existence and peace, but I guess I felt that there were things to be done back in my life. My granddaughter Carol had just been born, and my projects at work were not completed. I felt compelled to help out some environmental organizations that needed support. Our planet was crying out to be cured of this plague of abuse that we've inflicted upon it. There were just things that I felt needed completion."

Choking back his emotion again, he continued. "So with that, I felt myself being pulled back down that tunnel, gently swirling back down to that accident scene, back to all that chaos. They had placed my body in the ambulance by then and had put a soft, white sheet over my body. The doctor had pronounced me dead at the scene, and they were ready to drive me away to the morgue. To them, it was over. I felt the sadness there. They were good people, and I felt badly when I scared them in the next moment. My spirit eased back into my body, back from the Light. The first thing I did was breath in a great gasp of air. When I exhaled, I raised my head up, and the sheet tumbled off. Two of the workers screamed, and one hit his head on the roof of the ambulance. It must have been quite a shock to see a *dead man* stick his head out of the sheet. And with that,

I returned to this world. I haven't told many people about the Light, because I felt they would think I was crazy. I told my doctor, my priest, my daughter, and your grandma, because she seemed like a special person…and now you, because your grandma told me that you were very, very special, and I agree with her."

I did not respond with the awe I'm sure that most people did when Mr. DeVita was done with his story, and I knew he could tell by my blank expression that I was still skeptical.

Laughing, he peered at me. "You don't believe me, do you?" he said with a knowing smile.

This was my annoyance with science. It could be so rude, so cold. There was no vote with science; the rules were the rules. Mr. DeVita was this very nice man, trying to help me in my quest, telling me a very special, very personal story of a miracle, a miracle that I wanted so much to believe. But I had heard of these near-death experiences before. Those stories excited me when I heard them, and it still excited me as Mr. DeVita shared his experience with me, but, as a scientist, I had researched this phenomenon the first time I had heard about it.

A group of biologists studying the near-death experience believe it originates in the same area of the brain that creates dreams. They explain it away as a last ditch genetic reaction of the brain…dreaming, bathed in the bright light to jolt us back to wakefulness. They say it's a survival trait some people have inherited. It's just a theory, they stipulated. They also said that they couldn't eliminate the supernatural. That part left me some hope. How could I tell this very dear man that this miracle that he thought he had experienced was just a dream? And even if it were real, it was like the scores of people who told me that they'd seen ghosts. I couldn't go by hearsay. It had to be *me* that experienced the proof. I needed recordable data.

Damn you, science!

"Don't tell me, Annie…you've read that research by those scientists at the University of Kentucky, and what I had is just a dream hallucination to jolt me back to life."

"I didn't say that, and yes, I did read that research."

"Boy, you *are* a little scientist, aren't you? All my granddaughter reads are texts from her girlfriends and the back of the Captain Crunch cereal box. So, I wasted your time here, didn't I?"

"Oh, no! Your story was amazing, really cool. I hope it's true. A good scientist must keep an open mind, hear all sides. But your story doesn't give me any numbers to measure, just hope. And, they're your observations, not mine."

"Tell me, Annie. If that happened to you, what happened to me, would you believe in "magic," God, or whatever you want to call it?"

Bob wasn't angry. He understood my dilemma. He felt so confident in his experience. I wished I could feel the same. I thought he kind of felt sorry for me. "I don't know. I think I'd be pretty moved. I think that I'd believe, but I'd also be pretty skeptical."

"I see. Well, I told you my story. For what it's worth, you can add that to your data collection." Laughing and shaking his head, he continued, "Annie, will you do me a favor?" looking at me with smiling, genuine interest.

"Sure, Mr. DeVita. What?" I returned my own warm smile.

"When you do see a ghost, will you let me know, and then perhaps you can revisit my data…and revisit me. It would be very nice to see you again. You're a special kid."

"Sure thing!" I assured him, putting my hand out to shake his and seal the agreement. "It would be nice to see *you* again, sir," I politely said. "You're pretty special yourself."

"Please, call me Bob."

We spent the next hour talking about chemical engineering and cloning mastodons. Lots of time went by. Grandma was late picking me up and finally called me on the phone.

"I'm at the Duane's Food Mart. Could you put Mr. DeVita on the phone, honey?" She sounded a little nervous and shaken.

My grandmother had forgotten how to get back to Mr. DeVita's house, even though it was just four blocks away. Mr. DeVita gave her directions and grinned at me. I didn't think too much of it at the time.

"Forgetful much?" I joked when she finally returned, not realizing that this was the beginning of her Alzheimer's.

§ § §

I closed the photo album with a snap and rested my cheek on the cold plastic cover. Without lifting up my head, I reached into my pocket and took out my cell phone to make a call.

"Anthony?" I asked with desperation in my voice.

"Yes?" he answered in an urgent tone.

"Tell me something happy."

He paused a moment, to rearrange his mind from *help Annie, emergency* adrenaline level to *tell me a happy thought* mode.

"Ah…let's see…the Sun isn't going to turn red, swell, and destroy the Earth for about 4 billion years?"

I only offered him silence in return for that flippant bit of information.

"You okay?" he asked with real concern.

"Am I a bad, selfish person?" I choked out tearfully.

"Okay, what's wrong?" he asked urgently, his mind grinding back to emergency mode.

"I hate myself sometimes. I need proof for everything that I believe in…data for everything. I'm a cold, soulless, selfish science geek."

"What's the *bad* part?" he asked, trying to make me laugh.

"I was thinking about how my Nonna would be better off dead, that her existence is meaningless and that she should be gone. All of those poor innocents in that Home should just be put down like farm animals. What a horrific thought! What a horrible person I am!"

There was only silence on his end as he thought about my state of mind. He then had to filter it through his *Boy/Girl Translation Mode*.

"Number one, there is nothing soulless about you. Who else would do all these crazy things to try and prove that there is a spiritual energy in the universe? Annie, you're weighing dead cockroaches to prove the existence of a soul, for God's sake! You've spent nights in cemeteries enticing ghosts to appear. If this were four hundred years ago, you'd be tried as a witch!"

I tried and failed to hold back a giggle.

"And number two, I had the same feeling about those poor people, only I thought you'd be mad at me if I said something like that, especially about your grandmother," he confessed.

"You did?" I asked with surprise and some relief.

"I think that we are all *selfish* to a degree. We want the best for our short little lives. It's when our selfishness interferes with the well-being of others, that's the bad selfish. That's not you."

He told me how he had gone online the moment I told him about my Nonna's disease. He said the symptoms, the sharp decline in mental and physical abilities, shocked and saddened him. And, the idea there was nothing to do about it, that it was terminal and terrible. He thought, *why let them suffer and just wait for a terrible end. We even put our pets to sleep out of love!*

"I thought you'd think of me as a monster if I mentioned something like that," I confessed to him.

70

"Where was your idea of letting them die in peace coming from… hate or love of them? Do you care?"

"Love…yeah…love, of course I care. But I hate thinking about it," I said with resignation. I hadn't looked at the emotion behind the thought. I felt a little guilt lift with that insight, although the thought was still hard to relate to on a *loving level.*

"Me too," he said.

"So, I'm not a bad person?" I asked again, hoping for reassurance.

There was a pause. "I wouldn't…love you if you were," he said boldly.

I could only offer silence back. "You're a good friend, Anthony," I finally offered.

"I know," he said with a sad sigh of resignation. "A good *friend.*"

8

I WAS HAVING TROUBLE concentrating on school work. The photos had rekindled so many old memories of the past, and Nonna's fading condition at the nursing home had me worried about her future. My mind was trying to relate my feelings and fears, giving me more lucid dreams. The one I had last night really disturbed me.

I found myself alone in a room in a large mansion. The air was thick around me and smelled musty. There was perfect darkness therein. I held a long thin yellow candle which created a small globe of light around my head. I wasn't afraid of seeing a ghost, but I did sense some danger that alarmed me. Blending with the perfect darkness was also a perfect silence; even my breathing and careful footsteps were inaudible. I took two steps in a direction that didn't seem to matter, being as "blind" as I was there, and I heard steps behind me. Turning with a start, a hot breath blew out my candle, its warmth heating my neck.

I attempted to scream, "Who's there?" but the words were paralyzed in my throat. I spun round and round using my dead candle as a probing sword, cutting at the thick darkness around me.

"Who's there? Who's there?" I tried to call out, but those words were still locked in my head. That perfect silence remained unbroken. I waved the candle wildly now, as if trying to ward off a swarm of attacking killer bees, lost my balance, and fell to the floor. I felt so vulnerable...so alone, lying there helplessly. I screamed a silent scream and curled up into the fetal position to await my fate. My heart pounded in my chest and in my ears soundlessly.

"Stop!" I mouthed an empty scream as my candle was being tugged from my hand. I waved my arm around, again trying to feel what this presence was, when I heard the snap of a stick match followed by a sphere of glowing yellow-white flame. The match moved slowly to my stolen candle, relighting it. The perfect darkness was pierced. I squinted hard through the glow to try and see a face. It was Nonna! My heart eased.

She blew out the match and flipped it away over her shoulder. Bending low, she offered me her hand, which I gladly grasped, to help me back to my feet. I was still mute, but I thought the welcome word, "Nonna!" I was offered the candle back, which I gladly accepted. The flame's reflection danced in her eyes as if they were immersed in black pools of water. I held the candle out to her and hoped we could walk out of this darkness together. She refused to move towards it...or me. Her face remained unchanged, her mouth, a flat straight line of indifference.

And then...she blew out my candle.

Alone again in that perfect darkness.

When I awoke, my heart was racing, and I cried out. I looked around my room and listened, thinking what sound sleepers my brother and mother were, evidently not awakened by my cry.

It was the day before Halloween, and I planned to visit Nonna early in the evening so I was free to go with Christine and Caden on Halloween to visit the "haunted house" in the next town over, an old Victorian mansion that was up for sale. Caden had told me that her aunt was a real estate agent. A key had been given to her, as long as she promised not to have any parties there or bring any boys.

This year for Halloween I dressed as Nettie Stevens, the American geneticist who discovered the XX chromosomes that made a girl and the XY for boys. I wore a big, flat, feathery hat—she liked big hats—and a long purple crinoline dress that I found at the Salvation Army. Funny, no one was able to guess who I was. I thought the big hat would be a dead giveaway.

§ § §

"Toni, your friend is here to see you!" Daisy, the attendant, called out in that Jamaican accent that I'd come to find so endearing. "Grandma's watching television, sweetheart," Daisy said as she dried the dishes in the kitchen area. "My, my, just look at you. That is some fancy hat you're wearing today...and that dress. What's the occasion? Oh, wait a minute. Of course, it's Halloween and you are dressed up as..." She looked me over for a long moment, but obviously had no idea who I was.

"Give me a hint, sweetie, will you?"

"Okay," I said. What clue might help, but not give it away too easily? "Explained the difference between males and females," I announced, confident that she would surely get it with that clue, and I gave her a look of expectation.

"Oh, honey, you aren't one of those cross dressers, are you now?" she asked.

"No! I'm Nettie Stevens, geneticist. You know? XX for girls? XY for boys?"

"I'm sure you are, honey. If you say so…I'm sure you are." She sighed and scratched her head before she went back to drying and stacking dishes.

Anthony had always warned me that I lived in a world of science, thinking that everyone around me shared my enthusiasm and insights into the subject. He told me that many things I say and do sound and look strange in the real world outside of my laboratory, and people may come to treat me like I'm a little nutty. I guess being Nettie Stevens is one of those moments. Not one person had guessed. If I dressed as a famous movie or reality show star, they'd obviously know immediately.

"Hi, Nonna!" I announced cheerfully when I saw her sitting on the sofa watching the television with a few others. Never knowing what mood to expect from her, I always tried to permeate my hellos with cheerfulness.

There was a big squint of confusion in my direction. I had forgotten for a moment about my Nettie Stevens costume. "It's me! I'm dressed up for Halloween."

My Nonna recognized my voice. She turned and smiled at me fondly and took my hand. "I know you!" she said slowly with a broad smile. "You're a nice girl."

That was good enough, although her mood could easily change, but a good start was always better than a bad one. Either she was so meek and sweet and happy to get a visitor or so angry and sad. I had been screamed at the last time, again with the *How would you like to be here? I work all my life and you put me here! Where is my money! Where is my car! You can leave here but I can't. What did I do to be treated like this! I hate it here!* Then she cried. When I left, she was still miserable and in tears. Nothing I could say would break those sad, mad moods. They told me at times like that, I just had to wait for the medication to kick in. On the night after that visit, one of the caretakers called me at home.

"Hello. Annie Barone? Your grandma wanted me to call you. She said to tell her 'sister,' who was here today, to please visit again tomorrow. I assumed that she meant you. I couldn't help seeing her screaming at you. I think this is her way of apologizing."

In that simple phone message, Nonna found a way to sooth me. She was still my Nonna inside, even though she had trouble expressing it. I did visit the next day, and she was as sweet as sweet can be.

"What are you watching?" I asked as I cozied up next to her.

She just pointed at the screen.

We watched a fellow on the television named Lawrence Welk. If it's not an old TV comedy they're watching, it's Lawrence Welk, a band leader with a really thick German-Russian accent who played very old-fashioned music. I had Googled him. There were dancers and singers dressed in bright clothes, always so cheery and chipper. Six other ladies and Albert, who was still waiting for Benny, sat watching the screen, transfixed, seemingly lost in their thoughts. Mr. Welk was on television during the 50's through the 70's, and the old people loved him. I bet it was their respite from rock n' roll. His music probably reminded them of their youth.

I put my arm around Nonna and kissed her on the cheek saying, "Missed you." A smile was sent my way.

What a lovely face she had always had. It was lined and drawn now. It wasn't the slow progression of age for these people. Their faces were breaking down, perhaps from the sadness within. A hair dresser came in once a week to cut or perm their hair and do their manicures. It broke the monotony for them and did spruce them up, making them feel proud. Killed time too.

"You know, you're leaving me hanging with this supernatural stuff. You always said you'd help me solve this quest of mine," I said, pretending annoyance. I kissed her on the cheek again. "Only kidding. You'd help me if you could," I said.

There was a laugh and a nod, seemingly out of habit.

"Boy, I really do miss talking to you."

One patient who never talked blurted out, "Oh! That's my song!" as Lawrence Welk and his merry men started to play a song called "Moon River." It was like a portal had opened into her mind and rekindled a memory. I understood music could do that. As the lady hummed happily along with the band, I saw the glow of sweet memories lighting up her face.

"Shut up, you old hag!" Albert blurted out.

There was nothing that could break her trance, as she just ignored him and kept humming along.

I whispered to my Nonna, "I had a strange dream last night and you were in it. It seemed that I found myself in this big house..."

And then, I saw *her* again, across the way. It was that little girl with the parasol that was out in the garden weeks ago when I came here with Anthony. How could I have not seen her when I came in? Dressed in a little powder blue dress with a matching bow in her hair, she was such a cute vision.

There she sat with an old, white-haired woman in a wheelchair, who just nodded and stared. That little girl was holding her hand and talking to her. I guess it was her grandmother or great-grandmother. I turned back to my Nonna.

"Do you remember my name?" I asked, holding her hand. This was always my opening question, hoping beyond hope that she would remember.

All she could do was give me a half smile and point at me.

"I'm *Annie*. I'm your granddaughter, and I'll never leave you alone here. I miss you so much…our talks, all the things you taught me, your cooking…"

"I cooked," she said meekly. "Nice man would always told the house."

Her words had started to mix into nonsensical phrases. I had expected this from my readings about her illness. I could see in her eyes that she struggled with those words and knew that they were coming out wrong, but there was nothing she could do. Her thinking part of the brain was disconnecting from the vocal area. I could only pretend to understand, nodding and saying "sure" to diffuse her frustration.

"That's right. You were the best cook ever," I announced so the others could hear me, wanting her to be proud.

Little things she taught me and told me started coming back to me. I remembered something she told me once when I thought about quitting my ping pong team because I didn't think I could play well. *Never give up on yourself, Annie. Always love yourself and know that all things are possible.*

"Can't stay too long today, but I'll be back and we'll have fun together, just like always. But I have to go now. I'm going ghost hunting with two of my friends. It should be interesting. Who knows, maybe tonight's the night!"

"You have got to be careful, young Annie. You shouldn't mess with no spirits," that Jamaican voice bellowed behind me.

I looked up.

Daisy shot me a look of great concern from the kitchen where she was now chopping up celery.

"My friends told me that if I'm ever going to see a ghost it will be tonight. I'm pretty excited."

"Oh dear, Mother of God. Please dear, you stay away from those spirits. You stay home tonight. You be safe."

"Do you really believe in ghosts? Have you ever seen one, Daisy?" I asked with genuine curiosity.

"I've seen plenty back in my home Jamaica. As a little girl, younger than you, I got a visit from spirits that lived in our house back one hundred years ago. They were mad as hornets. We couldn't go back into that house till we got the Obeah man to come and send those demons to the dark place."

"Obeah man?" I asked with a tinge of excitement over a word that is associated with ghosts but that I had never heard of before.

Daisy explained to me about the Obeah man. Each village had one. He was their shaman, voodoo man, and spiritual advisor. For a small sum of money, he would handle all of your spirit needs, including sending the bad spirits back to the *Dark Place*. If they were powerful spirits, the sum of money would be greater, and they usually were.

"Don't know if I believe in that stuff, Daisy. I've tried and I'm trying tonight, but I've never seen evidence of ghosts, and I'm starting to doubt their existence. No offense."

"Don't worry about offending me, sweetheart, worry about offending those spirits. Stay home, dear, and go trick and treat. You do your home-work like a good girl," she warned with genuine concern for my safety. "This girl should stay at home tonight...right, Toni?"

My grandma just smiled and laughed.

"I appreciate your concern, Daisy, but I hope I do finally find a spirit tonight." I hugged Nonna and gently turned her face towards mine so she could see my face, see my eyes, and then I kissed her on the cheek, like I did each time I left her. "Remember me, your Annie." I implored as I stood up. "Good night, Nonna. I love you."

A smile came back my way. "She's here, you know," she murmured.

I just thought it was another of her nonsensical quips. "I know, I know," I politely responded.

"You stopped singing!" she demanded, pointing to the woman who was humming Moon River.

"Yes! That's right!" Albert blurted out.

"Now you guys be nice to each other. Enjoy the music," I laughed. Then I addressed the lady humming. "You sound beautiful! I love how you hum."

The woman smiled at me and waved. I felt more comfortable around the patients as I visited more and more. It was like a little extended family for me and Nonna. Oh sure, they had their moments, but they were sweet.

"Have a good night, Daisy. Thanks again for the advice," I called out.

"You listen to ole Daisy and stay home tonight...stay home, girl."

I turned and waved to her. Turning slightly, I watched that little girl with her grandma.

"*How very sweet,* I thought. If she's here next time I come, I should introduce myself.

§§§

Caden and Christine, the Goth Twins, met me with their bikes at school by the bronze statue of Rachel Carson holding up a starfish. On Halloween, the students usually costumed her as a traditional, good natured prank. This year some kids had put a witch's hat on her head and covered her starfish in that thin, stringy, spider-webby stuff and placed about a hundred little plastic spiders in it. It was simple but tasteful. As per instructions, the sun was just setting as I got there. They both wore garlands of garlic cloves and big bulky wooden crosses. Christine had a wooden stake in her right hand.

"Are you guys preparing for a Vampire Apocalypse? I asked. "It's ghosts I need to see, not Count Dracula," I said as I leaned my bike against Rachel Carson's shoulder.

"Oh, there's a ghost all right. But you never know what else we might run into. It's always good to be prepared," Caden explained. They offered me a garland of garlic.

"No, but thank you. I'll take my chances. Your aunt must really trust you to give you a key to this place."

"My Aunt Marge trusts *me.* That's why we have to be careful in there. We can't touch *anything.* Who are you supposed to be anyway?" Caden asked, squinting at me with concern.

"Guess," I challenged her.

"Don't know. Lady Gaga?" Christine guessed.

"Nettie Stevens."

"Who?" they both chimed in together.

"What song does *she* sing?" Caden asked.

"Hello! XX, XY chromosomes! Genetics!"

"Uh-oh, more of your science…we'd better go," Christine moaned while grabbing her bike.

We biked for about fifteen minutes until Caden pulled up to a long and high stone wall that spiraled up a hill. She explained that this was the old Swain House. An old woman died here after living in it for 95 years. Her nephew, who lived in London, was putting it up for sale.

"Maybe we can buy it and live in it," Christine said.

"Sure, you chip in five hundred thousand dollars, and I'll chip in the other five hundred thousand," Caden snapped back.

"Wow, you guys must get great allowances," I said, huffing and puffing after the long bike ride.

"Shhh. Let's go. I told my aunt that we'd be quiet," Caden ordered.

Clicking on her flashlight, she waved the beam across the wide driveway. We followed her slowly up the steep, cobblestone driveway that wound snake-like up a hill. When we got to the top, we laid our bikes down. It was hard to make out the property in the darkness that shrouded us. We were at the mercy of Caden's flashlight, or *torch* as she liked to call it, being a fan of BBC television.

Her beam was aimed on the house. It looked very old and elegant, made with lots of stone and green painted wooden siding. It was designed like a little castle. There were a couple of attic turrets that looked pretty spooky, but I'd seen *spooky* before...it was ghosts that I had come to see.

Christine pointed for me and instructed, "Back door, over there."

We stepped across the driveway, our feet crunching the dry, chunky gravel as we walked. Caden clicked in the key, and the heavy wooden door opened with, of course, an ominous squeaky creak.

"Light's got to be around here someplace," she whispered to herself, feeling around the wall just inside the open door.

Click. A small but welcome nightlight warmed the kitchen in a creamy off white glow. Christine poured a line of salt at the floor by the door and looked over at me, expecting me to ask again what she was doing.

I just nodded at her. "I know...keeps out demons."

Caden signaled for us to get close together in the center of the kitchen. "A girl died here in the late 1800's by falling down the stairs," Caden whispered as if someone, or something, was listening.

"Her older brother fell down those same stairs two years later. His name was Jacob," Christine pointed out. "Bet her ghost pushed him. He lives here, too," she added. "Right, Caden?"

"Shush!" Caden scolded. "You don't know that she pushed him on purpose. You'll get her mad at us."

"You don't know she didn't," Christine challenged.

Sighing, she looked away from Christine back to me. "Anyway, their ghosts are still here. I know you think I'm crazy with your science and matter and molecules and all that *E equals ms squared*, but I've really seen and heard stuff."

"It's E equals mc squared, and I don't think you're crazy. I wouldn't be here if I thought you were crazy," I reassured her.

I hoped ghosts waited for me to find them and felt this would be the night. It all felt so right. I felt like I was ready to open the biggest, most well-wrapped present on Christmas morning.

"Last time we were here with my aunt, after we went from the kitchen to the dining room, that door there, slammed behind us," she said pointing.

"Wind?" I asked, always trying to cover all the variables.

"There was no wind. Then I heard piano music coming from upstairs," she added.

"Was someone up there?" I asked, knowing what she would say.

Caden spread a beam of light up onto the kitchen ceiling and held up a hand directing us to stand very still. "No, no person of flesh and bone was up there. And there's no piano up there either," she eerily whispered.

"Whoa!" I whispered back.

"Tell her about the voices...tell her," Christine coaxed.

"After we had gone upstairs looking for the music, we heard a little girl's voice calling out for her mama. *'Mama...Mama...'* like that."

"Could it have been a bird outside a window?"

"Why are you questioning all of this?" she snapped. "I thought you believed me."

I had to remind myself to stop being such a skeptical scientist. I was starting to annoy them, and I needed to keep them on my side. *Don't be such a nerd.* Oh, how I'd love to believe, I really would, but I really needed *proof.* I had to be sure.

"Sorry," was all I said. The less talking the better.

"Well...okay. You'll get your proof here...tonight," she guaranteed. "After we heard the little girl, my aunt knocked on the wall twice, and something responded with *three* knocks."

"Hairs on my arms are standing up!" Christine stammered.

"That's good. That's the paranormal static electricity from the ghosts that's making your hair act that way. They must be near," Caden explained.

Opening a drawer and pulling out a black, waxy candle and a box of matches, she swiped the match over the rough edge of the box. It flared up and the candle was lit, a big wagging tongue of flame, dancing, illuminating our way.

"Shhh." Caden prompted us to move forward and led the way into the wide darkness of the living room.

81

"Why not turn on the electric lights in here or use your *torch*," I asked, moving close so I could whisper into her ear.

"It'll ruin the static electricity of the spirits and scare them away. If you want to see ghosts tonight, it has to be by candlelight," she explained, growing a little impatient with my questions.

I found myself in a Victorian living room, so musty and old, thick with dark furniture and heavy curtains. This felt so creepy, but I was not afraid; on the contrary, excitement filled me. Would I finally see a ghost? A halo of light surrounded us as we crept around that old living room. Suddenly a chill ran through my body. This was like my dream, walking in the dark with only a single candle to illuminate my way. Once I became composed and convinced myself that this was not a dream, I peered around the room and tried to see into the darkness that lay around us, the darkness that the candle could not permeate. I could make out the faint images on the painting that hung on the wall. It was of a grim old man, dressed in an ill-fitting black suit, perhaps the original owner of the house. The sofa and chairs were old velvet, overstuffed and soft. The thick, dark air was dense, musty, and still.

Caden stopped at the center of the room, beckoning us to stand next to her. Placing her finger to her lips, she silently instructed us not to utter a sound and called out in a long, loud whisper. "Jacqueline, hello. Don't be frightened. This is Caden. Remember me? I'm here with Christine and Annie. We won't hurt you. We just came to meet you. Annie especially wants to meet you because she heard what a beautiful, wonderful girl you are."

She turned to me and explained in a slow whisper how you have to introduce yourself and reassure a ghost that you mean no harm, otherwise she might not appear. Some ghosts are shy, some suspicious, and some are scared of humans.

"Aren't *we* the ones who are supposed to be afraid?"

"Shhh!" she scolded.

Caden whispered out into the darkness again. "Jacqueline, if you are here, knock three times on the wall for us to hear your presence."

My ears strained to the point that I could have heard an ant doing pushups, but there was no knocking.

"*Please*, come out and play with us, Jacqueline," she called out in her most reassuring voice. "Let's play a game, okay? I'll stomp on the floor a certain number of times and then you knock on the wall that same number. Okay? Doesn't that sound like fun? If you knock the same number as my stomps, you win! That sounds like fun, doesn't it? Bet you like to win."

"That's quite a childish tone. How old *was* she?" I whispered into Caden's ear.

"She was six years old when she fell down the stairs and broke her neck."

"Oh, oh my," I sighed sympathetically.

"Here goes, Jacqueline. Ready? Let's have some fun."

Her boot stomped onto the floor twice. We listened, straining again into the depths of the darkness. There was no response…nothing.

"Come on, Jacqueline. I know you can win. This is an easy game to play. We played this last time I was here with my aunt," she pleaded.

Caden banged down on the floor hard just once. Still, nothing but silence followed. The silence was suddenly broken by Christine's loud scream.

"Huh! What?" Caden jumped and yelped.

"Jacqueline just touched me!" Christine screamed.

I leaped back, momentarily frightened, but regained my focus and searched intently behind Caden for a ghostly form.

Caden turned with a start and saw Christine tapping on her shoulder silently with wide, frightened eyes.

"What?" Caden angrily hissed.

The frightened girl took her tapping finger and turned it upwards. "I…I heard something upstairs. I think our friend might be upstairs," she puffed out a barely audible whisper.

"Let's go," Caden hissed, waving her arm, signaling for us to follow as she walked towards a large staircase to our left. We stayed very close, as we dissolved into the darkness. I strained to listen again as we were quietly climbing up the warped hardwood stairs.

"Be careful on these stairs. They're old," Caden warned.

"You think?" I quipped.

At the top of the flight she waved the candle around. A long dark hallway beckoned straight ahead of us. Through the yellow mist of candlelight, it looked infinite in length. Another set of stairs lay to our right.

"There are about six rooms ahead," Caden pointed out, as if she had read my mind.

"Are we going up more?" I asked.

"No, they just lead to the big turret room on the roof. We're walking straight ahead to the second room on the right. That was Jacqueline's old bedroom," she whispered as if talking about an old relative.

The old wooden floor squealed under our feet as we moved softly with kitten's feet-like steps. When we got to the bedroom, Caden pushed the door open. A cold chill ran down my spine, and my heart pounded in my chest in anticipation, as before us lay a girl's room directly from 1889, bathed in the faint orange glow of the candle. It was like a "mind's eye" memory. I felt we were defiling this poor girl's privacy. A tiny bed of white linen was covered with old wooden and bisque dolls that must be worth a fortune now. There was a wooden rocking horse in the corner and a dresser with old metal and wooden toys. At the head of the bed was a big pillow that read, "Welcome to Atlantic City, New Jersey." We leaned our heads in to take in the sight, none of us willing to go in yet.

"Caden, is…?" I tried to ask.

"Yes. They left the room just the way it was when Jacqueline died that day. When the house passed on to the new owners, they had to agree to keep the room clean, but unchanged. Each new owner kept their word. No one touched anything. I don't know whether it was out of respect…or fear."

"Listen! Do you hear that!" Christine gasped, pointing into the room.

"It's just the wind," I pointed out unimpressed. "Hear it in the trees?"

"Oh," she sighed, a little disappointed and embarrassed.

"Shhh," Caden again instructed us. "I'm going to try again." Motioning for us to stay by the door, she took two careful steps into the bedroom.

"Jacqueline, we love your room. It's so pretty. I love the flowers on your wallpaper, and the dolls are so sweet. I'm Caden, and I've brought Christine and Annie here to meet you. Can you say *Hello* to us?"

Our ears ached attentively, but only registered silence.

"Jacqueline, could you knock on the wall? Let's play a game. I'll knock on the wall. *Da…da…ta…da…ta.* And then you return with two knocks, *da…ta,* okay? And you'll win the game. Annie would love to see you win."

"Me too." added Christine, looking around the room, hoping to get on Jacqueline's good side too.

"Shhh!" Caden protested angrily, shooting Christine a look of disdain. "Ready, Jacqueline?" she whispered again with her syrupy, child-like voice.

You could tell Caden was getting a little testy and impatient with her ghost, and us. Her promise of showing me a ghost wasn't looking too good right now. Angrily, she tapped on the wall with that old familiar beat 'Da…da…ta…da…ta.' We waited, daring not to breathe.

Please, Jacqueline, I thought. *Please knock.*

Repeating her knocking signal again only resulted in thick, frustrating silence.

"You can win, Jacqueline. Please," Caden begged.

Again and again she knocked, followed by the only sound that could be heard, the faint October wind outside.

"I really heard her that other time. I really did," Caden sighed apologetically. "Jacqueline!" she yelled out in frustration, momentarily losing her cool, but quickly composing herself.

"Jacqueline, I'm sorry I yelled at you, but I really, really wanted you to meet my friend Annie. I told her all about you. How nice you are and how sweet you are. It'd make her, and me, so happy to hear you. Please if you're here. Give us a sign!"

No sign came...nothing. I guess she didn't want to make us happy. *I knew it, another fraud, proof that there were no ghosts,* I thought. Science wins. Damned science wins again. Yet I resisted feeling sorry for myself. I tried to reserve judgment and tried to keep an open mind. Maybe this Jacqueline was frightened by me. Perhaps she could sense my doubt of her existence, like a horse senses fear. Who knows, perhaps she was out haunting another mansion somewhere or trick or treating—after all, it was Halloween. Maybe she had a thing for candy corn.

Caden let out a deep sigh of resignation. "Let's go. We're done here, girls." We were led down the stairs, still very carefully, but without so much ceremony. "I know they're here," she muttered to herself. "We heard them... both of them."

When we were firmly planted on the living room rug again, it suddenly dawned on her. "Both!" Caden remembered excitedly. "Jacob! I forgot about Jacob! *Jacob* might be here!"

Holding the candle high over her head, she called out optimistically. "Jacob, it's me Caden. We brought Annie, who would love to meet you. Pretty, isn't she, Jacob? And she's smart, with mousy brown hair, and she's not seeing anyone at the moment."

"Shush!" I blurted. "What are you trying to do, fix me up with a ghost? Are you nuts? And by the way, my hair's not mousy!"

"I'm just trying to lure him out," she whispered, gazing around for signs of Jacob's ghost.

"And you're using *me* for the bait?" I protested, also gazing around for the boy.

"A ghost would be better than ninety per cent of the boys in our class."

"Hmm, you have a point there...Hey! Wait...what was that?" I grabbed tightly onto Christine's shoulder and turned my eyes to the wall where the thick, musty curtains hung blocking out a big window.

"I heard it too!" Christine gasped, placing a shaking hand atop mine. "Over there!" she cried out, pointing in the area where a large ornate sofa sat in front of the window.

"Shush!" Caden ordered. "It's here…here. I feel it…I mean *him*…Jacob. I'm going to tap three times. If you're here, please tap back to us."

Pausing a long nervous moment, she knocked upon the wall three times slowly. It took just a second for the sounds to return to us. Three loud bangs on the wall! Caden and Christine screamed out. I listened and stared intensely at this profound moment of truth, this moment that could rock my view of the universe forever. Finally, my epiphany! *Be real, Jacob, be real,* I prayed.

"Jacob, is…is…that you?" Caden stammered with giddiness, surprised and shocked at her success.

Suddenly, I felt a moment of awe, and a chill ran down my spine as the ghostly figure of a boy rose up from the sofa. My mouth gaped as my mind spun in wonder. There was a whole new universe to learn about. Christine screamed and ran into the kitchen.

"Jacob! Welcome! Tell me…" Caden implored excitedly.

But before she could finish, a voice growled, "Jacob's going to suck your blood!"

It came towards us. We could see red fluid dripping from his eyes and nose. Caden screamed in terror and grabbed onto me. Suddenly two more figures rose from behind the sofa and let out blood curdling screams.

"Annie!" she cried, squeezing so hard I thought my ribs would crack.

In an instant, the living room exploded with lights that flooded the room, revealing three dancing flashlights followed by the howls of boys' screeches and laughter.

"What the…" I growled.

"You should have locked the door behind you," taunted the boy who had risen first. "You never know what kind of creatures might sneak in after you!"

"Snuffy Brodie! You idiot! What do you think you're doing?" Caden barked, aiming her candle at him like a sword ready to stab.

"We're channeling Jacqueline and Jacob and Casper," Jay Holimer taunted, waving his arms over his head.

"Yeah, Casper's the friendly one," said the third boy, whom I didn't recognize.

"You're pathetic!" Caden scolded.

I just stood crestfallen. My beautiful, scary ghost, it was right there—

my gateway to a whole spirit filled universe—and then, poof, some dopey boys ruined it.

"Hey, you're the ones who banged on walls and asked ghosts to come out and play. That sounds pretty idiotic to me," Snuffy shot back, shining his flashlight directly into her eyes.

"Yeah?" she barked, stepping toward him and slapping the flashlight from his hands. "Well, the ghosts are real, and you guys are just jerks. You could have scared someone half to death. You're not funny; you're idiots."

"Hey, Annie, if Jac the Ghost doesn't want to meet you, you can have my number," Jay shouted from across the room, breaking into gales of laughter.

"If it's your IQ, I have it already, moron...it's 37," I returned.

"Whoa! Burn! That girl got you, Jay! Actually, Annie, you're about two points too high," Snuffy taunted.

Christine, who had hidden under a table in the kitchen, finally came back into the living room after she had heard that all the commotion was produced by mere mortals.

"They aren't really ghosts?" she asked with tempered relief.

"No...just idiots," Caden explained, turning her back on the boys. "You guys better get out now. If my aunt, the realtor, finds out that you guys broke into her house, you'll be in for real big trouble."

"Yeah. I hear those realtors are tough," Snuffy mocked.

I crashed down upon the big, purple sofa, as far from the boys as I could get. The screaming and the arguing had just faded into noise. I had been silly to think that I was so close. There were no ghosts, just scary, stupid boys. Maybe Anthony was right. This quest of mine might just be a colossal waste of time

"Let's go, guys. I guess there are no ghosts *and* no sense of humor here," Jay instructed them.

"If we saw something *funny*, we'd have a sense of humor," Caden added angrily, pointing an accusing finger.

"Yeah, like your faces," Christine punctuated.

The boys marched by us laughing and giving each other congratulatory slaps on their backs. "We can take a hint," Snuffy laughed, tapping Caden on the head playfully as he led the trio into the kitchen.

"Girls have no sense of humor. A little Goosey Night prank, and they get their feathers in a ruffle," Jay called back as they disappeared out the door.

"Goosey night? It's Halloween, idiot!" Caden snapped.

"Let's egg *their* houses!" Christine demanded.

"Hey," she explained excitedly like a little light bulb had gone off over her head. "That probably explains why Jacqueline didn't respond to us. Those stupid boys probably spooked her. Want to try again?"

I could not believe that she wanted to try this again. *Be polite, Annie.*

"No, not tonight, it's getting late. I have homework…and a book to finish. Thank you for trying so hard," I said, checking my watch.

I reflected on Nettie Stevens and that "Y" chromosome that gives boys their XY maleness and how it makes boys so different—especially what they find funny, like burps and farts, scaring people, and things that are so infantile. Is there a *silly gene* on there…or perhaps a gene that stunts maturity until the age of twenty-five or so? I know their "Y" is so much smaller than our second X in our XX. Maybe they're missing out on some enzymes, because boys are so different. Wow, are they ever different.

"Okay. They are *here* though. I know it," Caden explained, again trying to convince me.

"Who? Who's here?" I asked.

"Jacqueline and Jacob. They are here…probably right now. The boys spooked them. I've seen them, really. You do believe me, don't you?" she implored.

"I believe that you think they're here," I flatly returned moving gradually towards the kitchen.

"Do we have to give you back those fetishes?" Christine asked with sad eyes.

I could see her turtle hanging around her neck on a string. She seemed to really like it. "No. You both went through the trouble of bringing me here," I reassured her. "They're yours."

"Thanks, and…ah you're not as geeky as we thought. You're pretty cool," Christine gratefully replied.

"Thanks, and you're not as weird as I thought. You're pretty cool too, both of you."

"Thanks. Yeah…I heard about your grandma, being sick and all. I hope she's okay," Caden said with genuine sincerity as she followed me into the kitchen.

I had to stop and gaze at her with new found respect and fondness. In that moment, she went from being this character in a haunted house to a caring human being right before my eyes.

"Thank you," I said with equal sincerity.

I stopped right in front of the door that had been left open by the boys, the cold night breeze blowing into the kitchen. "Thank you," I repeated. "Well, she's been better, not really herself, but they're taking good care of her at a nursing home. It's the Sunshine Nursing Home, you know, that old spooky looking mansion on Oak Street."

"What?" they both exclaimed, their faces registering immediate shock. They looked at each other, then at me. Christine looked like she had just seen a ghost...or worse, a vampire.

"Did you say the Sunshine Home?" Caden asked with keen interest and awe.

"Yeah...why?" I looked back and forth at their faces. "What's up?" I asked nervously.

"You...who are so fascinated by ghosts never heard of the Lupescu Mansion?" Caden quizzed.

I remembered that name from my first visit. The nurse told me about that rich family that gave it up so it could be used as a nursing home. Sounded like an Eastern European name.

"You're talking about The Sunshine Home, right?" I said.

"Yeah, that's what they call it now...ironic name change."

"No, I don't know much about the house. All I know is that it's a nursing home, a very old nursing home judging by the looks of it, donated by a rich family."

"Well, you should learn about it. We try to avoid it. We like benevolent spirits like Jacqueline and Jacob. That Lupescu curse creeps us out big time," Christine added.

"Curse?" I asked, giving them a look of interest. "What's that about?"

"You should read about it yourself, but be careful there. Be very careful," Caden warned, looking at me long and hard. "Once you read about it, I know that you'll try to explore and find out what or who's in there. Please don't. Come back here again one day with me, but don't...don't explore that house."

I looked past her as we stepped out onto that crunchy gravel driveway into the crisp October night. I looked long and hard.

What could be in that mansion?

THEY'RE HERE YOU KNOW

9

THE GOTH TWINS! You went ghost hunting with the Goth Twins?" Anthony asked as I quickly scarfed down my grilled cheese and apple sauce lunch so I could get back to the bio lab to work on my cockroach experiment.

"Shhh! They'll hear you!"

"They're sitting all the way across the cafeteria. They would need the hearing of bats to…" He gazed over at them, examining them like specimens in a jar, dressed completely in black, vampire-like, munching on carrot sticks and kale. "Maybe they can hear like bats," he mocked lowering his voice.

"Yes, I did go with them. They promised to show me ghosts."

"Let me guess…" Pretending to be deep in thought, he tapped his head like a psychic. "You went with them and wasted the night, not ever seeing a ghost."

"Look, I knew that you wouldn't like me doing my paranormal business with them, but I had to pursue every avenue," I confessed.

"But they're nutty, and they scare me," he said, glancing over in their direction again.

I looked over at Caden and Christine. I thought how, if only people got to know them, they wouldn't think of them as Gothic, vegetarian, vampiric, fetish hoarders. They were nice. They were kind of sweet.

I placed my hand on his chin and turned his head away from them and back to me. "Look, I wouldn't have even mentioned it you—it's my inquiry—but something very odd happened as we were leaving."

"I don't like you hanging around with them!" he said like he was my dad, which didn't thrill me at all.

"I'm not hanging around with them. They took me to see ghosts! And what if I *did* want to hang around with them? That's my business, not yours! Actually, they're very nice. Maybe you can learn something about tolerance from them."

I cut myself short because I didn't like the harsh tone I was taking with him, although I was taken aback by *his* tone. Now it was *his* turn to be the scolded puppy. He avoided eye contact as an uncomfortable fog settled over our lunch table.

"Not only did the girls know about the Sunshine Home, but they seemed really frightened by it. The Goth Twins, frightened by my grandmother's nursing home! That says a lot."

"Why?" he asked, grateful to be on a new topic.

"They wouldn't say. They told me to find out about the mansion myself, to research it."

Leaning close, he whispered, "I told you that the upper floors were very strange and amazing, like a whole different world from the care center on the first floor—very opulent and creepy. And that guy seemed pretty upset that I was exploring up there."

I looked hungrily at my Honey Crisp apple and decided to wrap it up and save it for after school. I had work to do in the lab. Without looking his way, I asked Anthony, "Would you come to the library with me one day to help me research the house? I think we're going to need more than the Internet. I think we're going to have to go through town documents and old newspaper records."

Suddenly a hand slapped down onto our table, interrupting our conversation. "Hi, guys!"

It was Chloe Rockerman with her usual vapid smile. She had to have something she wanted from us. She never socialized except when needing something from somebody.

"Hi, Chloe," I answered with a flat, yet polite tone.

"Just wanted to remind you two that Student Council elections are next week, and I hope I have your votes for President!"

Her mouth contorted into that big, fake smile that all politicians share with potential voters; there must be a gene for that.

"Why should we vote for you, Chloe? What can you offer us?" Anthony asked with fake concern.

I jabbed him hard in the ribs, knowing he was just baiting Chloe. It was a foregone conclusion that she would win. We were a school of future engineers and scientists, and few of us wanted to get into politics. I think a freshman boy was running against her just as a goof. Her opponent was promising that, if he won, he would have a swimming pool built on the school's roof, a particle accelerator built in the basement, and video games would be part of the curriculum. However, Chloe saw him as a real threat and was campaigning hard as the election approached.

Chloe paused a moment, as if trying to visualize her campaign speech. "Well, I've been an honors student for three years, and I was historian of the Chemistry Club last year. I'm trustworthy and honest and promise to do my best." The candidate smiled again at him.

"No, I mean…" he continued, holding his side where I had jabbed him. "What can you actually do for us? A swimming pool on the roof would be great! Perhaps ice cream making machines in each class."

Chloe's face broke into a frown. "Those things would be cost prohibitive," she sighed, thinking that we had fallen in with evil freshman's camp. "Those things are impossible."

"A good president would find a way."

"Chloe," I broke in, "you have our votes. You are a person of integrity," I assured her. "You were probably the best Chemistry Club historian that this school ever had."

A genuine smile broke over her face. "Why, thank you! Thank you, Angie," she gushed with great relief. Moving closer to me, she whispered, "I think I'll need every vote. That freshman is running a tough campaign."

"You'll do fine," I reassured her, "and, the name is *Annie*."

"Oh yes, *Annie*. That's right. Of course, Annie." Walking away nodding her head, she moved to the next table to beg for more votes. I hoped that she remembered their names.

"That was mean," I chided Anthony, nudging him playfully in the ribs again.

"Ouch!" he groaned, pretending to be hurt by my slight nudge.

"Forget that. Let's get back to what I was saying. Will you help me research the mansion?"

"Sounds very interesting. Sounds like a detective movie. How about today?" he said anxiously.

"I'd like to, but I'm going to visit Sunshine Home after school."

"Ah, the scene of the crime! Tomorrow then?" It was obvious that he was very anxious to get on my good side.

"No, that doesn't work either. I'm meeting with a psychic."

"A psychic? Why?" he asked sarcastically.

He knew very well why. I had told him that I wanted to see if they could really communicate with the dead. He was just teasing me, and this was not the day to tease. I just ignored his question and wrapped my apple.

He sighed.

"But we have to do this soon, before the weekend," I explained.

"You seem pretty excited about this investigation into the Sunshine Home."

93

I could sense that he was excited, too. He had seen the upstairs and was quite impressed. I was sure he was intrigued. Besides, he loved crime movies.

I corrected him. "Let's call it by its name, the Lupescu Mansion, and yes, I am. Remember me telling you that my Nonna had promised me a resolution to my spiritual quest and that she would always be there to answer my questions?"

"You mean your ghost hunt."

"Whatever. Don't you see, she's doing it in her own mysterious way. Somehow she must have gotten my mom to place her in this home to get me there."

"Why do you think that your grandmother wants to get you into that mansion? What's so important?"

"It's got to be haunted. Why else would the Goth Twins be frightened of it? The Goth Twins aren't afraid of anything."

"Maybe there's a math test waiting for them there," he said sarcastically, peeking their way again. He gulped down the last of his water and wiped his mouth with his sleeve.

"Recycle the bottle," I reminded him.

"I know, I know. I threw a bottle away in the garbage by mistake last week, and now you think I'm working for DuPont. I'm ecologically aware. Hey…how's the cockroach soul experiment coming?"

"That's why I'm rushing. I had a breakthrough on control of the insecticide's mass, so I'm free to assume that any loss of mass upon its death would be accounted for by the loss of a soul," I pronounced proudly.

Trying not to smirk, he stifled a fake cough.

I explained to him that, instead of spraying it in, I was going to take a very measured drop and apply it through a tube. Once inside the *death tank*, as I liked to call it, it would vaporize and kill the cockroach! It would be so much easier to control the mass of the insecticide that way.

"Aren't you worried about complaints, protests, and angry Tweets from PACT?" he said much too seriously.

"PACT? Never heard of them."

"You know, People Against Cockroach Torture. They're a very powerful lobby! Saw a heart-rending commercial on television the other night with them asking for donations. Little roaches looking sadly out of cages, destitute bugs hanging out in Roach Motels, people wearing clothing made of cockroach exoskeletons. It moved me to tears." His sarcasm dripped all over the table.

"How about People Against Annoying Boyfriends?" I offered clumsily, the word *boyfriend* sneaking out of my mouth before I had a chance to catch it and swallow it. Its awkwardness struck me speechless.

Anthony tilted his head towards me, trying to discern if he had heard the word correctly. There was an anxiousness in his face, while mine was red and perplexed.

"I mean…" I corrected with scarlet cheeks glowing, "*Against Annoying Friends.*"

There, awaiting me, was the coward's way out; I excused myself to avoid any more discussion on any topic, especially word usage. I rushed out, grabbing his plastic water bottle. I slammed it into the recycling can and hurried out to the lab. He just watched me as I walked quickly away, with a half-hearted smirk on his face. Knowing as a scientist that my use of the phrase *boyfriend* had many possible explanations but too many variables to jump to a conclusion, as a boy, he still smirked because he knew there was hope. Boys are well known as a species that holds onto hope much too long in these situations.

Later that day, Anthony told me that after the cafe door closed behind me, he felt a tap on his shoulder. It was Caden. There was a dark scowl on her face that her black lipstick and her newly painted on fangs elevated to "horror movie death scene" in his mind.

"Hey, I don't care if you are a junior. I don't care if you're going to MIT. It's not nice to call people 'nutty.' I think you're dull, and it scares me that my friend Annie hangs out with *you.*"

Then, she stomped away

"Holy…she did hear me!" he marveled to me. "It left me speechless. All I could do as she walked away was to utter meekly, *Yes, ma'am. Sorry.*"

"Good for her!" I laughed, applauding her.

§ § §

November could be such a gray and a sad month. After the brilliant festival of fall color, leafless trees, a chill, and clouds seemed to dominate. But what kept me going was that there would always be a rebirth come spring. Dead brown leaves crunched under my wheels like stale crackers as I biked to Sunshine Home, or, as I needed to refer to it now, the Lupescu Mansion. The cold chill of the air and the featureless gray sky hinted that winter was just around the corner, as was the mansion. It loomed in front of me now, looking larger and more ominous, but I knew that this might just be my holy grail, if, as the Goth twins had hinted, it was haunted.

The uncertainty of Nonna's mood each time I visited always numbed me a bit as I waited and pressed the button so they could unlock the gate. Would she be the sweet little lady who would smile at me and talk optimistically about her news that she had found a house to move into or about imaginary people who had befriended her and were going to help her out of her *situation*? Or would she be the angry old woman who thought I was some demon from her past and accuse me of all kinds of crimes against her and her pocketbook? There was a chill of foreboding each time that door opened, and it wasn't a temperature drop due to the presence of ghosts.

A new face greeted me at the door. "Hello, young lady. You're here to see whom today?"

The staff changes often. I was told that they switched hours or just couldn't take the sadness of the home and went to nurse in a place where the old people were less needy.

"I'm here to see Toni. I'm her granddaughter."

I could always tell by the response when I said *Toni* what kind of visit it was going to be…an on-meds or off-meds day. That look was the *canary in the mineshaft* for me. They predicted the mood of my visit, like in the old days, the death of a canary hung in a cage in a coal mine warned miners about poison gas exposure.

"Oh…" Her eyes looked downward. This was going to be a bad visit.

"Grandma's in her room right now, honey. Your poor grandma had an angry outburst this morning at breakfast with one of the nurses who tried to help her. Not a good day, I'm afraid to say."

"Thank you," I politely responded.

Sighing deeply, I girded myself as I approached her closed door. My chest tightened, and my breathing turned shallow. On the door was her name in big bold letters to help remind her that this was her room. There was a paper turkey that Kevin had made for her in school and a heart with glitter on it that I had made. The doors were rarely closed. Residents wandered aimlessly into each other's rooms out of curiosity or bewilderment. In their diminished states, they would take each other's things, not out of larceny, just out of confusion.

My Nonna had a photo of Fritz, a big German Shepherd, a wrestling trophy, and a photo of two African American boys posing for a football team photo on her dresser. I had no idea where they had come from. *My* photo that I gave her ended up in Albert's room for a week until I retrieved it and put it back on her dresser.

Before I could raise my fist to gently knock, I heard sobbing from inside and gently pressed my ear up against her door. I strained to listen. She was sobbing so hard. Between sobs I could hear her pleas. "Oh, God, why am I like this? Why did you do this to me? I'd rather be dead. What did I do to be here…like this?"

I moved away from the door, heartbroken for her, a prisoner in this place, a prisoner in her mind. Why should she have to suffer so much? Last week she had been so bitterly sad, and it was horrible to see her that way again today. It tore at my soul and made me feel so guilty. The nurses said if she didn't take her medication she had these moments of reality and reflection, little bursts of neurons that still had clear connections, and the awful truth just devastated her. There was nothing I could do or say when she was like this, so I moved away from the door. It was time to go.

As I went out, I spotted that girl again sitting by the old, white-haired woman. What a sweet kid, to visit here so much. That was so nice. But she wasn't talking with the woman today, just holding one of her hands as they both stared forlornly out the window. I guess this was just a sad day in the home for everyone. Then I felt a tug on my sweatshirt sleeve. It was a tiny old woman, round of face and body, her hair tied in a bun.

"They didn't give me toast. Could you tell them to give me toast with my coffee, please?"

"I gave you two slices of toast at breakfast, Dorothy," bellowed a voice from inside the kitchen area. "Don't bother the young lady. Go sit down at the table. I'll get you one more slice, but you know you have to watch your sugar."

"Thank you," the lady said to me with a smile.

A much taller and younger woman sidled up to Dorothy, touched her shoulder, and whispered loudly into her ear. I assumed she was another nurse, since she was so young, but to my surprise she was a patient there also.

"Do you think we can trust her?" she asked Dorothy, referring to me. They eyed me with interest and suspicion.

"Oh, she looks like a nice person. I'm sure we can."

"Then ask her."

"You think she'll do it?" Dorothy asked.

"Ask her," the taller woman prompted her again.

Dorothy turned back to me. "Could you bring me my car? It's in the driveway. Oh, Lord, I hope I didn't keep the engine running." Putting her hands to her face, she tried to remember if she had left her engine running. "Oh my, I hope I didn't forget to turn that darn thing off. They'll yell at me again, telling me I'm old and forgetful."

"Could you, please?" the taller woman chimed in, giving me a cheerful smile.

I was guessing that the two of them had an escape plot they were brewing, like *Thelma and Louise*. I had learned from the nurses just to placate their fantasies. "Just say *yes*," instructed the nurse who had come over to bring Dorothy back to the table.

"Oh...sure...I'll bring your car here later. Maybe tomorrow."

Dorothy sighed and smiled again at me. "See, I told you she looked nice," she reassured her friend.

"Okay, now you two come back to the breakfast table and finish your apple sauce," the nurse told them. Their medications were always in the apple sauce or pudding. It was sneaky but effective. "That would be some sight, you two trying to drive your cars again. I would pay to see that," she added with a wide grin.

They laughed, too. Dorothy waved and called me over to the table. "Could you ask them to get me a piece of toast? They never give me toast."

"Sure, I will, and I'll get your car, too," I answered, moving closer to the door.

"What car?" the tall one asked with a mouthful of applesauce.

"Leave the girl alone, you two," the nurse repeated. "Nobody comes here to see you two busy bodies; she came to see Toni. Go ahead, honey. Next time you come your grandma will be in a better mood, I'm sure. They all have their ups and downs."

I had to ask. "Ah...do you know anything about the history of this place. It seems pretty old."

"It is old, isn't it? Well I'm sorry, but I just started here a few days ago. Maybe Nurse Lauren can help you. I don't think that she's here right now, but I do understand that she's been here the longest," she said, placing a spoonful of apple sauce with pill into Dorothy's open mouth.

"Right. Okay. Thank you," I said, nodding and backing off, feeling guilty for my question. I didn't think I was cut out to be a detective. I peeked over to the stairway that Anthony had referred to. There was a fence blocking access to the stairs with a new sign, *KEEP OUT!*

"Next time," I whispered to myself.

"Your grandma is lucky to have a granddaughter who visits her. I guess not too many children want to come here to visit. It's tough for them to take, seeing people act this way," the nurse said with a curt little wave as she sunk her spoon into the apple sauce jar. "That lady is lucky to have you."

"I guess. Thank you," I answered with more than a hint of sadness as I reached for the front door.

As I rode away, the word *lucky* bounced around in my head like a rotten apple. *Lucky* was the last thing I thought she was.

THEY'RE HERE YOU KNOW

10

MOM LOOKED DOWN at the oatmeal that I had cooked—it was one of my specialties. My mom revealed a hint of pride as she announced that she had visited Nonna in the nursing home. Major achievement! I knew how hard it was for her to set foot in there.

"On my way home from work yesterday, I dropped off some cookies. I talked to grandma for a few minutes. She didn't have a clue who I was, and, to be honest, it took me a few moments to recognize her. Oh my, she's aged so much just in the last few months."

I nodded, knowing exactly what she meant.

"But she was pleasant, to my great relief. I know how she can get."

Reaching across the table, I put my hand on her arm. I told her how proud I was of her, and how Nonna really appreciated visitors even though she didn't seem to recognize them. It broke her tedium and made her happy that someone cared.

Looking up from her oatmeal, she put her hand on mine. "You're so strong. You've always been the strength in this family...how do you stand it there? I mean, I was there for about ten minutes, and I was so depressed and uncomfortable; all those sad people just...just waiting to die." Pulling her hand away, she looked back into her oatmeal. "I'm sorry, that was a terrible thing to say," she whispered.

"That's okay, Mom. Do you know I felt the same way when I first visited, and so did Anthony, but when you get to deal with some of the patients, they actually are pretty sweet and even funny."

"You're a good girl," she said touching my hand again.

"I've been told," I sighed, always wondering about the truth in that.

She pushed the oatmeal away, took a couple of sips of her coffee, turned, and gave me a long, loving look. "You've been so busy lately with school and science fair and visiting Grandma. We haven't had much time to talk."

"Yeah, I know."

"Still hunting ghosts?" she asked with a little smirk, along with a long, warm look.

"Yes, that's what I do. It's what I need to do," I responded in a very official manner.

Reaching over, she took hold of my hand again. "My little Annie, Ghost Hunter. I hope that you're finding time for fun things, too."

I placed my other hand atop hers. "Mom, I'm having a ball."

Standing up, she came over to me and kissed me gently on the forehead. "My little scientist," she said. Then she pulled back and gave me a look of disbelief recalling my science fair theme. "Cockroaches? Really?"

§ § §

Anthony was fifteen minutes late getting to the library for our research into the Lupescu Mansion. The library was just about empty except for three sixth grade boys off at a corner table giggling and pointing as they leafed through a copy of a magazine that I assumed had scantily clad women in it. It was Saturday morning, so most kids were either at indoor soccer or basketball practice. I'd never been an athlete, but I wouldn't embarrass myself if I played soccer or did track. In fact, I did play soccer one year, but the screaming parents freaked me out. I didn't like the craziness. I preferred hunting ghosts.

My finger tapped on the walnut library table impatiently, annoyed at Anthony's tardiness. I gave him a stern, teacher-like stare as he finally pushed open the wooden door and rushed towards me. He acted cheerful to ward off my annoyance at his lateness.

"Hey!" he said in his library whisper.

"Hey, yourself. You're late," I scolded.

"Time is relative—just ask Einstein."

He sat down across from me and studied my face to sense if I was *really* angry. His hands rummaged around in his jacket pockets, pulled out a bag with two cinnamon raisin bagels, my favorite, shoved one into his mouth, and held the other out to me.

"There's no eating in the library," I chided him, even though I appreciated the gesture, and the cinnamon smelled so good.

He waved the bagel under my nose. "Sniff," he suggested.

"Put them away!" I whispered harshly.

He pulled my bagel back, and then he took two giant bites of his and placed the two of them back into the paper bag in his jacket.

"You're hard to please, you know."

"You want to please me? Keep your appointments on time and follow library rules."

Squinting at me, he again looked into my eyes, as if trying to analyze the depth of my cranky mood. "Bad day with the psychic yesterday, huh?" he asked, remembering my appointment.

It was hard to hide things from him.

"How many have you visited so far?"

"Five, and they all were frauds!"

"I could have told you that. I could have saved you lots of time."

Ignoring his comment, I turned and pointed an instructing finger. "Houdini said he didn't believe in an afterlife, but I think deep down inside he believed it or wanted to believe it."

"Sounds like someone I know!" he chirped.

Ignoring that too, I went on in my proper library whisper, "Houdini tried to contact the spirit of his mother by going to scores of psychics, proving them all frauds and liars. As the world's greatest magician, I guess he knew all the tricks. Before he died, he made an arrangement with his wife to continue the search for the spirit world. His wife was to search out psychics to contact him after his death. To insure the truth, the two of them shared a secret code, a word that only the both of then knew, no one else."

Anthony put his hand into his lap. I heard the crinkling of the bagel bag. "What was the secret word?"

"His word was *believe*."

"Nice word," he said, as he snuck another bite of bagel.

I went on, "The great magician died on Halloween, and for years and years his wife went from psychic to psychic each Halloween. They would use all kinds of fakery, creating smoky images and false voices from the beyond, but if these "spirits" could not repeat their secret word, she knew that it was all fake. *Believe* was the key. Never did she find one true psychic."

"Why the Houdini lesson?" he asked with a bagel-filled mouth.

"Because I have a code I use with the spiritualists."

He swallowed the bagel down. "Oh yeah? Who are you trying to contact?" he whispered loudly with real interest.

"You!"

"Me?" he shouted.

I looked around. "Shush. We're still in a library, silly," I reminded him with mock sternness as I peered around the huge room to see if indeed anyone was even there to disturb. Those boys off in the corner were still in a rage of hormones over their magazines.

"Me?" he hissed again at a proper decibel level. "But I'm not dead."

"I know. That's why I use you. I went in to see Madam Kayla yesterday. She's downtown on Main Street. As always, when I visit these people, I'm teary eyed when I enter, holding a handkerchief and a picture of you when you were in kindergarten to remember you, my dear departed brother."

It was the cutest picture of him. He was standing on the top of a big concrete turtle that was in the playground at PS 27. He stood up straight and tall—tall for a five-year-old—a Burger King crown atop his head, hands on his hips, smiling proudly as if he had just scaled Mount Everest.

"But I'm not dead!" he whispered with insistence.

"Shush, or you will be. So I tell them that you were my brother, Clive."

I could see the word *brother* dim his eyes a bit.

"I weep and the lady consoles me. It's the same each time I visit one of them. This one, Madam Kayla, wanted to know about you, and I told her how you were a dim witted child and how you wandered away a lot."

"Great, I'm so flattered by your image of me."

"And one day you took your bike and rode it to the railroad tracks, listening to Justin Bieber on your iPod."

"Justin Bieber? Yes, Annie, kill me now," he said, horrified at the thought of being a "Belieber."

"Yeah, you had the volume so loud you didn't hear the train coming, and before it could stop…here, I get really choked up…the train ran you over. Madam Kayla, like each in turn, hugged me or held my hand to console me."

"I hate you," he hissed.

"That's not what the psychic said," I related in a sing-song teasing voice.

"What do you mean?"

"Well, after all the crying and consoling—they're very good at crying and consoling—Madam Kayla took your photo and clutched it firmly in her hands. Her eyes were closed tightly, and her face tilted towards the heavens. Then *you* came to us. Madam told me in hushed tones that Clive was in the room with us, that he was a little scared of being here, but he was happy to see me, his beloved sister. Then, she went silent for a short while, grimacing and nodding, as if you were communicating with her. Sighing, she wiped away more tears from her eyes and told me that Clive didn't want me to feel guilty that I didn't watch him close enough that tragic day and let him ride away from the house to his doom. She told me that you forgave me. Thanks, Clive. That's so sweet of you."

Anthony released an annoyed groan.

"I was told that you didn't feel any pain when you died and were in peace now."

"I didn't feel any pain? I was hit by a train! What kind of moron psychic is this?" he asked, taking another bite of his bagel.

"I was told that you love me very much and always will." Peeking up at him, I smiled. His cheek turned the appropriate shade of crimson. "She said that you look over me and protect me every day like a guardian angel, and you support me in my decision to become…a nun."

He choked on his mouthful of bagel. "A nun?"

"Yes. In our little pre-chat these so-called psychics always try to grill me before they do their spiritual stuff. This way they get some clues into what I might want to hear from the deceased. I told her that I went to St. Dominic's High School, how I'd like to teach someday, and how I admired the nuns. I guess that was supposed to be her big reveal."

"So, she was a fraud?"

"You think, Clive?"

"Do you call them out on their lies and deception after they give you all their fake information and insights?" he asked.

I had thought of doing that, to be real dramatic. I thought of screaming at them in front of their clients and accusing them of being frauds, telling them that they were leeches feeding off the lonely and broken hearted. But, I chickened out each time. It would be mean. I guess it does bring consolation to some to *hear* from their loved ones, even though it's fake. I guess fake love is better than none.

"No, I just thank them and leave."

"Am I always a brainless brother?" he asked grimacing.

"No, sometimes you're a foolish sister or an adopted brother. Once you were a conjoined twin. You were Sheldon, and my other brother was Leonard. But no matter who you are, you always forgive me and always love me…very much."

I smiled at him, waiting for the inevitable change of complexion that would make a chameleon envious. Then came that sad look that said, *why do you torture me like this?* Then he spoke in a very serious and soft whisper that made me lean closer to him.

"What if you found a *real* psychic? Who would you ask her to contact?"

I pulled back, my face flushed with discomfort. "That's…um, I don't know. It's not important." I lied. "Hey, we'd better get to digging into the Lupescu family history. Where do you want to start?"

He just looked at me for a moment, disappointed in my not answering his question, but he knew not to take it further. "Well, the Internet is the obvious starting point. I know that the town keeps its records of death certificates and newspaper stories in the basement. They go back hundreds of years."

"The Lupescus were Polish. Can we get information about them here?"

"If it's not on the Internet, we might have to contact the town where they came from in Poland. They probably have records of them there."

So, we began our search. I went on the library computer, while Anthony went downstairs into the basement to look at newspaper articles and death certificates. A few more people came into the library, mostly older people. They came by to take out a good book or to just spend some time reading. Finally, the librarian went over to those kids in the corner and gave them an ultimatum to either quiet down or leave the library. She took their magazines away and they left.

I typed in "*Lupescu family*" and got some fascinating choices.

Lupescu Family exiled from Romania

Lupescu Family rise to fortune in Poland

Lupescu Coal Industry

Polish Coal Strike and Massacre of 1863

Haunted Mansions of America

Of course, I researched them all, jotting down important bits of information that I could share when Anthony returned from the basement. "Haunted Mansions of America" would be saved for last. After about an hour, the librarian came by my cubicle.

"Finding everything okay, honey?" she asked.

It was nice of her to be helpful, but I also knew that she was probably checking to make sure I was on an appropriate website. They didn't trust teenagers. That was okay because *I* didn't trust teenagers either.

"Everything is fine. Thank you very much," I reassured her in my *honey* voice.

My research was finished after another fifteen minutes, just as I saw Anthony appear from the basement, or, as we referred to it, *The Dungeon*. Out of breath, he sat down next to me and looked at me with wide, anxious and excited eyes.

"Wow!" we both said simultaneously.

An elderly gentleman reading the *London Times* shot us a nasty look. We both lowered our voices to a hush.

"Wow," we repeated in a barely audible whisper.

"You want to go first?" he asked anxiously, placing two pages of penciled notes that he had taken on the table.

"Sure!" I explained excitedly. "The family origins were from Romania. *Lupescu* meant *Son of the Wolf.* They became notorious in the 15th century for taking money from both the Hungarians and the Turks, who were at war. They took their money to assassinate important leaders. They made lots of money but also lots of enemies.

Nodding, his face turned very serious. I cleared my throat.

"Now get this: it was rumored that in 1476 they assassinated Vlad III." Looking at him, I anticipated amazement that never came.

"Vlad III...You know, Vlad the Impaler!" I stressed, nodding my head as if he should have known that name.

"Whoa!" he gasped, knowing *the Impaler* reference.

The *London Times* guy shot us a nasty look again.

"Whoa. I know Vlad the Impaler, the origin of Bram Stoker's *Dracula*."

"*Dracul*," I corrected him in my very best Transylvanian accent. "That novel is entitled *Dracula*. All the movies say Dracula. But in Romanian it's Dracul."

He stood up slowly, ominously hovering above me, and spread his arms out like caped bat wings. "You are under my spell. Show me your neck. I am Dracula!" he threatened in a hushed Romanian accent.

"It's Dracul, and sit down!" I looked around embarrassed.

"Yes, please sit down!" the paper-reading man barked.

"Whatever...hey, this is heavy stuff," he added with great concern, as he sat back down.

"Vlad's former rival, his brother Radu, was given control over his territory, and the first thing he did was to banish the Lupescu family. They were banished with the curse of the House of the Dragon, a curse that would place a black cloud of bad luck wherever they went. They tried to settle in Hungary, but they were hated there as well for their treachery. After some time, they settled in the Silesia region of Poland. For centuries, they made a living through murder and thievery. Some of them settled down, bought properties, and built castles. In the 1850's they started mining coal on their lands, and they became filthy rich."

"Sounds like the curse didn't work," he pointed out.

"They paid their workers next to nothing for mining twelve hours a day under dangerous conditions. In 1863 the workers went on strike, only to be massacred by the Lupescu family's army of lackeys. That ended the strike, but the people of the region were appalled by the Lupescus' violent actions. With pitchforks and torches in hand, thousands marched to their doorsteps and forced them to leave."

"To America!" Anthony chimed in knowingly.

"Yes, Sigmund Lupescu moved to Pennsylvania, bought up land, and did what they did best, mined coal. Ironically, he was like a 'fossil fuel vampire,' ruthlessly sucking coal from West Virginia and Pennsylvania and destroying hundreds of hills and mountains while strip mining."

"That explains those murals upstairs I told you about. Then In 1893 Sigmund bought the mansion here where the nursing home is now." Beaming with pride, he unfolded the scribbled pencil items that the detective work down in the dungeon had uncovered.

"This is what I found down there. Sigmund was eighty-two years old when he had the mansion built, a wedding gift for his new bride, Krystyna, who was shipped over here from Poland by her parents. It was an arranged marriage. Poor, beautiful Krystyna was all of sixteen years old," he added.

"Sounds like true love to me." I imagined such a horror. I knew, as a teenage girl, you dream of marrying the perfect boy: handsome, kind, witty, smart, and at least born in the same century as you. What a heart break that must have been for poor Krystyna.

"Yeah, not quite *true love*. Sigmund was considered the most ruthless of all the Lupescu clan, the one who ordered the massacre in 1863. His favorite saying was, 'You can always hire new workers, but profits are fleeting and precious.'"

I interrupted him, not needing notes. "On the site for *Haunted Mansions in America,* it stated that the Lupescu Mansion is possessed by two spirits that wander the upstairs corridors. People have said that they've heard footsteps, sighs, and crying. Some people have said they've even seen two shadowy figures floating against the backdrop of those huge murals that you mentioned. What do you think? Are good ole Sigmund and Krystyna wandering the halls reliving their marriage made in heaven?"

"I think the marriage originated quite a bit lower than *heaven*. Sigmund paid off the parents and forced the poor girl to come to America, kicking and screaming. They had to have a guard travel with her to make sure that she showed up at the wedding. I made a copy of their wedding picture."

Leafing through his papers, he found the photo and slid it over to me. I felt so horrified, this hulking old man next to this poor wide-eyed waif.

Krystyna was all adorned in white frills and ruffles and bows. Her face, which was turned downward, was covered by a veil. No doubt she was weeping. Sigmund, on the other hand, should have had a veil. His face was long and oval shaped, with a large crooked nose like an Italian plague mask. Wrinkles and bags enveloped his face, and at what should have been a moment of joy, he scowled at the camera with piercing, hateful eyes.

"The newspaper said she was *kidnapped* twice, although it was suspected that she ran away, only to be returned by Sigmund's army of thugs. Then in 1895, she disappeared."

"Disappeared?" My eyes pulled away from the horrific image of Sigmund that was drawing me in hypnotically. "What do you mean, *disappeared*?"

"Police report from May 19th, 1895. The case of the missing person, Krystyna Lupescu, has been closed. Person not found," he read with a dark tone.

"Do you think she finally got away from him?" I asked hopefully.

"Small chance. An immigrant girl like that in a strange country and Sigmund with all his tentacles of power. It's very unlikely."

"Wow, *tentacles of power*. Good one."

"I could pretend that I made it up, but it was a phrase from the newspaper," he confessed.

"Do you think he killed her?" I whispered, looking around as if Sigmund might be sitting two tables down.

"Nobody ever turned up. Krystyna was never heard from again. It was a quick investigation that Sigmund I'm sure made go away by paying off the police. His young wife just disappeared, the report said."

I glanced at a copy of Sigmund's obituary. It said that he had died in 1905 at the age of 101.

"You know, only the good die young," Anthony sang, after he noticed what I was reading.

I put my head down and thought for a moment.

"I didn't make that up either, it's from Billy Joel, I think…" he confessed again.

"I know! Shhh. I was just thinking. If there are two ghosts up there, it can't be Sigmund and Krystyna, can it? That girl hated him. The Haunted Mansions site said that family members tried to live in the house over the years but were made to feel very uneasy and unwanted at night by *odd happenings*. Finally, the mansion was donated to create a nursing home by the last of the Lupescu European relatives. She thought that a good deed might cleanse the house and the family name."

"Maybe Sigmund's keeping her hostage up there for all eternity."

I thought for a long moment. "Or maybe there's more to the story than we've uncovered so far."

11

NONNA, HAVE YOU *brought me here to this house to show me my answer?* I thought as I pedaled hard on my way to the mansion.

I got off the bike and looked at the nursing home in an entirely different way now. The huge witch's hat on the main turret of the mansion now seemed so appropriate. My eyes were drawn to that upper floor, so foreboding, now that I knew the story, but so important to me. I couldn't help but think about that poor girl and what she had gone through. I paused at the gate. For me the whole place had consisted of my Nonna's room and the dining and living room; now there was a whole universe on the third level. It seemed like a living, breathing organism now, this huge, otherworldly beast.

I wanted to size up the beast, so I walked down the alley that ran along the side of the mansion, Magee's Alley. There were still old cobblestones there. My feet started to tingle thinking that Sigmund Lupescu and Krystyna had walked on these very cobbles. My neck strained upward, and I saw for the first time the great stained glass window that Anthony had seen from the inside. When I reached the end of the alley, I tried to peak into the backyard, but an eight-foot wall prevented me. It looked like Sigmund liked his privacy. I looked for some sign, some evidence of Krystyna's ordeal, until I remembered that this had happened over one hundred years ago. I went back through the gate, up onto the porch, and to the back door where a nurse was waiting for me.

"Well, hello, young lady, I've been told all about you and your grandma. You're both kind of celebrities here. Grandma is in a much better mood today. They do that you know. One day they're sweet as pie, the next, well, you have seen that yourself. Today's a good day."

"Oh, thanks. It's nice to hear that's she's in a good mood. My name is Annie. What's yours?" I reached my hand to her.

She smiled, pulled off her latex glove, and extended her hand out to me. "Annie, it's nice to meet you. I'm Lauren. I work in various nursing homes, filling in as they need me. I haven't been here for a few months. It's good to be back. I think this is my favorite home. Come on in. We can use some company today. Oh, what's in the bags?"

I answered hesitantly, not knowing what she'd think of my idea. "Well, I was hoping to use the kitchen and make cookies—pizzelles. They're flat crispy Italian cookies, kind of like little waffles. I brought my own pizzelle iron. Would it be okay? May I do that?"

"Only if you let me taste one when you're done. I think it's a wonderful idea," she agreed with a warm smile, putting her glove back on. Then she whispered to me in a solemn tone, "Don't expect too much help from Grandma."

I nodded. I knew that all too well. I didn't have to be told.

"Yes, I know. Thank you, Lauren. Nonna gets the first pizzelle. You get the second one. Okay?"

"Okay," she smiled and nodded back.

As I entered the living room, I saw most of the patients sitting on the large sofa watching *I Love Lucy*. I sat down on the arm of the sofa next to Nonna and gave her a kiss on the cheek.

"Hi, Nonna, it's me, Annie."

There was an immediate smile of recognition. "It's *you*! Oh, how nice. Where have you been?" she said with that generic tone that saddened me so.

Tapping the shoulder of the lady sitting next to her, she proudly announced, pointing to me, "This is my niece."

"Very nice to meet you," the lady responded. "You're very pretty."

"Oh, thank you. So are you."

I gazed about the room. I saw the haggard faces of the women and men, wrinkled and drawn not just by age, but also by confusion and sadness. I looked at them, imagining that each was probably such a vibrant person when young, like my Nonna. They probably took great pride in the way they looked and acted. Now they were just confused phantoms of their former selves, unrecognizable as they looked into the mirror trying to figure out who the drawn, blank-faced strangers looking back at them were. Perhaps amid all their confusion and pain, their essence was still burning inside, unable to be expressed. I just wanted to tell everyone, *They're here, you know.* They're not gone. They're right here if you look deep enough, look with your heart. So, I made up my mind to see them all as their beautiful selves.

"What do you have in the bags?" the woman asked excitedly. "Are they my things?"

"Oh, no, this is for my Nonna and me. We're making cookies today!"

"Oh," she sighed with disappointment.

I turned away from her, sadly and quickly. I thought for a moment to ask her if she'd like to join us in our baking project, but this was supposed to be quality time for Nonna and me, and two confused baking assistants would be too hard to bear.

"Did you hear that, Nonna? We're making pizzelles today? You and me, like I promised, like the good old days."

"Okay, get yourself up from the sofa and help your granddaughter make cookies," Daisy, piped up as she walked by.

"Hi, Daisy!" I called out and waved as she went by. It was nice to see her familiar face.

I had told her all about my visit to the haunted house after she demanded to know a few days after Halloween. She was happy to hear that there were no spirits there, good or evil, just silly boys.

"I'd love to try one of those cookies when you're finished, little Angelfish," she said with a smile, looking back at me.

Angelfish? I guess that was her nickname for me. Well, it's better than *Science Geek*, which was my nickname in the sixth grade.

"You've got it!" I called out as she disappeared into a patient's room.

I helped Nonna up and directed her towards the kitchen area. The poor woman was stooped over and walked very slowly, almost hobbling. Many of the patients were in wheelchairs now. This horrible disease, after a while, took their balance away and their ability to walk. There was a lot of falling. I really hated this disease. I was glad Nonna could still walk... for now. Out of the corner of my eye I saw that ten-year-old girl again, reading the newspaper to Albert. What a saint this girl was. She was the true Angelfish. I turned and gave her a quick wave when she looked up from the paper with a shy smile. She returned a hint of a wave to me and went right back to reading to Albert.

When we got to the kitchen, I started to explain to the caretaker who had just finished washing the breakfast dishes what we were going to do.

"Oh, you go right ahead. Miss Lauren told me to expect you two. Hey, Toni, are you going to make cookies with your granddaughter today?" she said ever so sweetly.

Grandma smiled and nodded.

The caretaker dried her hands after she had put the last cup into the cupboard. "If you need anything, just let me know," she whispered to me.

"Ah...can I ask you something?" I asked hesitantly.

"Why, sure.

"Have you ever been upstairs?" I motioned to the stairway.

"No, honey. We don't go up there. Nobody goes up there, except the administrators sometimes."

"What's up there?" I asked innocently.

Shaking her head, she responded, "Don't know. Don't care. I have enough work down here." She changed the subject. "Now with that said, can I help you with your baking?"

"Thank you, but I think I'm pretty well set."

"You have fun, Toni!" she said, patting Nonna on the cheek as if she were eight years old. If she would have done that to my grandmother three months ago, I would have been so annoyed, but now I knew she *was* like an eight-year-old. They all were.

I pulled my hair back so it was tucked in behind my ears and out of the way of our cooking. I craned my neck to check myself out in the reflection of the mirror in the living room. I always thought that when I did this it made my ears look too big. When I said that, Anthony always said that my ears were perfect. He was just being nice. They did look big. I took the old pizzelle maker out of the bag. It was one that Nonna had given me for Christmas when I was ten. I emptied the next bag out onto the table as she watched, fascinated by all this new stuff.

"Let's see flour, sugar, baking powder," I checked off the list. "Baking powder, you always told me, Nonna, baking *powder*, not baking *soda*."

She just smiled at me.

I thought I was over the heartbreak of seeing this shell of her, but it still hurt to see this dynamo of a lady so meek and relatively unresponsive. I thought that she'd go on forever, that there'd always be time to share her energy. It used to be so much fun to bake cookies with her.

"...eggs, anise, vanilla...we'll make both kinds, anise and vanilla... and butter and confectionary sugar."

Out of the next bag came the bowls, the sifter, the measuring spoons, and the spatula.

"Okay, here we go. Can you crack six eggs and put them in the bowl for me?"

Placing the egg in her hand, she looked at it curiously and then looked up at me with a quizzical 'what do you expect me to do with this' look. Without a clue, she squeezed it hard, and the egg shattered, yolk and clear goo dripping from her closed fist onto the table and the floor.

With a towel, I wiped all the egg matter off the floor, the table, and her hand. "Okay, you did good...you broke it. Not exactly like we needed, but you did break the egg! You did good!" Always so patient and supportive of me, it was now time I played that role for her.

"I'll handle the egg cracking. Can you pour the flour into the sifter? It's four cups." I handed her a measuring cup of flour. "You pour it in, and I'll sift it, okay?"

She just stared at the white powder, and a moment later she held the cup up to her lips and attempted to drink it.

"No grandma, it goes…" My voice cracked as I witnessed her helplessness.

"Can I help?" a soft voice asked from behind me. Turning, I saw the little girl who seemed to always be here with the residents.

"Can I help you with your cookies?" she asked again.

"Why, sure. Ah…I see you around here a quite a bit. My name's Annie." Extending my hand, I noticed some egg yolk dripping off my thumb. "Oh, I'm sorry," I said, pulling back my hand and quickly wiping off the egg goo.

"Oh, that's okay," she giggled. "My name is Amanda."

"Nice to meet you, Amanda. You must be a very nice girl. I've seen you here quite a bit helping the residents."

Shyly, she just nodded and bowed her head.

"My Nonna taught me to make these cookies and lots more. What a great cook she was. These cookies are called pizzelles." I looked around the room and asked, "Is your grandma here?"

Her head remained down, and there was a long silence. I wondered what she was thinking about just then.

"No, she passed away a while ago," she whispered sadly.

"Oh, I'm so sorry. And you still come here to visit the residents? That's so incredibly nice. You are beyond sweet."

"Thank you. You are, too," she replied, raising her head up and smiling at me. This girl was so beautiful, with long, brown hair and jade-like green eyes, and so dear. I could have hugged her to bits.

"Well," I said, sighing, "This is my Nonna. Her name is Antoinette. Everybody calls her Toni."

She smiled and said, nodding, "I know."

I had forgotten that my grandmother was a bit of a celebrity here. When she was nice, she was the sweetest thing to everyone, but when she was in one of her moods, watch out. Either way, she had made her mark.

"Looks like she won't be able to actually help much with the baking."

"That's why I'm here," Amanda chirped up helpfully.

"Good. Did your grandma like the anise or the vanilla pizzelles?"

"Loved vanilla!"

"My Nonna too! So, vanilla it is."

With that said, we went to work making the pizzelles. I had Amanda put the butter in the microwave to liquefy it and then cool it in the frig. I added the eggs, flour, butter, baking powder, and sugar and mixed it all together. She poured in the cooled butter. Placing the measuring spoon into my grandma's shaky hand, I guided it over the mix.

"Okay, Nonna, you put in the vanilla."

Wildly shaking her fist, she sprayed it all over the mixture.

"Very good! You added the vanilla. What a big help you are!"

"Molto bene!" Amanda giggled.

I looked over at her. She must have heard me say that to my Nonna on one of my visits.

"*My* grandma would say that to me," she said happily.

"Molto bene!" I repeated to grandma touching her cheek softly. She smiled and nodded.

We took turns mixing the vanilla in under Nonna's amused, watchful eye. My pizzelle iron had been heating up.

"It's ready!" I announced. "Amanda, you put in the first lump."

Scooping up a tablespoon of the mix, she gave it to my Nonna. Her hand and grandma's hand tapped the lump into the pizzelle iron. I pressed down on the iron, waited thirty seconds, and then opened it up.

"Scoop it out with the spatula," I instructed.

Carefully Amanda guided the thin pizzelle that was embroidered with the flower design of the iron onto one of the sheets of paper towels for cooling. The house quickly was filled with the sweet smell of fresh pizzelles. Most of the residents were oblivious to what we were doing as they stared at the television, but some sweet souls sniffed the air gently and turned to us with hints of smiles. It seemed that the smells of fresh cookies opened, if just for a moment, an avenue to a memory. Maybe a memory of when they made cookies with a parent or grandparent or maybe the first time they taught their grandchildren to bake. Our pizzelles opened a few sleeping neurons, and for a moment they were alive again. Odor was such a powerful memory trigger.

Thirty pizzelles were laid on the counter awaiting the final touch. This I knew Nonna could do. I gave her a shaker filled with confectionary sugar. Each one was to be covered with a scattering like the dusting of snow.

"Shake it on!"

Her shaky hand did the trick. Clouds of the powdered sugar lightly covered the cookies. I picked up some of the powder that missed and sprinkled it on the bare spots. Then I placed a dab onto Amanda's nose.

Giggling, she picked up of some of the powder and rubbed it onto my cheek. Nonna smiled and laughed, causing laughter from the other residents.

In "retaliation," I patted both of Amanda's cheeks with sugar. Giggling, she put a handful right square onto my cheeks. Her face was as white as a ghost, as was mine, and we laughed joyfully, uncontrollably, exorcising our sad spirits. Just for today the house was sweet.

I stopped and turned to look at Nonna, who still tried to shake the very last of the sugar onto the pizzelles.

"Don't be sad," Amanda consoled. "You made cookies with her today."

It was like she could read my thoughts. I smiled, nodded, and gave her a hug. "Thank you for helping."

I gave the first cookie to Nonna, the second to Lauren, and the third to Amanda. Daisy was still busy somewhere.

"Oh, Lauren, can I ask you something?"

Her eyes shone at me as she took her second bite of the pizzelle. "You sure can," she sweetly replied.

"Is there a way that I might visit the third floor of this house one day?"

The shine drained from her eyes, as if I had turned a switch off, and she drew in a surprised breath, coughing on the confectionary sugar. I could see a sternness blanket her face, but she quickly regained her composure.

"Now, why would you ever want to do something like that, honey?" She tried to sound very casual.

Feeling the depth of resistance in her voice, I didn't want to give too much away. "Oh, no big deal, I had heard that this mansion had some beautiful statues and paintings up on the second and third floors, and I thought it might be a good research project for my art class."

"Well, no honey, that area's off limits. We have a couple of offices up on the second floor, but most of the rooms are decrepit. The third floor is crumbling, so no one is allowed up there anymore. It would be too dangerous.

"Oh, okay," I said, backing off physically and verbally.

Putting her half-bitten pizzelle down on the counter, she started to walk away.

"Have you ever heard of any stories about ghosts up there?" I asked. I was feeling brave and wanted to put some bait out there to see if I got a nibble.

117

There was a pause. Even though her back was to me, I could see it tense up and feel her mind working to create a composed response.

"Why, those silly rumors. No, dear. Don't you know there's no such thing as ghosts?" she replied with a measured tone.

Molto bene.

12

"IS HE DEAD?" Ms. O'Meghan asked, tapping on the plastic case where the cockroach lay motionless.

"I think so," I responded hopefully, also tapping on the plastic.

"You know, Annie, this is really weird. In my twenty-five years of teaching, I do believe this is the most bizarre project that I've ever seen."

"Thank you, Ma'am," I replied, not really sure if she was complimenting me or insulting me.

Ms. O'Meghan knew all about my effort to "bring science to its knees" by finding proof of the spirit world. Like all my science teachers, she wished that I wasn't so obsessed with the topic, seeing "great inquiry potential" in me and hoping I would become more of a traditional science student.

"You see any loss in mass?" she asked, still staring in at the roach, looking for signs of life.

I kept peering at the digits on the scale and didn't see any change whatsoever. "No, not a bit," I sighed disappointedly.

"No, me neither. I wish you'd have done something more traditional."

"Like a paper mache volcano with baking soda and vinegar?"

Paper mache volcanoes. There was something I had done once that I'd never confessed to anyone and wouldn't in the foreseeable future. It was my darkest secret. I was so ashamed and embarrassed by this act of sabotage. It was both dangerous and cruel, something a *boy* might do. Now *that's* embarrassing. I might, on my deathbed, reveal this to whoever is at my bedside, except if it's Mary Chu.

Mary had built a paper mache volcano for our fifth-grade science fair. I was such an elitist, I thought it was a real baby project and so beneath Mary, who was brilliant. I think I was a little jealous of her, too. My project was on the behavior of anti-matter, brilliant stuff if I do say so myself, but all the kids seemed so excited waiting to see the foamy goop come out of Mary's stupid volcano as she mixed baking soda, red dye, and vinegar. So the night before the science fair, I snuck into the high school chemistry lab and took some chunks of sodium. That day, I placed the sodium chunks into her volcano on top of her baking soda. Sodium, when exposed to water, reacts violently and explodes.

When poor Mary proudly poured in her vinegar, which is mostly water, it didn't erupt, it exploded, sending fiery sparks and burning bits of paper mache flying everywhere. Screaming, terrified people went running in all directions. The fire department was called to investigate, but no one was charged after a lengthy investigation. I just couldn't confess to such a dark crime. I was so ashamed. I made Mary my best friend over the next two years to make it up to her. I consider myself a fair person, so I'm not proud of that day. Even Nonna didn't know about it. I had always hated science fair volcanoes. Now I loathed them.

"No, you know what I'm talking about, something where you get concrete data, data that could be helpful to our understanding of science."

"What would be more helpful than finding proof that the soul exists, that's there's more than just matter and death out there?" I asked forcefully, tapping hard with frustration on the plastic tank.

"Well, according to your observation, there was no weight loss. Have you reached your conclusion that there is no soul?" she asked with finality in her voice.

"No. I need a bigger animal or a more sensitive weight scale. The percentage of loss was just too tiny with the cockroach," I said stubbornly. I opened the case, took the dead roach out with forceps, and flipped the dead bug into the trash can.

"Doesn't he get a burial?" she asked with her head bowed in mock solemn respect.

I shook my head. "It was a *she*—she had an ovipositor."

"Look, Annie. I'd love to help you. As a sophomore, you know how important this science fair is to you and your grade. You've picked something really…"

"Weird. I know. I've heard that from multiple sources," I snapped.

"I just don't want you to get frustrated. Well, let me know if I can help with anything."

I forced a smile. "Thanks. Could you call someone in industry and get me a super sensitive scale. Souls can't weigh a heck of a lot."

Laughing, she joked, "Yes, I know some very light souls that work in government. I've got to give it to you, you don't give up easily."

"Thanks," I returned, removing the not-so-sensitive scale from my chamber.

"I'll be in the class next door if you need something," she reminded me as she left.

"Damn cockroach," I whispered to myself, staring at the stiff little martyr in the trash can.

"You need a bigger cockroach!"

I turned quickly. It was Caden.

"Preferably one the size of a refrigerator," she added.

"I think they come in petite size only."

"I think I can get you a bigger one than the one you just dusted," she promised, lifting it out of the trash by its antenna and flicking it back in.

"That would be great. Could you also make sure it's got a soul?"

This girl who could act so bizarrely seemed different today. Caden seemed like a normal person, except that she wore purple lipstick and so much black eyeliner she looked like a raccoon. Around her neck hung the largest gothic cross I'd ever seen, with which she could probably wipe out half of Transylvania, accessorized with two large earrings of dragons worming through the orifices of a skull.

"Making your First Communion?"

She ignored my joke and asked sympathetically, "No soul yet, huh?"

"Nope. A bigger roach just might do it, plus a more sensitive scale. Souls can't weigh a lot."

Then out of the blue she asked, "How's grandma?"

It took me a couple of seconds to attach the question to the character that stood before me. "Okay, I guess," I said in a tentative voice.

"That's good. That's good," she added with sincerity.

"Well, not really," I confessed. "It's like she there, but not there. A lot of her mind is gone."

"It's like she's a shell of her former self," she nodded empathetically.

"Yeah, that's right, a shell," I agreed, warming up to her sincerity.

Then she presented me with a bag that she had been holding when she entered the lab. She told me that it was filled with chocolate cookies that she had baked for me and for my grandmother the next time I visited her. I didn't know what to say as I gratefully took them from her.

"I...I...that's so very sweet. I can't thank you enough," I offered sincerely, placing my hand upon her shoulder.

Nodding, she didn't bother looking up. "I had an aunt who had Alzheimer's when I was ten. I was afraid to go near her. She spoke gibberish and just stared into space most of the time when I was there. We only saw her on Christmas and maybe her birthday. Even though she was my favorite aunt, she seemed like a stranger. I don't like to think about it. That's why I can feel for you. I know what you're going through, and it makes me sad."

"Thank you, that's sweet. It is hard, breaks my heart really, but I have to pretend, for her sake and mine, that nothing has changed, and she's still my Nonna."

A fog of sad memories for both of us that filled the room, uniting us and rendering us silent. I knew now that Caden was going to be a *forever friend*. I wouldn't tell her about the volcano, but I knew that I could tell her a lot. Finally, she broke the fog.

"I suppose you researched the mansion."

"I did. Found some interesting history, that poor girl just disappearing like that."

"She didn't just *disappear*."

"What do you mean?"

"Old man Lupescu did her in—and her boyfriend, too," she accused with certainty, as if she were there a hundred years ago and witnessed the whole tragic event.

"Boyfriend? I didn't read about any boyfriend."

"I'm sure you didn't. That's why I'm here. I have to fill you in about what really happened."

"What really happened?"

After she looked around the lab and peeked out into the hall, she sat down at the teacher's desk and proceeded to fill me in on the rest of the story. The beautiful Krystyna had a suitor back in Poland when her dad received the request and the very generous payoff for her hand in marriage to the elderly Sigmund. Krystyna was very much in love with a young Polish university art student named Vitas. When her father gave her the news of her move to America and her promised marriage to the ancient Sigmund, she ran off with Vitas but was soon captured and returned by thugs hired by her father. Vitas was beaten and warned to stay away from Krystyna. She was brought to America under heavy guard and delivered to Sigmund.

"How terrible!"

"Yeah, poor thing. After the wedding, she was forbidden to leave the grounds, hence the high wall he had built around the mansion. A *slave* was what she was, miserable and desperate. But Vitas, not afraid of Sigmund's power, followed her to America."

"Ah, he really loved her," I gushed.

"Yeah, twice he was able to get to her and free her from the mansion, but each time they were found. They forced her to come back, but Vitas, who was clever and driven by love, was able to escape the vengeful grip of Sigmund. Captive again in the house, Krystyna still was able to communicate with brave Vitas by sneaking up to the third floor and signaling him with a candle. One night, Sigmund and Krystyna were supposed to attend a dinner party. Krystyna pretended she was sick, even went so far as making herself vomit, which probably wouldn't be hard to do if you were married to Sigmund. That left her alone."

"Boy, you have much better sources than I have," I pointed out enviously.

"When Sigmund was gone and the servants were asleep, she signaled with her candle from the third-floor window for Vitas to come and get her to take her away once more. She opened a first-floor window for him to come in. They kissed, and she went to get some of her belongings when they heard the open window slam shut. They thought it was one of the servants."

"It was Sigmund, wasn't it?" I guessed anxiously.

She ignored me and went on explaining. "They both froze in silent fear at that point. Krystyna put her finger onto Vitas' lips, and with her other hand pointed to the stairway. They crept up the stairs as quietly as they could. When they got to the third floor, it was thick with musty darkness. Knowing that Vitas would not be able to see her finger point in the black sea of that room, she turned him and gently pushed him towards the turret room, the room under the witch's hat. Once they were inside, she pulled him close. She could feel his heart pounding in his chest with great fear, so she held him closer and kissed him. Suddenly, a burst of candle light blinded them. Vitas was knocked to the ground by a heavy fist to his face. Krystyna was slapped by a dry, bony hand and cried out as she fell to the floor."

I had always listened to stories with my thumb resting upon my lip; it was a bad habit germ-wise. I felt my thumb shaking as I anticipated what would come next. I kind of knew what was coming.

"It was Sigmund and two of his thugs who had set a trap for the two lovers. There was no beating or warning this time. Vitas and Krystyna were bound together with heavy chains while their mouths were gagged with dirty rags covered in coal dust. Over a two-day period, Sigmund had his thugs build a small three foot by three foot, six-foot-high room, walled with a double layer of bricks."

"You finally have what you've always wanted, my dear, Krystyna. Now you and your Vitas will be together forever." Caden mimicked the sinister voice of Sigmund, which gave me the creeps.

"They were thrown into the small room, eyes wide with anguish and terror, as they saw the very last of the bricks laid down quickly and heartlessly, sealing their tomb. Sigmund reported her missing the next day, saying she had run away for the third time. The fiend hired a detective agency to go through the motions of searching for her. He was never accused of a crime, and of course she and Vitas were never found." A long, silent moment followed as Caden seemed to be visualizing their horrible fate in her mind.

"Krystyna and Vitas' spirits have been wandering that upper floor for all these years," I offered.

Caden nodded at me. "*Someone's* up there. That's why the relatives gave the mansion up so easily. They were scared out of there. They moved back to Europe and donated the house to a nursing facility to care for Alzheimer's and dementia patients."

"You really think they're up there?" I asked, hoping they were there.

"*Something's* up there."

I walked back and forth between lab tables pondering what I could and should do to get up there. Sure, it creeped me out, but…*ghosts*! How could I pass that up?

"Would you come with me one night to go up there, to the third-floor witch's hat? You still owe me a ghost," I said dangling a little serving of guilt over her.

"No! Absolutely not," she said with certainty.

"But why not? I mean, look at you. This is your kind of thing." I was hoping that she would take that as a compliment.

She placed both her palms onto a table and leaned her body with great intimidation towards me. "I…don't…do…vampires," she announced, saying each word with an assured finality.

"What?" I asked, a bit surprised by this girl who did her best to look like Dracul's niece.

"I don't do vampires!" she confirmed with concrete conviction.

"But it's Krystyna and Vitas. I'm sure they're lovely people. They're not vampires. No one associated with the…" Then it dawned on me. *Sigmund!* There were rumors about some of the family members, especially Sigmund, but not enough evidence.

"I just don't like the idea that the Lupescu ancestors were involved with the murder of Vlad lll, Dracul. Just that connection freaks me out," she explained.

I smiled at her pronunciation of *Dracul*. I'd have to remind Anthony how I had been correct about that.

"Vampires freak you out?" I asked with a tone of disappointment. I could tell that she sensed me looking her over and wondering about the unspoken paradox, *then why do you dress like one?*

She got up from her chair, took two steps towards me, and stopped. "In five years, I'll cringe at pictures of myself if I haven't burned them by then. I intend to be a chemical engineer like my mom. That's why I'm in this school. Don't think for a moment that this," waving a hand in front of her, "is Caden Pennington."

I thought for a moment. All this time I'd been looking at Caden, judging her from my perspective, and all the while I'd been pretty wrong. I should have and would now look at her differently. *Hey! That's my point about the universe!* We look at it with certain technologies and equipment, defining scientific laws and principles. Perhaps there's a perspective that we haven't used yet, a different way to look at matter and energy. Maybe it was at least a lot deeper and mysterious than we think. Looking at Caden superficially was like looking and judging the ocean from its surface, not seeing and comprehending the great mysteries of its depth. I could see her depth now. I wanted to peer beneath the universe's surface as well.

"I didn't mean anything by…" I stammered nervously.

Her hand flashed to stop me. "No. I'm not insulted, Annie. You asked a good question. All this zombie and ghoul satanic stuff is funny and fun, and it gives us a reason to hang out and to dress cool."

Her tone dropped an octave and turned into a harsh whisper. "But I *do* believe in vampires." Her voice had so much conviction that a chill ran down my spine.

"But Caden, *vampires?* That's…"

"Weird, you mean like your ghosts? '*The strength of the vampire is that people will not believe in him.*' That's a quote from Professor Van Helsing."

"Van Helsing is a fictional character," I pointed out.

"I still think it's a pretty profound idea and true. People think you're a bit odd looking for ghosts, don't they?"

There was a bond of empathy between us; we both had the courage, some people might say the foolishness, to believe in the unbelievable. Who were we to judge each other? We were in the same creepy boat.

"So, I can't go with you on this ghost hunt. I might find more than I bargained for. I won't go near that house. Please understand."

I nodded my head and smiled. "Okay. I got it. No problem, I…oh my goodness. That window!"

"What! What's wrong?" she asked.

I covered my mouth with a trembling hand, thinking back to three weeks before when I'd left the home after visiting Nonna. It was late and already dark. I had seen a flicker of light up there in that window in the witch's cap. I didn't think anything of it at the time, but now…I explained what I had seen to Caden.

"West window under the witch's hat facing the street, right?" she asked with certainty.

I nodded slowly. "Yes."

13

BUT SHE'S A nut! Plus, she scares me. She has hearing like a bat!" Anthony had expressed his doubts about Caden's story about the mansion and his annoyance over me even speaking to her.

"And how would anyone know about all those details? *Krystyna put a finger on his lips. They kissed. Their eyes were wide with terror.* There were too many intimate details. It sounded like she was writing a soap opera script. No, I would not believe her. Look at her!"

He looked over at my lunch tray and my two pieces of pizza crusts. I never eat the crust, just the cheese and the sauce. He moved his right hand, his fingers creeping like a clumsy spider towards my crusts.

"No!" I snapped. I pulled the tray quickly away. "I'm saving the crusts for my roaches." He quickly withdrew his hand as I shot him an angry look.

"Stop judging her by the way she looks. That girl made cookies for Nonna! Okay, maybe she added those intimate details to spice up the story. Hey, she's a good storyteller."

I, too, was a bit concerned with the colorful details she had mentioned. How would she know about that? My mind wandered. If this were a novel, Caden could be the reincarnation of Krystyna who had designed all this to make us go up there and free her and her lover from their brick tomb. That would have been cool. But this wasn't a novel; it was real life. So what if she overelaborated her stories? She was a colorful girl. I liked her details. I liked when they kissed.

"You just *want* to believe it."

"Maybe I do! But she still knew the main details, and, Mr. Detective, they corroborated your findings. Krystyna disappeared without a trace, didn't she? Sigmund was an evil old man, wasn't he? His ancestors killed Dra-cul," I said, stressing the pronunciation to remind him that I was right about that name. "...didn't they? *And* they have closed down the witch's cap third floor, haven't they?" I pulled my lunch tray a little further from him. His hand spider had been creeping toward my pizza crust again.

"It could be coincidental data that proves nothing. You're still a scientist, aren't you, or will I be buying you a gargoyle nose ring for your birthday? Oh, and I checked," he added meekly, "it *is* pronounced Dracul."

I grinned triumphantly. "Yes, I still am a scientist, and as curious scientists it is our duty to investigate these pieces of data and reach a conclusion." Many of the greatest scientific breakthroughs were not discovered until after painstaking work. They were serendipitous moments, moments when scientists had the light of wonder shine on them, when they would just say, 'Wow!'

"We have to see if Krystyna and Vitas are up there. We have to prove there is a spiritual realm."

"Well, if…wait a minute…what do you mean *we*?" He crooked his head and squinted his left eye at me, nervously awaiting my answer.

I sat up very straight and rigid. "You're not going to let me go up there alone, at night, are you?" I asked, challenging his friendship.

He shook his head to digest this new challenge that he, until now, hadn't known that he was a part of. "I thought you were going to investigate the ghosts with your new BFF?"

I cocked my head upwards and glared at him. "No, she doesn't do vampires"

"Vampires? Who said anything about vampires? Now you're investigating vampires?"

I matter-of-factly reminded him of the possible connection with Vlad and how that freaked Caden out. The air was getting very tense between us.

"I didn't think anything freaked a freak out," he whispered under his breath.

"Vampires do. And she's not a freak! Stop saying that. You know, you can really be mean sometimes," I said angrily. "She's going to be a chemical engineer, you know!"

"Yeah, well, Dr. Frankenstein was a transplant-medical engineer, didn't stop him from making a freak," he continued with a combative tone, just before gulping down the last of his Gatorade.

I stood up like a shot, an angry shot. The mood had risen from tense to stormy. "You're not being very nice today. I was hoping that you would help me, but I guess you're too cool and smart. I thought you were different from the other boys. I guess I was wrong."

With that, I picked up my cafeteria tray.

"And I guess I'll go investigate the witch's cap alone. Thanks! Thanks a lot…*friend*!" I turned my back on him, slammed my trash into the garbage, recyclables and all, and stormed up to the biology lab.

§ § §

Each time now that I rode up to the mansion, all I could see was the witch's hat. This house that I had thought so beautiful and like a second home seemed mysterious and threatening now. All I could I think of was that monster Sigmund and the horrible things he had done to poor Krystyna and Vitas. I had a guilty rush of excitement thinking that this was part of a destiny — my destiny, maybe created by Nonna or not, to give me my ghost, finally.

Today, as I locked my bike onto the bike rack, I started planning the search. It would not be easy. I was surprised that Anthony had made it up the stairway to the second floor undetected that time. That they found him wandering around up there made them even more vigilant now. There was a small fence at the foot of the stairway with a new warning sign, "WEAK STRUCTURAL FLAWS IN THE STAIRS. KEEP OFF," and I noticed more eyes following my movements down the hall when I visited. I'd have to try to get up there at night. All the residents would be medicated and sleeping, and I'm sure they'd have a small skeleton crew there till dawn. How could I get in undetected? How would I get up to the third floor? I'd have to think about it some more.

"Well hello, my sweet little Angelfish," Daisy said greeting me. "Not a good day. Not a good day at all for grandma. We had to give her something to calm her down because she was a little too agitated and got into a screaming fight with one of the other ladies, even kicked her. Just needs to rest. Ole Daisy had to put her to bed."

"May I look in on her?" I asked in a hushed murmur. The image of Nonna screaming and kicking seemed incomprehensible to me, but I knew that Alzheimer's could cause the incomprehensible.

"Oh sure, my sweet one. Just be extra quiet," she said softly, touching my shoulder to show her support for me.

As I strode through the living area, I could see the same people staring at the television. Some were murmuring to themselves, some were fast asleep in their wheelchairs, and some were at the tables eating a snack or searching through their pocketbooks for their lost freedom. I peeked down the long hallway at the great stairway to calculate how far it was from the living area. No Amanda today. I guessed she couldn't always be there.

There seemed to always be a couple of new faces. The disease seemed to be gripping more and more victims. The new ones were always very confused and angry as to why they were there and not with their families. They seemed to feel that they were maybe just going to stay there for a few days. Truth was, I'm sure, that their loving families just couldn't care for them anymore, the wandering, the dangerous things they did in their forgetfulness. Their love was still there, but the patience had eroded. Some faces went away. The nurses told me that some were just admitted for a few weeks to give their caretaking family a break, or they got sick and had to go to a facility that could better care for their ailments.

I searched around for Albert, the cute little guy who thought that I was his brother Benny.

"Where's Albert?" I asked with a loud whisper, turning back around to Daisy, who was busy folding sheets.

She hesitated, and I could tell that there would be sad news.

"That dear man is with the Good Lord, Angelfish. His suffering is over. Albert took a bad turn last week, just stopped eating, and now he's gone to his eternal home, Sweetie. I guess that his brother Benny finally did come for him."

My eyes welled up with tears, more for my grandmother's fate than poor Albert's. Daisy looked at me and cupped my chin with her big hand.

"Don't you dare shed a tear whenever any of these sweet ladies and gentlemen are called home. They all sit here praying inside for that glorious day. You can't hear them, but that's what they want. It's the only thing they can hope for, sweet release. So don't cry for Albert, Angelfish; that man is whole again. That man thinks clearly once more."

I blinked back my tears and nodded at her.

She gave me a wink. "Go see grandma," she urged, pointing down the hallway.

I eased Nonna's door slowly open and found her asleep in her bed. "Rest," I whispered into her ear.

I gazed around her room. There were cards that Kevin and I had sent or made for her, a few of her paintings, some photos of complete strangers, and a chess piece that she must have taken from another resident's room. There was both something peaceful and heartbreaking as she slept.

I wonder if she dreams, I thought. *And if so, are her dreams confused and tormented, or was she there in them, logical and clear, only to awaken again into this nightmare stupor of delirium?*

"Mind if I do some homework here, Daisy?" I called out as I poked my head out the door.

"You gonna do your homework *here,* Angelfish?"

"Ah, yes. I want to sit with her while she rests just to keep her company."

"This is an odd place to do your school work, Angelfish."

This, of course, was an excuse I made to stay as late as they would allow me. I was testing them to see what their time limit for guests would be. Their rules said nine PM, but it was important to see if I could stretch that, and I needed to get a sense of the night crew.

Daisy walked over to check on Nonna, who was still deep asleep. "You can do your homework here, sweetie. Just don't expect any help from the men and ladies here, and especially don't expect anything from old Daisy. What are you learning about?" she asked, craning her neck towards my books with genuine interest.

"Well, I have a social studies paper on the contribution of Persia to our knowledge of the stars, and in Astronomy I have a report on singularities—you know, black holes."

"Sweetie, you are a genius girl, aren't you? You can be assured there's no help coming from ole Daisy tonight. Now, if you're doing your times tables or any Jamaican history questions, give me a call," she added laughing.

"I will call you right over, Daisy," I assured her.

Daisy went back to her duties folding sheets and then would be preparing the residents for their bedtime. I had taken out my computer and researched my papers. It was so quiet, even peaceful there, as the three ladies on call gently got each of the residents ready for bed. I got a lot done. After about an hour and a half I walked back out into the living room and beckoned Daisy after I saw that she was pretty much finished with her work.

"Daisy?"

"Yes, Angelfish?" she called over. "You have a times table issue?"

I laughed. "No, I'm good."

She came over and sat down next to me. "All my darlings are in bed now, but that doesn't guarantee that they'll stay there."

"What do you mean?"

"Oh, they can get up all hours of the night and wander. We have to corral them back."

I nodded my head and started piling my books up, trying to act casual. "When do *you* go home?"

"Well, on this shift, we're done at nine o'clock. Why you asking?" Her tone didn't sound suspicious, just curious.

"Just curious. You people work all different shifts, don't you?" I yawned and patted my mouth, pretending that the question was not that important.

"You know that. Sometimes you'll see me in the morning and now here I am. Working on different shifts gives us different routines with the lovely ladies and gentlemen here. Some shifts are more stressful. Night's pretty peaceful. Why all the questions? You doing a school report on ole Daisy?" Laughing, she fluffed up her hair a bit. "If you are," she went on, "I have some much more interesting bits and pieces to share with you, but I can't tell you *everything*! No, no, couldn't do that!" She laughed again.

I felt I was being pushy, not casual enough. I opened my astronomy book and started leafing through it. "No. I'm just trying to get a sense of the place, you know, since my Nonna lives here now. How many people are on the night crew?" I asked, trying to sound very casual, glancing at my book.

"Only need two a night. Main job is to hunt down the creepers and return them to their beds."

"Creepers?"

"Yes, the creepers. They're the ones who get up in the middle of the night and plan on going home or calling their long-lost husband or wife on the phone, or they just like to wander." At that, she instinctively peeked over my shoulder at the far corridor to look and see if there might be a creeper.

I tried to envision this place at night with people popping out of bed walking around. It sounded scary. It ruined my peaceful image of a night at the Sunshine. "What happens if there are no creepers?"

"Well, the crew will watch some television and peek in on the sleepers to make sure that everything is fine."

"Hmm…sounds pretty easy," I said, making mental note in my head.

"Not if they get a wild creeper, sugar. Oh my, that might wake up the whole house. Oh, the yelling and screaming…my, my, what a sight." She laughed and swayed back and forth as if visualizing the chaos that would ensue. Then she composed herself so as not to wake up any sleepers.

"But *usually* it's pretty peaceful and quiet here late at night?" I asked, trying to get reassurance.

"Yes. I guess it's usually pretty dull here at night," she agreed.

"It's eight fifty, young lady!" a nurse called out from the kitchen. "You should be leaving in a few minutes."

I closed my book and checked my watch. *Hmmm*, I thought, *pretty firm with the time.* I collected all my stuff and clutched it close to my chest as I slowly rose up from the sofa. "Okay, nurse, thank you," I called out.

"You need Daisy for any more questions, Curious Annie?" she asked.

"Nope, I'm done for tonight. Thank you," I said, sounding like the host of an interview show ending a session.

Daisy laughed that hearty, good-natured laugh. She went over to the television, which was still on with the sound way down low, even though no one had really been watching it for an hour, and clicked off *The Andy Griffith Show*. Barney Fife had just been looking for his bullet in his top pocket.

"That Barney's a funny man," she chuckled to herself, and then turned to me. "Next time your grandma will be feeling better, and you can have a nice visit with her."

As the nurse held the door for me, I asked as I walked by her, "Was that little girl Amanda here today?"

"Sorry, don't know an Amanda, honey."

This nurse must be new, I thought. "Okay thank you. Good night," I said politely. "Good night!" I called out to Daisy.

"Good night, Angelfish!" she called from some far corridor.

§ § §

I was up in my room working on my black hole report when the doorbell rang. I heard mom answer it. "Oh, hi! Yes, she is."

I heard a faint, apologetic male voice.

"Oh, it's okay, you don't have to apologize. Come on in." There was a pause before my mom called up. "Annie, Anthony's here to see you! Can I send him up?"

I slowly walked over to my door, craned my head out, and called down in a loud and angry voice to be sure that Anthony, and I guess the neighbors, could hear me. "No! Tell him that I ran off with the Goth twins to Transylvania. I'll be back in two years."

There was a long silence. In my mind, I could see her contoured face trying to figure out why I would say such a bizarre thing. Then, "What? Don't be silly or rude."

I paused a moment for effect. "Okay, send him up," I agreed with a heavy sigh.

"It's late, can't stay too long," she added.

"Oh no, *he* definitely won't be staying long!" I assured her and him.

He plodded up the stairs slowly. I could feel the fear in his footfalls. Entering my room meekly, his eyes were glued to his feet, avoiding any eye contact with me. He knew that they had to be my angry eyes. I approved of his humble body language. It was an appropriate entrance for someone looking for forgiveness.

"Sounds like you're still mad at me," he said remorsefully with his sad, puppy dog face.

"Somewhat," I sighed, to continue his torture for a few more moments.

"Well, I'm really, really sorry. I know I should be more tolerant of those girls. It's just the way they look…"

I quickly turned my head away from him and walked to the edge of my bed. I sat, still with my head turned away disapprovingly. "I thought this was going to be an apology," I interrupted.

He sighed, "Okay. They look fine. It's *me,* I'm too judgmental." He carefully chose his words as he added, "They are creative and expressing themselves in a way that I need to be more understanding of. There are many kinds of people in the world, and I need to appreciate that."

"That's better," I said matter-of-factly, finally turning to face him.

"And I was wrong. I'm sorry. And I know that 'sorry' is not enough from past dealings with your famous anger, so I thought a bit and I will make a special gesture of repentance. I was thinking of flowers."

"No, flowers will not do it this time," I interrupted. I pointed to the seat at my desk deigning to let him finally take a seat.

He sat with a sigh, a smile shyly appearing. He probably felt that this gesture meant that peace was at hand.

"I know, I was just *thinking* of flowers. My gesture was that I will accompany you when you go looking for the ghosts on the third floor of your grandma's home."

Hmmm, I thought. I had assumed he would come with me all along anyway. I was hoping for something more, like a supersensitive scale or a humongous cockroach. But I knew in his mind this was a big leap. I paused a long moment to make him nervous.

"And, I will help you plan it!" he blurted out, upping his gesture.

"Oh, and flowers," I added from my position of strength at the bargaining table.

"I thought that you didn't want flowers this time," he said with a grin, probably knowing he was close to a deal.

"Oh, they're not for me. They're for your new friend, Caden," I said with a grin.

He rose up from the seat. "You're kidding, right?"

Seeing the scowl on my face, he knew that I was not kidding and conceded. "Okay, flowers for Caden. I could get her dead…"

"Anthony!" I scolded.

"Well she is Goth. All right, I'll get her something nice. Are we good now? Are we friends again?" he asked.

I waited another long moment for effect. "Sure, we're good."

I stood up and walked over to him with extended hand. We shook. His palm was sweaty from the tension. "I'm glad that you're going to help me plan this search because I've been casing the joint…"

"Casing the joint? You sound like Humphrey Bogart," he laughed. A fan of the old black and white crime movies from the 30's and 40's, he knew all the important dialogue.

"…and I'm seeing some problems," I pointed out.

"Like us going to jail for breaking and entering?" he said seriously.

I went back, picked up my plush, bearded lizard from the floor, hugged it, and sat back down on my bed. "No. We're kids. We can cute our way out of any problems. For one, they close down to visitors at nine o'clock, and there are always people on duty till morning, obviously."

"How about ghosts killing us?" he asked sarcastically.

"Why do people think that ghosts are automatically scary and killers? They might be nice. Besides, Vitas and Krystyna seem like very sweet people, so I'm sure their ghosts are very sweet, too."

He walked over and sat down next to me on the bed. "What makes you think that it's Krystyna and Vitas?" he asked sardonically.

"What do you mean?"

"What if it's Krystyna, and it's Sigmund there tormenting her forever in the witch's hat?"

I had never thought of that. Actually, I had, but I'd quickly erased it from my mind.

"Or…" he added

"Or what?" I asked anxiously.

"Or, maybe it's Sigmund and Vitas battling each other for all eternity, both searching for their Krystyna."

14

THE HOLIDAYS THIS year were terrible when Nonna fell and hit her head a week before Christmas. This was that stage of the illness where her legs and coordination were failing her. I had been taking her for short walks to try to strengthen her legs, holding onto her so she wouldn't fall. One day when Amanda was there, she held onto Nonna's right side while I supported her left. That girl was an angel.

I knew that I was fighting against the inevitable. Soon, she'd be one of those wheelchair ladies. I didn't want to think about it. At the nursing home, when you hit your head, they send you to the hospital to be checked. Nonna just had a minor concussion, but she couldn't afford to lose any more brain cells than the disease had already taken. Nonna stayed for a few days for other tests, and then they brought her back to the home.

I sent four more cockroaches to the Pearly Gates, and each one still registered no weight loss, even a big fat one that Caden had trapped for me at a Greek-Chinese restaurant. I made a note to myself to never eat there.

Something else happened that surprised me, not the event itself, but my reaction to it. I was told that Jennifer Moretz had asked Anthony to go with her to the junior prom. My Anthony! And that was the part that surprised me. When I heard about it, I felt a twinge of jealousy, well, maybe more than a twinge. He had been like a brother to me, my future partner in crime, so I should have been happy for him. Jennifer Moretz was a very pretty and sweet girl, so why was my first thought when I heard the news to substitute her for one of the cockroaches in the Death Chamber? I was confused.

After our little Christmas at our house, we packed up cookies and cakes and presents for Nonna and drove over to the Lupescu Mansion. My mother was confused that I called it that, but I couldn't help it, and I couldn't help peeking up at the snow-covered witch's hat and its frosty window. This would be Kevin's first time seeing Nonna, and I had to prep him.

"Kevin, you have to imagine that she's hiding away deep inside her mind, and this isn't really her. Think of this woman you're meeting as a sweet old lady whom you just want to make happy."

He pushed me away sobbing nervously.

When I entered the home, it was decorated for holiday cheer. Christmas music was playing, and, of course, a Lawrence Welk Christmas Special was on the TV. There was an eight-foot tree that was sparsely decorated. There were tiny plastic trees on each of the tables and a menorah on the fireplace. I was prepared for the place to be filled with sons, daughters, grandchildren, and great-grandchildren honoring their loved ones, trying to make the day festive for them, but that wasn't the case. There were two other families there. Even on Christmas, most of the residents sat in the chairs, heads nodding downward or eyes fixed to the television screen with no visitors and no Christmas.

"Well, Merry Christmas to my sweet Annie," Daisy called out from the kitchen.

"Merry Christmas, Daisy," I returned cheerfully.

"Who's that with you, Angelfish?"

"Angelfish?" Kevin muttered with disdain, looking up at me.

"This is my mom and brother Kevin," I said, ignoring his look.

My mom waved cheerily. "Merry Christmas, Daisy. I've heard a lot about you," she said with warmth and sincerity. Mom appreciated the care Daisy was giving to Nonna.

"Merry Christmas. You have a real angel for a child there, you know," she called out.

"Thank you!" Kevin sarcastically responded. I poked him hard.

Daisy made her way over to us. "It's so nice of you to come on our Lord's birthday. It's a shame, a real shame that so many of these sweet ladies and gentlemen have no visitors. We do try to make each one feel special. God bless you for coming."

"Thank you," Mom responded, "and thank you for being so nice to Toni and my daughter."

"You must be looking for your grandmother. The sweet lady's right over there," Daisy said, pointing to one of the tables where she chatted with another resident. "Won't she be so glad to see you," Daisy assured us. Taking my mom's hand, she led us over to her table. "Toni, look who's here!"

Nonna turned away from her chat. Her eyes brightened when she saw me. I came often enough that she had a sense that I was someone special to her, and if she was in the proper mood, her eyes gleamed with appreciation.

"Oh, hello!" she chirped out. "It's my friend," she pointed out to Daisy, referring to me.

"Mom and Kevin are here. They came too," I announced, guiding the two of them closer with a little push.

Mom, hating the place, came about once a month for a few minutes, so there was no look of recognition. Kevin was a complete unknown to her.

"Merry Christmas, Mom," my mother said, bending down to kiss her on the cheek.

"Yes, I like it too," she responded with a smile.

"Kevin's here also, Nonna." I repeated, pulling Kevin by his coat sleeve from behind mom's back.

"Merry Christmas, Nonna," he said, never raising his eyes to meet hers. She smiled and patted him on the head. "What a nice girl," she gushed.

"Mom? Can I go home?" he cried as he started to tear up. "I don't want to be here."

My mother took him by the hand to the lobby and had a long chat with him. I was sure she was reassuring him that they weren't going to stay long and how much Nonna would appreciate this, and she probably added a bribe as well. I couldn't blame him. I was older and very much wiser than him, and my first few visits here had been terrifying.

I sat next to Nonna and gave her a kiss on the cheek.

"Hi," the lady who was sitting with her said, looking for attention as well. This was a new patient.

"Oh, I'm sorry," I apologized. "Hi! Merry Christmas to you."

"I don't know why I'm here. I'm going home after dinner."

"Oh. That's great," I happily assured her.

"Yes, right after dinner they said I will be going home. I don't like it here. It's not my real home," she whispered into my ear.

I nodded as I turned my face around to Nonna. I saw Amanda three tables over reading a book to one of the women residents. As she read the book, the old woman just looked intently at her and nodded, not understanding or caring what was read, just caring that someone had taken the time to read to her. *This girl's a saint!* I thought. *On Christmas, she's here.*

But then I felt a surge of sadness for her. Where was her family? Why wasn't she with them on Christmas? Mom and Kevin came back. I noticed a five-dollar bill tucked into his shirt pocket.

"We have some presents and cookies and cakes, Mom," my mother explained, holding up the bags and placing them on the table.

"Mom, that's Amanda over there. What a great kid, always here, almost as much as me. Hi, Amanda!" I called out. "Merry Christmas! This is my brother and mom."

My mom waved in her direction. "Hi," she said weakly, not looking over.

Amanda lifted her head, waved back, and went on reading. Lily, one of the workers, brought mom and Nonna some coffee and brought juice for Kevin and me. We opened the cookies and cakes, enough for everyone who wandered over to the table. These people liked treats and loved attention.

We gave Nonna her gifts, dull things really: a night gown, a new hair brush, some comfy slippers, and some pants. It didn't matter really. She just got a kick out of ripping off the wrapping paper, which she did slowly and awkwardly. After the first one, I had to assist her with the others.

"Oh, what lovely gifts you got, Toni," Lily said as she scooped them up. "I'll put her name on them and put these in her room," Lily reassured us.

Proudly, Nonna beamed at all the attention that was coming her way, especially when so many others there had been forgotten. Kevin kept tapping mom on her shoulder whispering desperately. I guessed the five-dollar bribe had run out of time.

"Mom, we're going to go now. It was so nice seeing you," my mother said, bending to her and kissing her cheek.

"Oh, yes, I'll be going home, too," she replied with certainty.

"Give her a kiss, Kevin," mom insisted, "and tell her you love her."

Kevin reluctantly shuffled up to Nonna's cheek and gave her an air kiss somewhere in the neighborhood of her cheek. Its length could have been measured in nanoseconds.

Mom gave her another teary-eyed kiss on the cheek. "Bye, Mom. Merry Christmas. We love you," she said, choking back her emotions.

"Yes, I like vanilla too!" the lady next to us added.

"Mom, can we please go now?" Kevin added with urgency.

"Just wait, Kevin. Wait for your sister. Say goodbye, Annie."

"Mom, you were going to stop at the store before going home to pick up stuff for the company coming over tonight, right?" I asked.

"Yes. Why?"

"Well, I'd like to stay for about twenty more minutes. Can you go pick up what you need for tonight and then pick me up outside at about a quarter after?"

"I guess," she said, flashing me an uncertain look.

"Come on, Mom!" Kevin whined as he yanked at her sweater and pulled her towards the door.

As they left, mom stopped by each of the workers and shook their hands, thanking them for the great care they had been giving Nonna. Money was given to each of them as a holiday tip.

"I wish I could give you more. You do so much for these poor people," I heard her say tearfully to them.

"Will you stay?" Nonna asked me, with uncharacteristic alertness.

I smiled at such a clear request. It was one of those perfect neuron touching moments that got rarer as the months passed. "Sure, for a little while more."

"But why?" she asked with concern.

"Because I love you," I replied, cupping her face in my hands.

"Oh, that's good," she responded with an appreciative smile.

"I have this for you," I announced. I reached into my pocket and removed one more present. I unwrapped it for her. It was a small wooden angel that held a yellow star over her head with both her hands. This angel had a joyous smile on her face as she looked up at the star, almost triumphantly. I placed it in front of her on the table.

"It's a nice girl," she commented, as she picked it up.

"You know who that is? That's me, your Annie. In some mystery of destiny, you have brought me here to show me spirits. I will be triumphant in my quest." I glanced up at the ceiling. I'd never felt as strongly as I did about my search as I did now. After that, the universe would expand into so many levels for me. I would believe in angels. Who knows, maybe I'd even believe in Santa Claus. I gave her a kiss on the cheek.

"I'm going to put this in your room. Don't let anybody take it."

When I returned, I went over to see Amanda.

"Merry Christmas," she piped up.

"Merry Christmas!" I replied cheerfully. It was so good to see her. I sat down next to her.

"This is Jessica Johnson. No one came to visit her. Her children live far away. Jessica never gets visitors. I'm her visitor for today," she explained, pulling a brush gently through her hair.

"I have to ask you. You are amazingly nice to be here. You are so precious and good, but it's Christmas. Shouldn't you be with *your* family? You're nine years old, and you're all alone on Christmas."

"I'm not alone. I'm here with Jessica, and now you."

"But your family?" I asked, my face contorting quizzically.

"Oh, I was with them. It was a very nice Christmas. I got exactly what I needed," she said with a smile.

"And it's okay with your family that you're here? You're only nine," I said, taken aback by the freedom they gave this little child.

"Oh, yes, they love me."

Okay. Who was I to question her family? There were all kinds of families. I guess she really was some kind of saint.

"Next time we're here together, let's talk. I'd like to get to know you better. You seem so special. Wow, my brother's nine, and he's such a goofball. You're...so...cool."

She giggled. "I would like that," she responded in a sweet whisper. "I would like to talk more."

I craned my neck to see what she had been reading.

"I'm reading my very favorite book to Jessica, *The Little Prince*."

"Oh, I know that book. My Nonna read it to me once. She loved it too. It's a very good book," I said excitedly.

"You want to read it to Jessica?"

I looked over at Nonna, who was busy talking to a worker who had just brought her some pudding.

"Jessica," she said, tapping her on the shoulder to get her attention back, as Jessica had turned to watch snowflakes that were gently floating down outside the window. "Jessica, this is my good friend Annie. I'm going to let her read to you, okay?"

The woman just looked at me with a blank expression. Amanda passed me the book. "Let's see. We were on page seventy."

Handing the book over to me, she put her little finger on the spot where she had stopped. I took the book from her and smiled into her crystalline eyes. I cleared my throat.

"Goodbye," said the fox. "And now here is my secret, a very simple secret: It is only with the heart that one can see rightly; what is essential is invisible to the eye."

"What is essential is invisible to the eye," the little prince repeated, so that he would be sure to remember."

"Arthur, get down from those stairs!" a nurse shrieked as she raced across the living room to the hall in a panic. "Lily, come quickly. Help me get him!" she called back out.

I put the book down and looked at Amanda. I rushed over to the stairway as well. Arthur, a fairly tall man and not as old as the others, had gotten one leg over the barrier that blocked the stairs.

"Step back, Annie. It'll be okay. We've got him." Lily warned with concern for my safety.

Arthur gave them a little tussle, but he soon relented as the women grabbed him and his long leg and brought him back.

"Now Arthur, you know better than that. What were you trying to do?" the nurse scolded.

"They're up there," he said with a chilling certainty. "They're going to take me home."

"Well if you fall on the stairs, Arthur, *we're* going to take you to the hospital," the nurse warned him. "Lily, take Arthur over to the chair to watch some television, and strap him in, please," she instructed, holding him tightly, her hands locked onto his shoulders.

Lily nodded. "Come on, big guy. Don't go messing with our Christmas cheer by getting hurt," she said.

"They're up there," I whispered to myself, but I guess loud enough for the nurse to hear.

"There's no one up there, Annie. They all think someone is going to show up and take them home. Don't pay any attention to what he said."

But that was all I could think about, *they're up there*. My head started to ache. I needed to get up there to the witch's hat. I needed to find the ghost that I knew just had to be there.

I gotta go, I thought.

I went back and hugged Amanda goodbye, and she gave me a kiss on the cheek.

"Thank you for reading to Jessica. I love you," she whispered in the melodic voice that only a nine-year-old girl could possess.

"I...love you too," I said a bit hesitantly.

I went to Nonna and hugged and kissed her goodbye. "I'll be seeing you soon. Merry Christmas. I love you so much."

I quickly said thank you and goodbye to Daisy and the others and went outside to wait on the corner for my mom. The whole visit was a blur right then. The only thing that spun clearly in my mind was one phrase: *They're up there.*

143

15

THEY'RE UP THERE! That's what the guy said," I reminded Anthony for the seventh time.

"I know. I know," he repeated for the sixth time. He seemed fixated on the periodic chart that hung front and center in our lab.

"But the guy has dementia," he reminded me as he washed out a beaker that held my cockroach food. "You've heard four other patients say that, including your own grandmother."

"Four others saying the same thing is even more compelling evidence," I pointed out to him.

"Or 'they' are the figments of their imaginations, the imaginary people who are going to come and take them home or come and give them their car keys."

"I read something on Christmas at the home from *The Little Prince*. I was with Amanda reading it to a little old lady."

"Who?"

"Amanda, that little girl we saw in the garden that day. One passage said, *It is only with the heart that one can see rightly*. Their minds are going, but maybe they have the ability to tune into another dimension, spirits and all that. Maybe they see rightly. With their minds gone, perhaps they are seeing with their hearts."

"This is not the Annie that I met at the seventh-grade science fair, winning first place, the fierce advocate for the scientific method, the scientist. You're making some wild conjectures," he said with a hint of disappointment in his voice, placing the beaker back onto its rack.

"No, I'm still a fierce advocate for testing and data as evidence. It's just my hypotheses are a little more outside of the box now. And we're going to test this hypothesis very soon. I've come up with a plan," I said confidently.

Sighing, he rolled his eyes with annoyance.

"You promised, remember?" I reminded him, with a pleading edge to my voice. "I really need you to come along with me on this."

"I know. I know," he sighed with resignation.

Over my shoulder, he still stared at the periodic chart. He looked at it so intensely I thought that perhaps he might burn a hole in it. It was the left side he seemed fascinated with—Family One, the first vertical row. "What's with the periodic chart? You can't seem to keep your eyes off it."

"Ag," he murmured. "Silver."

"Oh, are you planning on giving silver jewelry to any girls?" I said with a slight bite. Those words and my jealousy surprised and shocked me, but I went with it anyway.

"What?" he said squinting his eyes.

"So, what's with silver?" I asked.

"Well, I gave Caden those flowers as you suggested."

"Any other girls you know got flowers from you lately?" I asked with a cattiness that embarrassed me as soon as the question left my lips. It was like I couldn't control the words coming out of my mouth. There was no brain/mouth connection. It was scary weird.

"Ah…no!" he insisted with a double take and a bemused look.

"I'm sorry, go on," I uttered, trying to recapture my composure.

"Well, she was happy with the flowers; she thought I was nice. This morning after math class she gave me these for us."

Reaching into his pocket, he took out two small silver crosses that dangled heavily from their chains. "They're solid silver. She said that if we're going to the third floor, and especially the witch's cap, we should wear these for protection. Then she walked away quickly like she was scared or something. Protection from what?"

"Vampires. Silver crosses annoy vampires," I alerted him.

"Well, vampires annoy me, so that would make us even."

I reached out and handled the crosses. They were heavy silver and seemed quite old. "That was very sweet. Now, what do you think of her?"

"I still think she's weird, but a sweet kind of weird."

I leaned towards him and put the cross around his neck. He squinted at it uncomfortably as if I had just given him a very gaudy tie to wear.

"Are we really going to wear these?" he asked with annoyance.

"Sure. Why not? It was nice for her to give them to us. The least we can do is wear them for her," I said placing my cross around my neck.

Sighing, he took his chain off and placed it into his pocket. "Later," he said.

"Speaking of weird, I'm a little worried about that little Amanda," I said, changing abruptly to another topic.

"Ah…okay," he muttered, giving me a blank look.

"I mean she's the most adorable thing and so bright and smart, but

146

what's a nine-year-old doing at a nursing home so much? I'm afraid she has a terrible home life, that or no friends."

Taking out his silver cross from his pocket, he tried it on again as he half listened to me.

"Are you listening?" I asked impatiently.

"Oh, yeah, sure. Some girl at the home has no life," he said by rote. "This does look pretty cool, doesn't it?" he said, caressing the chain.

"Her grandmother was there, I think, but she must have passed away. The kid's always there, talking to different residents each time, reading to them, singing with them, even feeding the ones who can't or won't use utensils."

"Yeah, yeah, great kid," he muttered, still handling the cross.

"But she's *nine*. You know what I think? I think she's one of those IQ geniuses. Remember that kid in grammar school that was one year behind me. I think his name was James, IQ of 203."

"Wow, that's a big number for an IQ, even in our school," he said. "I remember him. Went to Stanford, didn't he, at eleven? That was so cool."

In the fourth-grade, this boy James had mastered four languages and was playing chess on an international level. Nobody played with him. They thought he was weird. I felt sorry for him one day and offered him one of my brownies. Instead of thanking me, he went on and on about the chemical bonding in the theobromine molecule that makes up chocolate and the history of chocolate from the Mayans to present day manufacturing. My goodness, he was so hard to take. The next year they skipped him from fourth grade right up to high school; our teachers had nothing more to offer him in our school. He spent just a year and a half in high school and was shipped off to Stanford University...at eleven years old.

"Yeah, that's impressive all right, I guess, but sad too!" The poor kid had no friends. The other children made fun of him all the time. There was no childhood for him. It sounded pretty sad and lonely to me.

"I bet he'll grow up to do impressive things," Anthony predicted.

"Yeah, if he stays sane," I added. "I'm worried that my Amanda might be one of those kids, and she's trying to relate to someone who will listen to her, people who won't ridicule her."

"*My* Amanda?"

"Yes, we've bonded, told me she loved me. At least *someone* loves me," I added before I could stop myself.

Anthony just stared at me with a penetrating look in his eyes. I could see how nutty the things that I was blurting out seemed to him. I wished I had a "ten second delay" on my brain these days. These remarks just seemed to explode from my mouth. I was surprised how jealous I was over Jennifer asking him to the prom. When would he tell me about Jennifer? Why would he have to tell me? It was his life. It wasn't like I was his girlfriend or something. I really had to stop being so catty. Hey, we were just friends, buddies. Annie and Anthony, BFF's. I had to change the subject quickly.

"Well, it's time to hunt down the ghosts. I'm thinking next week," I announced quickly.

"To go into the witch's hat? Really? Next week?" he questioned.

"Yes, next week. I've worked things out. We have to be there after ten o'clock when the night crew has made their checks on the residents and settled things down. There will only be two of them, and they are probably less vigilant than the day crew."

Standing up, he walked around the lab table considering my idea. "Okay, how are we going to manage to be there after ten o'clock? You said the couple of times you did your homework there they kicked you out at ten minutes before nine."

"I took care of that," I announced proudly. "Quadrantids!"

"What?" he asked confused. "That's a meteor shower. What does a meteor shower have to do with your plan?"

"Correct. The Quadrantids meteor shower takes place next week," I stated. "I gave an Academy Award performance last week, tears and everything. I told them that Nonna and I were into astronomy, which was true. And we loved staying up late some nights to view meteor showers, which was true. I told them that we'd viewed every annual meteor shower, which was true...except for January's Quadrantids shower."

"Which was a lie," he pointed out before I could.

"Acting. I was playing a role, not lying. That's different than lying. I told them it was our goal and dream to view each and every meteor shower, to reach completion. It was here that I cried. I told them that this could be our last chance to see the one and only shower that had eluded us."

"How many times have you seen it really?" he asked with an accusing grin.

"Two times. Anyway, then I blew my nose. Nurse Casey gave me a tissue to wipe away my tears. I asked her if I could please have a special dispensation to have me and a friend stay there past the visitation hours so we could see the Quadrantids with her. My voice got real crackly and weak. I really impressed myself, made me think if this science thing doesn't work out, maybe I could go into the movies." I raised my head and turned my profile towards him.

"Yeah, as an usher, or you could sell popcorn. What did she say to your request?"

"Well, she thought for a moment and asked how late we would need to be there. I told her about ten. That's when the meteors are first visible in the east. I figured I had been there so often and helped out so much that they had to trust me."

"Trust you to deceive them?" he said ironically.

"Remember it's…"

"Acting. I know. Go on," he prompted, checking the clock on the laboratory wall.

"Offering me another tissue, she patted me on the head and said, 'Sure, why not? Sounds very sweet. Just don't keep grandma up too late. You're a good girl.' I gave her a hug and through a torrent of tears thanked her."

"And meanwhile you were thinking, 'Yippee, I get to see a ghost, a spirit!'" he quipped.

A big broad grin broke over my face. "Correct!" I reached into my briefcase and pulled out a list. "Now, you have to bring your telescope case," I instructed him.

"You don't view meteors through a telescope. They're too fast. You know that."

"I know. Just bring the case; it's for effect." I looked back at my list. "We're going to need it to hide lock cutters in. That door to the witch's cap might be padlocked. We can also use it for any other equipment we bring to collect data."

"Any dynamite or flame throwers?"

"Too extreme. I think the lock cutters will be enough." I looked down the list and then around the room trying to visualize any other things that might come in handy.

"You've really thought this through, haven't you? I hope it works," he said, checking the clock again. "I think we should go; it's getting late. Your roaches are fed and tucked in."

I craned my neck and looked over at the roach pen at my sleeping future victims. "Yeah. Thanks for helping me clean the roaches' habitat… and my plan *will* work. Let me finish, so it's clear in both our minds. When we come in from outside, after watching our meteors, I'll put Nonna to bed, and you'll sneak into room 13. That's where poor Albert lived, and it's still unoccupied. You'll unlock the window and open it up a crack. Leave the lock cutter and our equipment, take the case. We'll sneak back in after they see us leave."

Anthony sighed and scratched his head. "You know how nervous we're going to be?"

I stood up and put a reassuring hand on his shoulder. "We'll do fine. I'll bring a small tape recorder to record any sounds we might hear up there and a thermometer to measure any temperature drops," I said, noticing the thermometers by the scales on the counter near the window. I thought for a moment. "And the silver crosses."

He patted my hand and stood up slowly. "Well, I hope this works, and I hope the ghosts are pleasant," he said, walking over to get his coat from the back of one of the lab chairs.

"Oh!" I shrieked with excitement, rushing over to him and punching him playfully in his shoulder.

"What's wrong?"

I was giddy with excitement. "I almost forgot. Do you know where the Quadrantids will appear in the sky?" I asked him with a gleam in my eye.

"Where?

"Out of the constellation Draco, the Dragon."

I loved irony.

"House of the Dragon, Dracula," Anthony muttered half to himself.

"Dracul." I corrected.

16

THE NIGHT WAS chilly, but not overly cold, so we decided to walk to the mansion. It had been a fairly mild winter so far. Most importantly, it was a clear night with a crescent moon, a good one for viewing meteor showers, not that this was our prime objective.

"What'd you tell your mom about tonight?" Anthony asked anxiously.

"I told her that I was staying late at the nursing home to show Nonna the meteor shower. Why?"

"You told her *that,* and she believes and trusts you?" he questioned with disbelief.

"Sure! Doesn't your mom trust you?" I asked.

"No, of course not. I'm a teenager, and she's a mother. It's her job not to trust me."

"So what did you tell her?"

"I told her that I was studying late with Jason."

"Hmm." I rolled my eyes at him.

The streets were quiet, and we didn't talk much as we went along. There was one moment when I felt a sudden need to grab Anthony's hand, but instead I put my hands in my pockets as we proceeded down the street. We stopped two blocks away from the Lupescu Mansion and gazed at the witch's hat with fear and reverence. The moon's sliver of light painted the hat with a dull glow. I took a deep breath and sighed.

"Here we go."

All the lights were on in the home. It was only eight thirty, and many of the residents were still up and about. I was ready to hit the buzzer with my finger to open the magnetic lock on the gate when I heard a car horn blare behind me. We both turned and noticed a black SUV parked on the street about twenty feet behind us to our right.

I ignored it and prepared to push the buzzer again.

The horn continued beeping, and the car rolled towards us. I moved very close to Anthony and grabbed onto his shoulder. When the car was directly behind us, he pulled me behind him and turned to face the car. The passenger side window rolled down, and a face darkened by the shadows of the night leaned out the window.

"Hey, you two, get in here," a voice commanded.

I squeezed on his shoulder so hard I was afraid I might dislocate it. I could feel him tensing up.

"Hey, it's me, Caden. Come on in!"

I let go of Anthony's shoulder, and he stepped back a foot or two. We looked at each other and together moved towards the open window.

"Hop in the back!" she anxiously directed.

We followed her order and got in. She was dressed in black pajamas with eye black under her eyes and black driving gloves. Atop her head was a black beret.

"What are you doing driving a car?" Anthony asked.

"Yeah, you're only fifteen," I added.

"It's my mom's car."

"You stole a car from your mom?" he squealed.

"Shush! I didn't *steal* it. I borrowed it. It's like a pet—it's a member of the family. Anyway, she's out playing bingo. The car was lonely."

"But you don't even have a permit. You're not allowed to drive," he pointed out. His head wagged back and forth looking out the window for a police officer.

"Says who?"

"Ah, the state, the county, the law, the police. You better be careful," he said, still looking out for the law.

"Ha. I'm a very good driver. I don't need their permission."

"You drive a lot?" I asked, a little dumbfounded.

"Just in emergencies."

"This is an emergency?" I asked suspiciously.

Caden turned away from us and peered up at the witch's cap. Then she pulled a silver cross from her pajama pants pocket and reverently kissed it. "Yes. *Do not* go up to the third floor. I'm sorry that I ever told you about it," she begged.

"Too late, I have to do this. This could be a big moment for me."

She turned back to us and leaned over the back of the driver's seat with wide, watery eyes. "I left out why the family donated the house for people with dementia and mental problems. The last Lupescu to live there went crazy after she visited the third floor and saw something horrible that freaked her out. Couldn't and wouldn't explain what she saw. Killed herself two months later. That's when they closed down the third floor. Please don't do this," she pleaded.

152

"Now hold on," Anthony shot back angrily. "I've been tolerating this ghost stuff for Annie's sake, but all this stuff you're feeding her is just hearsay. There were no witnesses for most of your story. Records tell us there was a very old man, a very young bride, a boyfriend, and a disappearance. All the other stuff is just fiction. There's no proof any of the happened."

She balled her hand up into a tight fist and banged it on the top of her seat. "The last resident *did* go insane. Explain that!" she added defensively.

"The last resident was very old! All these people in this house have dementia. They're always imagining things."

"Annie, don't go in, please," she pleaded again, holding her hands in a prayer-like gesture.

I turned from her begging eyes to Anthony's hard, analytical stare. "Anthony, what if the stories are true?" I asked softly, treading gently on his anger.

"Of all the things I lo…like about you, one of the best is what a good science head you have. You look at the universe demanding proof and facts. You see through all the fakeness and superstitions. You see the world clearly and truly. You appreciate the beauty of its laws and predictability. Now you're falling for mumbo jumbo. You've stopped looking at things like a true scientist." He was lecturing to me like a dad.

"But I don't want it all to be predictable. I want to hold onto hope that besides the laws there is something spiritual or supernatural out there."

"Well the universe can't be what you want or hope it to be or need it to be; it just is. You think that it's harsh, that it's defined by finite laws. I think it's beautiful. You used to think it was beautiful, too."

I didn't want Anthony to think I wasn't a good scientist. I had always taken pride in that. It was important to me that he liked and respected me. I got teary-eyed and sad, grabbing his hand.

"I know I've said this so many times, but that's why I'm here tonight. To observe and look for evidence like a good scientist. I'm using the scientific method. The present laws of science are firm, but maybe there are laws we don't know exist yet."

There was a contrite sadness and desperation in my voice that he empathized with. A hint of a smile cracked his tense expression. "I'm still with you tonight in the witch's hat, Annie. Don't worry. We're in this together." Taking my hand, he patted it.

"Well, if you won't listen to reason…" Caden began.

I saw Anthony's eyes bug out. *"Reason?"* he shrieked.

I could read his unspoken thoughts and squeezed his hand hard. His head was ready to explode with frustration. I could feel him shaking.

"Then at least do you have your silver crosses?" she asked in desperation, knowing her warning would go ignored.

"We do," I assured her.

Bowing her head and shaking it, she gave in with an air of defeat. "Okay, then if you really have to do this." Raising her head up again, she looked at Anthony, lecturing him sternly. "You take care of her. Remember the greatest strength the vampire possesses…"

"I know. I know….is that no one believes that they exist. It's also the greatest strength the Tooth Fairy and the Easter Bunny have," he mocked.

"But they don't exist! Vampires do." she growled.

I squeezed his hand even harder forcing him to look at me and wince. "Well thanks for the warning, but we have meteors to watch," I explained while opening the car door.

"Yeah, drive carefully," Anthony quipped as he followed me out into the night air."

"Be careful!" she shouted to us. "Find me at school tomorrow and tell me what happened." With that, she drove off, much too quickly for an underage driver in a stolen car.

§ § §

"Annie, I was told to expect you. Nurse Lauren told me all about your outing with grandma, and personally I think it's very sweet." The attendant at the door was all smiles. "I'm Stephanie…and you are?" she asked turning toward Anthony.

"Anthony. Can we come in?" he asked rather impatiently.

"Why sure, come on in out of the cold," she warmly invited.

We came in to a very peaceful scene. Many of the residents were in their rooms, while the rest sat with vacant eyes in front of a barely audible television.

Stephanie leaned close to us and whispered, "We haven't given your grandmother her medication yet. We're going to wait until you are done with your stargazing. Well, let me tell you this. I don't know too much about shooting stars, but this sounds like fun."

"Ah, yes," I responded, also impatient to get going. "Can we see my grandma now?"

"Why sure, sweetie. George, he's the other overnight aide, has taken out your grandmother's coat, gloves, and scarf and placed them on her bed. You can help her with those whenever you're ready to go see your stars. What's in the case, young man?"

Anthony turned with a start and dropped the case onto the floor with a *bang,* he was so nervous.

"I'm sorry," he said, more to me than to Stephanie as he clumsily picked it up. "Oh…ah…it's my telescope. You certainly can't see shooting stars without a good telescope."

"Well, that's one thing I know!" Stephanie laughed.

Anthony and I looked at each other and rolled our eyes.

"We're going to go see grandma now," I announced, trying not to sound overly anxious, but failing terribly.

"Sure. I hope you don't mind if I'm not too helpful with this. I have some of the residents to deal with before bedtime and loads of paperwork. Nurse Lauren said that you're as smart as a whip, so I guess you won't be needing me."

"Oh, trust us, we don't mind," he reassured her a little too heartily.

I cleared my throat at him, and added, "Yes, ma'am. We'll be fine."

We slowly walked down the hallway to Nonna's room. I went in as Anthony kept walking down the hall with a brisk and nervous step to room 13, where he was to unlock the window, crack it open just a bit, and place the lock cutter and my equipment under the bed.

Nonna sat on the edge of her bed staring at the photos and stuffed animals on her dresser. I eased down next to her.

"Hi!" I chirped merrily.

Turning, she smiled at me with that usual hint of recognition. I was just that girl who visited her often, talked with her, and kissed her hello and goodbye. I leaned close to her cheek and kissed it. Closing her eyes, she smiled warmly at my kiss, a consistent, rare joy in her dreary days.

"We're going to see some meteors, Nonna. Last time we watched them was the Perseid shower. Remember, August, about two years ago? We watched them on the beach at 2 AM in the morning. That shower was a real beauty."

"Beauty," she repeated weakly with a slight smile.

I turned and whispered to her. "Then, we're going upstairs." I looked up, pointed, and made a thumbs up sign. "We're going to see what's going on up there. I think that this could be the night. Oh, I hope I see a ghost. You know that I do."

155

"Ghost," she weakly repeated.

I heard footsteps in the hall. It was Anthony. "Hi," Anthony whispered.

Not acknowledging his greeting, she just went back to staring at the photos on her dresser. Anthony sat down next to her and put his arm around her. I just had to smile at that sweet scene.

"Pretty girl, isn't she?" he said to her, pointing to my eight-year-old self in a photo where I held up a first-place trophy for the county science fair. I had pigtails then.

"Pretty," she repeated, nodding her head and smiling.

Reaching out, he brought the photo over closer to her so she could see it better. Then he placed it into her right hand. As her hand shook, the photo fluttered like a captured butterfly trying to get free. Moving the photo closer to her face, she gently kissed it.

"Pretty," she mouthed in a hushed, prayer-like voice.

I sunk my face into her sweater arm and cried. "Oh, I miss you so. I love you with all my heart. I hate what this thing, this disease, has done to you. I hate it."

Anthony let me sob for about a minute, and then took the photo from her hand and placed it back on the dresser. Coming over and sitting next to me, he pulled me away from Nonna and closer to him, so I could sob into his sleeve for a minute or so.

"We've got to do this now," he whispered into my ear.

I sniffed and nodded, wiping the tears from my eyes. "I know," I sighed, looking longingly at Nonna.

Getting up, he silently swung the door open and explained to me that his mission was accomplished in Room 13. Target window was opened just a sliver and the lock cutter, tape recorder, and thermometer were safely under the bed. George, the night guy, was over in the other corridor, just starting to ease the people into their rooms. He had heard poor George was having a shouting match with one lady who was not having any of *this bedtime nonsense.*

"Good," I said as I stood up and patted his chest. "Well done. Nonna, let's get your coat on. We're going to see a meteor shower, just like the time we were on the beach."

"Pretty," she answered, still gazing over at my photo on the dresser.

Once she was wrapped up nice and warm and toasty, we eased her into her wheelchair and escorted her out through the living room, out the door, and onto the front porch. I felt like such a delinquent. It felt exhilarating!

"Moon's over there right in the southwest," Anthony pointed out.

"Good, it won't interfere with the shower so much," I returned, maneuvering her wheelchair around some porch chairs. We wheeled her to the center of the front yard.

"How long are we going to stay out here?" he asked.

"Till we see some meteors. I know why we're really here, but while we're here I want to share this moment with her. We reveled in these meteor showers. They were important to us. One autumn we climbed Slide Mountain in New York State and camped up on the top so we could view the Leonid Shower without any street or house light glare. It was magnificent. It *rained* meteors. No fireworks display could ever compare."

I wiped my teary eyes again. Turning our eyes skyward, I pointed up over the dark silhouette of a tall church steeple.

"Remember, northeast, Draco the Dragon."

"How can I forget?" he said, pointing a little more to the right.

We patiently scanned the sky for five minutes or so, waiting for our prize, fiery pieces of ancient comets. Airplanes and bright stars would momentarily catch our attention.

"There!" Anthony pointed out proudly.

"I saw it! Nonna, did you see it?"

A white streak scratched the blackness of the sky only to disappear in a fraction of a second.

"All that time drifting in endless space only to be annihilated by our atmosphere into a fiery speck," he mused.

"Yeah, but what a glorious way to go," I added, staring up where one had fallen just seconds ago.

Another one shot by.

"There! See!" I knelt next to Nonna and eased her head in the direction of the show. I held her cheek next to mine, propping her face steady.

"And another!" crowed Anthony.

We were seeing three or four per minute, which was pretty good. I wasn't sure Nonna was getting any of this, but we were here together, just like on the beach and Slide Mountain, and that was enough…that we were here together under this shower of stars.

"Next one, make a wish, Nonna! You too, Anthony! Ready?"

"Wow!" we both exclaimed.

One etched a sharp streak of red across the sky right at that moment, as if the sky were saving the best one for our wishes.

"Don't tell your wish, Nonna. It won't come true if you do. Anthony, did you wish for something?"

There was a smile on his face as he looked over at me. "You bet I did."

"Yeah, me too," I quipped.

We watched a few quick flashes of silvery white streak down from the heavens.

"This is better than I expected," he gleefully pointed out.

"It's nice, very nice," I agreed.

Then a thought hit me. "I wish Amanda were here. I bet that she'd love this. I can't wait to tell her about it," I sighed loudly.

"Who?" he asked, giving me a quizzical look.

"Amanda, that little girl, remember," I casually reminded him.

We had been watching for almost a half an hour. It was when one meteor streaked across the sky and shot behind the witch's hat that I was brought back to our reason for being here. He glanced at me, having seen it too. I pulled my head away from Nonna and pointed at the witch's hat. It was time. When I looked back to her, her face was still looking up and gazing out into the sky.

I leaned over and whispered in her ear, "Pretty."

"Pretty," she mouthed back.

When we wheeled her back into the warm air of the home, Stephanie was there to greet us. "Well, did you see your shooting stars?" she asked expectantly.

"We sure did, right, Nonna?"

She just stared ahead and smiled.

"That's great. Well, how nice it was for you kids to do this for her," she said, eyeing us both and nodding her appreciation. In her hand, she had a little cup of apple sauce spiked with Nonna's medication. "Here, Toni. Let's have a couple of spoons of apple sauce," she asked with that baby voice that I hated so much.

At first Nonna refused, but eventually she took two big spoonfuls.

"That's my girl! Well, Toni, you've had some special night. Now say goodbye to your two grandchildren."

I didn't bother to correct her. They really wanted to get the place closed down, so they could relax. I guess I couldn't blame them. I leaned down next to my grandmother and kissed her firmly on the cheek.

"I hope you liked the show," I whispered to her. "Night, Nonna."

Anthony just waved to her.

Stephanie took her wheelchair and started towards her room. "You two can find your way out, right? Don't forget to close the gate. Okay?"

"We're fine. Thank you." I grabbed Anthony's hand and backed him towards the door.

"Yeah, thanks," he called out, allowing me to lead him to the door.

The nurse left, moving down the hallway. We left out the door onto the porch again. This was it. My heart was racing now. We moved stealthily across the lawn and positioned ourselves beneath the bush outside of room 13. From there we could see the stream of light shining from Nonna's room. We knew that it would be a while till she was ready for bed, so we just waited.

That meteor shower above us was still going on. I rested my head against Anthony's shoulder as we gazed skyward. We saw a couple of really nice meteor flashes. One lasted for a good five seconds. His warm shoulder felt good.

"What'd you wish for?" I asked in a whisper.

"I ain't telling," he whispered back. "What did *you* wish for?"

I giggled. "I can't tell you, but I'll tell you what I almost wished for."

"Well, what did you *almost* wish for, Annie Barone?"

"I almost wished you wouldn't go to the junior prom with Jennifer Moretz."

"What?" he whispered with surprise, much too loudly and harshly.

We both looked around and waited a minute to see if anyone inside had heard. When we felt it was all clear, he continued in a quieter, calmer tone.

"What makes you think that I'm going to the prom with Jennifer?"

"That's the rumor round school."

"Well, it's a *wrong* rumor," he corrected sternly. "Jenny hinted around with me to see if I had a girl I was taking. I told her there was someone, but I doubted that she would want to go with me."

"Who?" I asked quietly, but it came out angrily.

"You! But I know it would seem too much like a *date,* and I know how you'd hate to ruin this wonderful platonic relationship we have," he barked quietly but with an effective sarcastic bite.

I let out a giggle of relief. I snuggled closer to his cheek, raised my face to his, and kissed him quickly and gently upon his lips. I could only imagine his blushed and surprised face in the darkness of the night.

"Was that a platonic kiss?" he asked with giddy expectation as our lips parted.

"Plato was very overrated, *and* I'd love to go to the prom with you," I answered, smiling into his eyes.

"Well, how about that! A wish granted. I guess I need another shooting star now," he sighed gratefully.

We kissed again, much longer this time.

This kiss was much better than the one we had shared in the movies. I guess that some things just take time. *Just like Krystyna and Vitas,* I thought. *Krystyna and Vitas!* I thought again, but this time with less dreamy and romantic overtones. I felt in my pocket for the silver cross. It was there.

It had been a clear night, but a few big gray clouds started moving in behind the witch's hat blocking out the stars and the meteors.

"It's not supposed to rain or snow tonight, is it?"

"No," I assured him, but the clouds lowered and moved to cover more of the sky.

"If this were a novel or a movie, I'd say that these clouds are a much too obvious sign of evil lurking," Anthony joked, "impending doom."

"Don't say that," I scolded, not joking. I bit down on my lower lip. "Do you have your cross?"

"Yes. You don't expect me to actually wear it, do you?"

I took mine out of my pocket and slipped it around his neck. "Please?" I asked sweetly, placing my finger softly under his chin.

Smiling down at me, he took his cross out and hung it around mine.

Nonna's light clicked off. Now the hallway just had the dim, orange glow of a nightlight. We still waited for the two night people to get settled, probably in the living room, probably to read or watch television. After five minutes passed, Anthony nodded to me. Going first, he silently opened the unlocked window and stepped inside, then reached out, grabbed my hands, and helped me into the room.

As we closed the window, we waited to hear if there might be some reaction to our entry. All we could hear was the television in the living room. It sounded like they were watching *The Godfather.* I heard something about, 'making him an offer he can't refuse.'

After we finally felt safe and undetected, Anthony slid the lock cutter from under the bed and handed me the tape recorder and digital thermometer so I could hang both around my neck. My heart was racing so much that I was afraid that Stephanie and George might hear the lub-dubbing of its beat. I took a long, deep breath and followed Anthony out the door. We walked down the hallway with soft kitten steps. When we got to the base of the stairway, we looked at each other. Motioning for me to go first, he helped me get my one leg over the barrier, then the other. His legs were long enough to just step over it.

As we crept up the lavish stairway, the faint light from the hallway slowly died away. Midway up, we found ourselves in a thick, soupy darkness. I put my hand around his waist the rest of the way up.

When we got up to the second floor, Anthony took out a very small flashlight to give us some light to follow. "They won't be able to see the beam from downstairs. We'll need a little bit of light up here," he whispered.

His flashlight's beam wobbled around the room. He tried to avoid the windows as he showed me the gigantic murals on the opposite walls and the opulent statues and furniture. Even with the tiny stream of light, the darkness hung heavy like a black fog. I took his hand, holding on to it tightly.

"Come this way," I said. I led him to a sofa that I had spied through the beam of light. "Sit with me here a minute," I said, leading him by the hand to the sofa. I patted the cushion next to me inviting him to sit.

"What are you going to do? I thought the ghosts were on the *third* floor?" he asked.

"They might be here. It's dark and creepy enough. Let's introduce ourselves to them. Caden said that you have to make them feel at ease, so they'll trust you and show themselves."

"What if it's Sigmund? I'm not sure I can trust *him*," he hissed, gazing about the darkness.

"Then have your cross ready." I felt for my cross to be sure mine still hung around my neck. I drew in a long breath.

"Hi, Krystyna and Vitas, I'm Annie, and this is Anthony." I called out in a hushed but clear voice.

"Do I have to say something?"

"No! Shush!" I said, placing a finger on his lips. "Krystyna and Vitas. We're very nice people. We would never hurt you. Can you please come out and meet us?"

Then we sat and waited. My ears strained, my heart pounded, but nothing followed my introduction.

"Krystyna, Vitas, is there something that we can do for you? We know your story. Can we help you?" I repeated.

A silence filled with slight board creaks and whispers of wind followed. Thick, silent air begged for a reply, but silence was all that was offered.

I bowed my head and sighed in frustration. I turned to Anthony and took my finger from his lips. "Be honest with me. Is this stupid? Do you think that there's any chance of seeing ghosts?"

"Well, you know my feelings on this, but it's not stupid to you. If it's important to you, then it's important to me," he assured me. He paused a moment. "Damn, maybe science *can't* explain everything."

He took my hand and stood up, pulling me up with him. "Come on, Columbus, let's go to the witch's hat. Maybe that's where the show is," he whispered in my ear. "Maybe that's the New World." I clicked on my little tape recorder.

We followed the floating puddle of light from his flashlight to the padlocked door. Lifting the lock cutter, he squeezed it, biting hard into the metal lock. It cut it a tiny bit. Again, he squeezed the cutter, grunting and groaning like a weight lifter trying to jerk the barbell up over his head. This time the lock snapped.

"Wait, won't they know we were here when they see the broken lock?" I said, pulling gently on his arm.

"Not a problem," he announced triumphantly. Out of his pocket came a nearly identical lock he had bought at a hardware store. "We'll replace it when we leave."

"But it's not the same combination," I pointed out.

"Do you think *anyone* ever goes up here? It's to keep people out, and someday if they do discover that it's a different lock, who would care?"

"I guess. It was smart of you to bring the new lock. I wish I had thought of that," I said gratefully.

The cutter was gently set down on the edge of the Persian rug that covered the floor. He took my hand and looked directly into my eyes with earnest. "You ready for this?"

I nodded.

With his other hand, he removed the broken lock, placed it on the rug, and then slowly opened the door. It opened painfully, stubbornly creaking and moaning. This door had not been opened in a long time, perhaps many, many decades. When the door was opened just enough, we squeezed in. The air was thick and musty with the smell of mold and age. That beam of light floated in front of us and revealed a single spiral stairway. Not like the wide, grand stairs that we had climbed earlier, these were narrow rusted metal, designed for single-file only. My heartbeat rose to my throat. A cold chill paralyzed me. Just as the light exposed the stairway, we heard footsteps slowly, invisibly ascending in front of us.

Anthony dropped the flashlight.

We stood in darkness, frozen at the sound of the phantom steps going up to the witch's hat just in front of us, perhaps to meet us there.

Then the footfalls stopped.

"Did you hear that?" Anthony asked with real urgency.

I could only nod.

"You...you, want to go up?" His voice quivered.

"I'm...I'm here to see a ghost. Yes, I do," I reassured myself...almost.

I thought there'd be more euphoria when I finally got to confront the unknown. I had forgotten that the unknown could also be terrifying. Hesitantly, we both looked at the narrow staircase. With trembling hands, he picked up his tiny flashlight.

"You go first," I prompted. "You have the light."

"Thanks," he returned sarcastically.

Carefully we proceeded. We paused with each step, listened, and tried to peer deeply into the darkness all around us. My senses and adrenaline were at peak alertness. I looked and listened with so much focus, I felt like I was all eyes and ears. My lungs and heart, however, reminded me that they were there also with the heavy gulping of moldy air and the major lub-dubbing. My systems reminded me that, with all my intellect, I could feel terror. Fear was primeval. It was part of who we were when evolving, and it was still part of us today. Shaking uncontrollably, fear gripped me as we continued upward.

The child-like brain in me wanted to tug on Anthony's sleeves and say, "I want to go home now. Let's go home." But, the scientist, the searcher, knew that this had to be done, this had to be discovered, so I went on.

"I think we're at the top now, Annie. Watch your step," he cautioned, shining the thin beam of light at my feet. I probed with my foot; it was indeed the top floor made of creaky wood.

We were now in front of that famous window that I had been gazing at for months. Finally, we were inside the witch's hat, looking out. The sky was cloud covered, so only a faint hint of moonlight shone through the dust and grime encrusted glass. Who or what was it that had walked up here in front of us?

The beam shone around a small room that was maybe only twice the size of my bedroom. It was pretty much empty, except for an old metal bed frame, a tiny dresser, an old wooden chair, and dust, lots of dust and cobwebs.

"Look!" I jumped and yelped.

"What?" he shouted.

Our beam of light exposed the right-hand wall. It was brick, old thick brick. The other three walls were covered with faded floral wallpaper.

"There it is," I marveled. "So I guess he did seal them in together. It's true. It's all true!"

"Maybe...Maybe."

I didn't bother looking at my thermometer. The temperature had certainly dropped, but after all, it was winter and we were up on the drafty third floor. Too many variables to prove anything.

I hugged him hard and long to drain some of the tension and fear from my body and transfer it to his. It was okay to hug him now—officially he was my boyfriend.

"What now?"

"We have to reassure them again, Anthony," I said, intently staring at the brick wall.

We stepped back and sat down carefully on the edge of the bed frame to be sure it could handle our weight. It creaked and complained under the strain, but it held up.

"We really heard footsteps right in front of us, didn't we? And there was no one there. This is creepy, I mean, really creepy," Anthony marveled, more to himself than to me. His flashlight bobbed nervously along the ancient brick wall.

"Krystyna, my name is Annie, and this is my Anthony," I started in a very weak, unsure voice that cracked. "We've heard your story and would like to meet you and Vitas. We understand your sadness. Please come to us and reveal yourself."

Only silence followed. We waited, only to be met by more silence.

Desperation filled me. "Please, Krystyna, you don't know how important this is to me. I need to see you. I need to know that your existence is possible. We don't want anything from you. We just want to know that you are here."

Again, we strained to hear and see.

"Footsteps?" Anthony questioned again out loud as if trying to solve a math problem.

"Please, Vitas, Krystyna, we're willing to help you," I begged.

Silence followed—dense, deafening silence.

"There's nothing here. You were right. It's all just..."

"Oh, the hell with this!" Anthony finally exploded. "Sigmund, you pathetic, disgusting piece of garbage! Show yourself, you dirty, carbon-footed ghoul. We know you couldn't get Krystyna in life, so you hold her here in death! I dare you! Come out, you coward! Come out now!"

I tugged on his arm to stop. "What are you doing?"

"Well, if they aren't…"

I muffled my scream, but it didn't stop the terrible chill that ran through me. I heard it clearly.

Footsteps. Again. This time coming *up* the stairs to us, slowly.

"Sigmund!" I yelped to Anthony, squeezing his arm so hard that I was sure I had cut off the blood flow.

Standing up in front of me, Anthony shielded me heroically, but I could tell he was scared himself. Pointing his weak, little light shakily at the doorway, he turned to me. "Here comes your proof, Annie, I just hope…"

Steps approached slowly but louder. And then, there in the orange glow of partial moonlight stood a shadow, a menacing figure of a man.

I tried to scream, but couldn't.

Anthony took a step back and fumbled at his shirt, pulling out the silver cross. I grabbed onto his waist and closed my eyes. The thing came closer.

"Sigmund? Don't hurt us!" he shouted, half demanding, half pleading. Holding the cross straight out in front of him, he directed whatever protective force it might have at the intruder.

"We just came to see a ghost! We're just kids!" he pleaded.

The creature emitted a growl seemingly caught in its throat.

"Do you know where my car keys are?" it asked slowly and meekly. "I'm going home tomorrow, you know. I'm a good driver."

My eyes sprang open. I knew that voice. Anthony turned around to me.

"What's going on? This isn't Sigmund!" There was a mix of relief and disappointment in his voice.

I composed myself quickly. "No, it's not Sigmund…it's Arthur. He's the new patient I told you about. Remember I told you he tried to climb up here on Christmas. It's Arthur."

"Do you have my cars keys?" he implored again.

I felt both relieved and crushed that our visitor was flesh and blood, that it was meek little Arthur and not the terrible Sigmund. In that moment, I surrendered all hope of contacting Krystyna, Vitas, and Sigmund; now my concern was being caught by the workers. We hadn't figured that a patient would come up to visit us. Anthony let out a big sigh of relief and sat down next to me on the edge of the bed frame.

"Well, what do we do now?" he asked, exhausted.

"Let me think a moment," I said, trying to change gears from terrified teenage girl to geeky problem solver. Arthur just stood there staring out the window, perhaps looking for that car he'd never drive again.

"Okay. He's what Daisy called a *creeper*. We'll just have to get him to creep downstairs."

I went up to the man who five minutes before I thought was an horrific ghoul. "Hi, Arthur. I'm Annie, Toni's granddaughter."

"Do you have my car keys?" he asked, as if for the first time.

"No, but the keys might be downstairs," I assured him.

"That's nice," he smiled.

"Will you walk down with us, and we can look," I asked in that nursery school voice that the nurses used with their patients.

"That's nice," he repeated.

Like all the Alzheimer's patients, Arthur was a little unsteady on his feet. It must have taken him forever to get up here. We guided him down, Anthony in the lead supporting him and me behind propping him up. When we got to the second floor, Anthony closed the door slowly to limit the moaning and creaking and replaced the lock. I picked up the cutter and tiptoed down the stairs into the hallway to see if either of the workers were around. The hallway was still awash in its dim orange glow. I leaned out to see to the very end of the hallway. The living room light was bright, and the television was still on. I heard "Drop the gun. Take the cannoli," from the movie still playing on the television in the living room.

"It's all clear," I whispered urgently after I got back to the second floor.

"Come on now, big guy," Anthony instructed. "Let's go down, one more time."

Silently we took each step. Because we were whispering in hushed tones, Arthur followed along, asking for his car and keys in a faint, matter-of-fact voice. Finally, we reached the first-floor hallway. Anthony hopped over the fence then motioned me to take most of Arthur's weight as he strained to get each of Arthur's legs over the fence. Once over, Anthony helped me to get over. I looked down the hall to make sure that it was still clear.

"I'd bring you to your room, Arthur, but I don't know where it is, and I'm sure that you don't know either. Anthony, here's the cutter. Go now and get out of the window. I'll follow in a few seconds."

Nodding, he disappeared into room 13.

"Okay now, Arthur," I instructed and pointed, turning his face towards the living room and Don Corleone. "Go down there to the living room. Your car keys might be there. Anyway, George and Stephanie will take good care of you. Bye, Arthur."

I gave him the slightest push to send him on his way. He made his own way slowly, but steadily. I waited until he showed me that he could walk safely on his own. Once I felt confident about him, I ran into the room. Anthony was waiting on the other side of the open window.

"Easy now," he said, supporting me as I clumsily climbed out in haste.

Once we were safely outside, Anthony gently shut the window. Before it closed, I heard Arthur's voice call out from the living room. "They're up there, you know."

"Arthur! Yeah, yeah. They're always up there. You're a real creeper, aren't you? Come on, buddy. Let's get you back to bed."

Two long blocks of walking went by before either of us said a word.

"*Carbon-footed ghoul*? Really?" I finally asked with a smirk of relief.

"Hey, he did spread a lot of coal into the world and contributed to a lot of ecological problems. I tried to insult him to get him to appear. Instead, we got Arthur."

"You were very brave up there," I gushed, grabbing onto his shoulder and resting my head on it as we stopped for the traffic light.

"Very brave against what? A sweet little man with dementia," he laughed modestly.

"You didn't know that. You thought that it was a ghost, or a *carbon-footed ghoul*. You were brave." I could see him blush even in the dim light of the night. My smile faded.

"But it wasn't a ghost, was it? You were right all along. There was nothing up there. I think I'm done now. Experiment over, data is all in. It's time to draw my conclusion. The two big moments this year when I was convinced I would finally see a ghost were defeated by fading handicapped minds…Arthur's…and the boys' at the Halloween mansion." I stopped and gazed up into the night sky that had partially cleared again, revealing the stars. *It was all just protons and neutrons.*

"Maybe it was just the wrong night," he said, feeling my disappointment and trying to console me.

As the traffic light changed, and we continued across the street, I said, "Nah, doesn't matter. It's funny you know. On Christmas night, I helped Amanda read *The Little Prince* to one of the ladies. The part I read said, *It is only with the heart that one can see rightly, what is essential is invisible to the eye*. That's such a beautiful thought," I sighed. "I guess it's true when it comes to love, but as a scientist, to discover the truth, you do need eyes and ears. I'm done…science wins. Conclusion: *This* is all there is; we're looking at it."

I surprised and embarrassed myself by suddenly bursting into tears. Anthony hugged me and let me sob into his chest. I remembered another old saying from a story or a movie or something: *God always answers our prayers. Sometimes, the answer is 'No.'*

"Annie, just one thing about my *ears*," he spoke with a mysterious edge, not at me but into the night air.

"You have nice ears," I half sobbed, trying to compose myself.

"No, no, what I heard with my ears. What *we* heard. Those sounds of walking, invisible steps right in front of us, *up* to the witch's hat *before* Arthur came up. We both heard them. I can't explain those. Can you?"

I quickly took my tape recorder from my neck and rewound it to find the moment of those mysterious steps. Had we imagined them?

No, it was not our imaginations. We heard them faintly, but clearly on the tape.

17

I CAN EXPLAIN THOSE footsteps now," Anthony announced to me with a mix of pride and disappointment as he sat down with me at our usual spot in the science lab, next to the cockroach Death Chamber, or as Caden had nicknamed it, *The Bates Roach Motel.*

Winter had turned colder and snowier as the season drifted into February. It had helped alter my mood. I had resigned myself to a godless, soulless universe where science was the master, where everything could be explained as matter and energy, and where what couldn't be explained today would be revealed as soon as another Newton or Einstein blossomed from some future generation. I was depressed about the fact that our existence was finite and that love fades. *That only with the heart that one can see rightly* seemed as flawed and trite as the tooth fairy. It seemed now that *it was only with the senses that truth could be discovered.* I borrowed that from Plato. At least he was good for something.

I went for long walks and read a lot of book, science books.

Anthony had been away for two weeks on a trip with the *Future Nobel Prize Winners Club*—really, that's its name. They went to MIT in Boston and stayed in the dorms and took part in classes. It sounded really cool.

"You can? You can explain it," I asked. I guessed that I still hung onto those mysterious footsteps as a thin reed of hope for ghosts. "Go ahead, hit me with the science," I demanded coldly, putting my seventeenth dead cockroach down onto the lab table. I could feel that thin reed ready to snap.

"We were in the electronic engineering lab at MIT when one of the college seniors asked me to go up a flight of metal stairs to retrieve a diode in the storage room. As I approached the stairs I heard footsteps, but there were no feet coming down the stairs."

"Yikes! Did you freak?" I asked.

"You bet. I yelped and went running back to Michele, the senior, and told her what had happened. The whole class laughed at my obvious panic and fright. Michele explained this phenomenon happens all the time with metal stairs if they are situated just right. If someone is walking on the stairs a flight above or a flight below, the vibration of their footsteps creates a harmonic reverberation that makes the adjacent stairway reflect the vibration of those feet. I tried it, and it worked. What we heard that night was the reverberation of Arthur lumbering up the stairway from the first floor. It's science."

Crack. My reed broke.

"I'm sorry. I know these revelations hurt."

"Oh, it's okay, Anthony. You know…*the truth shall set you free.* Actually, I feel like a weight has been lifted from me."

"It is an amazing universe out there, a lot of beautiful theories and marvels. It's *all* like a miracle," he said trying to cheer me up.

"Yeah, I know," I sighed as I crumbled stale bread crumbs into my cockroach bin.

"How are the roaches? Any mass loss?"

"Nope, it's done. My conclusion is due next week."

Even though Anthony had been able to get me a more sensitive scale, there was still no loss of mass with each cockroach death. I had a chart full of zeroes.

"Remember, after all, you were using cockroaches, for goodness sake. Who'd expect a roach to have a soul?" he pointed out, petting one of the roaches as the bug enjoyed a big crumb of stale bread.

"Not necessarily a soul. I needed something unexplainable to be lost, to rise up. A ghostly cockroach with tiny angel wings would have been nice."

We dismantled the chamber together.

We took the remaining dozen or so cockroaches out to a garbage dumpster and gave them their freedom. I didn't want to go down in cockroach history as a totally heartless fiend. Surely I would be reviled, but at least some high-minded roaches would say, *Yes, she did do horrible things to cockroaches, but she did set the last twelve free.*

Ms. O'Meghan said that she believed my grade would be quite good. She still thought that I was a strange girl, but my experiment, though offering very challenging variables, was controlled extraordinarily well. At least the experiment was not a complete waste. Maybe next year I'd make a paper mache volcano that erupted with baking soda and vinegar. Only kidding.

§ § §

As March came, my visits to see Nonna became more depressing as she became less responsive to me — no anger, no happiness, nothing; she shook more and smiled less. There was barely any recognition of me as someone special to her.

"Do you want to help feed your grandmother?" Nurse Lily asked as I neared the table during a dinnertime visit.

"Sure," I replied, always anxious to help. Lily seemed relieved because there were three other residents who needed to be fed.

"Hi, Annie," Amanda sighed.

I hadn't seen her when I came in. She was next to a very big woman helping feed her.

"Hi!" I said cheerily. I hadn't seen her since two weeks ago when we had taken turns reading *The Velveteen Rabbit* to one of the residents.

"How are you? How have you been? How's school?" I asked, still curious about this dear girl.

"Okay. I guess," she said, preoccupied with her feeding procedure, patiently holding the spoonful of sweet potato at the woman's clenched mouth until, like a baby bird, she opened her lips just wide enough for her to slide the tip of the spoon in. Once in, reflex took over, and the food was swallowed.

"Hi, Nonna. I love you," I whispered and massaged her now very thin and delicate shoulders.

Amanda peeked over at me and smiled.

"Looks like a delicious dinner!" I sang to her. "Let's see, mashed sweet potatoes, diced chicken, peas, and rice. Yum."

I filled the spoon with some tiny bits of chicken, and Nonna accepted the food much more readily than Amanda's lady. I was grateful for that.

"How is your experiment with the bugs going?" she asked as she held a glass of apple juice to the lady's lips.

"It's done. I'll probably get an A, but that really wasn't my goal."

"A's are good," she pointed out like a proud aunt.

"I guess," I agreed reluctantly, like a depressed niece. I had told her weeks ago, to her amusement, about our ghost hunt in the mansion. I figured that I could trust her.

"No roach souls. No spirit energy," I sighed. "I think I give up. I gave it my best shot."

"Maybe you've looked in the wrong places for your answer," she quipped.

"Hey, you're a kid. I'm nearly fifty percent older than you. I'm old enough to be your older sister. I'm a little more experienced in hunting ghosts. Trust me, I've looked in the right places, the *wrong* places, and I've found them all empty."

"Okay, sorry."

"No problem," I laughed. "But I really have tried hard."

We stopped talking so we could focus on our dinner guests. After about five minutes, Amanda put her spoon down and shook her hand to relieve her cramped fingers.

"You know, they stop remembering to eat," she said morosely. "That's what's happening now."

"I know," I said, trying not to think about it.

"Then they stop remembering to breath. That's how it will end for them," she said sadly, looking from patient to patient.

I slammed my hand down on the table hard enough to startle everyone and cause dishes and glasses to bounce. "Why did you have to say that? I know that," I exploded angrily.

"I said it because you have to know. You have to get yourself ready for when that comes. It won't be nice, Annie. I'm not trying to make you sad. I just want you to be ready for when it happens. Please don't be mad at me."

Then I remembered that this very gifted little girl had probably gone through this heartbreak with *her* grandmother and was just trying to protect me.

"Sorry," I said meekly, apologizing to everyone at the table for my anger. "Sorry, Amanda. I know you mean well. I just hate to think about it," I whispered, still trying to keep the image far from my mind.

"I know. I know," she said, grabbing my hand gently for support.

I was angry because I longed for a miracle; I hoped to walk in one day when Daisy would come running up to me, hug me, and say, *A miracle, Angelfish! Your grandma woke up today and she's back to normal. All her memories are back.* I'd go into her room. We'd smile at each other, hug for what would seem forever, and I'd take her home with me…forever.

I had been able to feed Nonna about half of the food, while Amanda had only been able to give her lady about a quarter when a worker came, took the plates away, and brought some chocolate pudding for them.

"They like their desserts," the worker chuckled.

How right she was about desserts. Our spoons made quicker work of the pudding.

"What do you want to be when you grow up?" I asked Amanda, still trying to figure out this amazing and mysterious girl.

"Not sure…a writer, an actress, or a doctor," she listed as her eyes seemed to be peeking into the future to see what it might offer.

172

"I vote for doctor. You're so smart and so good with people."

"Thanks, how about you?"

"I had thought that I'd get into genetics…cloning and stuff. I would have loved to bring back animals and plants from the past. I wanted to see a mastodon. That would be so awesome, but I've changed my mind. I've decided to go into medical research. I've decided to cure this Alzheimer's disease, to find where it's hiding, pull it out of that place, and crush the damned hateful monster once and for all."

"Sorry," I added. "Bad word."

Smiling broadly, she replied, "No problem. I bet you can…I bet you will."

I got up to help Nonna over to her wheelchair to watch a little television as the workers cleared the table. Amanda came up next to me and hugged me.

"It's getting late, very, very late. I have to go," she explained apologetically.

"I hope I see you soon."

Smiling, she nodded. "I love you," she said, hugging me again.

"And I love you, too."

§ § §

It was hard focusing on school work over the next couple of months. Nonna was declining pretty fast. The woman that Amanda had been feeding that night had passed away two weeks after that meal.

It was a Sunday afternoon in early April when I saw my Nonna alive for the last time. Her eating had pretty much stopped. A few spoonfuls of yogurt and pudding and a few sips of juice were all she could manage when I came to help feed her, which was pretty much every night now. I knew the time was coming close. She was just *there*, no responses to anything, except annoyance when I tried to feed her more than she would accept.

I would just talk about my day in school and go on and on about all the things she had taught me and all the things we had done together. If there was nothing more than *that*, it was okay. I needed to make every moment count. On that Sunday in April, she lay in bed motionless, just mumbling inaudible things and breathing slow, sporadic breathes. I read *The Little Prince* to her. Those themes of love and leaving were more real to me as I read to her. Amanda was not there. I wished she were. What a comfort she would have been. I stayed as long as they allowed me.

"Annie, you should be going pretty soon," Nurse Lily said softly, stroking

173

my shoulder. "Let grandma rest, and you rest too. I'm sure you have school work to do."

I was left alone with Nonna. I leaned in close to her ear. "If you can still hear me and understand, I love you. I love you forever. I know you told me once that you would give me the answer, you know, about spirits and ghosts and God. It's okay. I guess the answer is *No.*"

I gave her a soft, drawn out kiss on her sunken cheek, in case it would be my last kiss for her forever.

It would be.

§ § §

My next day started out poorly. It was announced in home room that we were all to proceed to the auditorium where Principal Myhre was going to speak to us. We all pretty much knew what the subject would be. Someone had set off a stink bomb, sulfur dioxide, in the freshman hallway at dismissal on Friday. We would get yelled at, and she would ask that the culprits confess. If they didn't, we'd all lose some privileges.

I never got to the auditorium.

"Annie, Annie Barone," the secretary came up to me whispering and pulling me out of line. With a weak voice she told me that I should get my things and that my mom was coming to pick me up in the office.

There was no need to explain.

I had hoped Nonna would stay with me for at least a few more days. I had always wondered how I'd feel at this moment, how I'd react; I felt nothing, just numbness.

I eased into the car with my mom; her eyes were red from crying. Mine were not.

"You okay, Annie?" she asked with genuine, loving concern.

Nodding, I just stared out the window.

"You know it's for the best, don't you? She didn't want to live like that."

My eyes remained fixed on the blur of the scene outside the car window, nothing of substance coming to my mind.

Those were the only words during the ride home. Kevin was home from school with a headache.

"You know Nonna died last night, Annie," he announced as I came through the door.

Breezing right by him, I went into my room and closed the door. Crying was in order, I knew that, but I had cried after each visit to the nursing home, and cried when she stopped walking and when she stopped talking, and most of the nights when she stopped eating and now, she was gone. My tears had gone with her. I just lay on my bed and stared at the ceiling. Mom was right, of course, her suffering was over, but over in return for what, nonexistence? I could not comprehend the light that was my Nonna gone from the universe forever—all that energy, all that love. How cold and empty the world would seem without her.

I reached over for a teddy bear dressed up to look like Albert Einstein that she had given me years ago, and I held it close to my breast. On his little t-shirt was an Einstein quote—*The most incomprehensible thing about the universe is that it is comprehensible*. I hugged the bear closer to my chest as we both stared up at the blank, off-white ceiling. Suddenly my eyes sprang open, and I jumped from the bed and raced down the stairs.

"Are you okay?" my mom asked, surprised and concerned by my burst of energy as I ran by her.

"Remember…remember she told us that she wanted to be cremated and wanted her ashes sprinkled in three places: in the ocean off the Jersey shore, atop Slide Mountain in the Catskills, and in the hills of Sala Consilina in Italy where she was born."

"Yes, but the last one will be a tough one," Mom confessed.

"But we'll do it, right?"

"Sure, Annie. We can't let her down."

"And we'll have a memorial for her, right? At the funeral parlor before she's cremated, with photos and her paintings so people will know how wonderful she was and how much we loved her?" I frantically asked.

"We will, honey. I've arranged for that on Wednesday."

"Good. Good. I'm going to look through the photo albums and get a bunch. We'll put them on poster boards. Order lots of flowers, especially daisies, she'd like that," I said as I raced by my mom towards the stairs again.

"Sure, honey. Her paintings, flowers, photos…"

"And her favorite songs!" I shouted back at her.

With that I raced back up the stairs and climbed into our attic where the photo albums were stored. We had so many photos of her, our trips together, holidays, picnics. There was an old black and white photo from her wedding. Then I found a very old, dusty album that I had never seen before. It was small and tucked into the back of a larger one. I opened it carefully and gently.

It contained very old photos, ancient photos of what seemed to be the Italian countryside, with lots of people I'd never seen before: kids, ladies dressed all in black, men with bushy handlebar moustaches. A single photo fell from the others and danced down like a butterfly onto the attic floor. I bent low and picked it up. It was a photo of a little peasant girl.

Immediately an electric shock went through me. My hand shook as I peered closely at it. I shrieked, "It can't be! It can't be!"

"Annie? You okay up there?" my mom called up to me with concern.

I couldn't answer. As I looked closer at the child in the photo, my mind swam with this juxtaposition of lives and time that could not possibly be real. I careened down the stairs clutching the photo. I thrust my shaking hand out to my mom, showing her the photo.

"Who...who is this?" I begged, out of breath as she took the picture from my trembling hand.

Her matter-of-fact reaction stunned me.

"Ah, that's a cute one. I'm glad you found that. We definitely have to put that one out at the memorial."

"What do you mean? Who is this? Who is she?" I stuttered in near panic.

"Why, that's Nonna when she was just nine years old over in Italy. Wasn't she adorable? Cute photo. Very cute."

"Mom!" I screamed incredulously. "Mom, this is Amanda, my little Amanda from the nursing home."

"Who?" she asked, handing the photo back to me.

"The girl! Remember I told you about her. I...I...pointed her out to you on Christmas. Remember, she was across the table."

"No, honey, I don't. Oh, I do remember you pointing out a sweet little lady with white hair in a bun. I waved to her, but there was no girl there. No, I would have remembered that."

"Mom? You really don't remember seeing her?"

"No, I don't...I...oh, funny thing, you know your Nonna's middle name was Amanda. That's a coincidence, huh? It means *love* in Italian."

"This photo is *Amanda*!" I insisted. How could my mom not remember her but remember the old lady?

I pushed the photo deeply into my pocket. "I have to go!" was all I said to my mom as I dashed out the door.

I leaped onto my bike and pedaled as fast as I could. I headed to the Sunshine Home. About halfway there, my cell phone rang. I stopped the bike to answer it. It was Anthony.

"Annie, I just heard. I'm so sorry about your Nonna. What can I do?"

"Anthony, Amanda, the girl we saw that day, the little girl holding the blue parasol in the garden. You remember her, right?" My voice was panicked now.

"Ah...no, can't say I do," he replied, a bit confused.

"Don't do this, Anthony. We were leaving the nursing home one afternoon, and I pointed her out to you. She was sitting at the table with two older ladies."

"I do remember the two ladies, but no girl. I do remember you mentioning a little girl who visited there...ah, Amy or Angie..."

"Amanda!" I barked back and clicked the phone off.

I continued to race to the home as fast as I could ride my bike. When I got there, I threw the bike down and pressed the buzzer hard and often. Magnets clicked open, and I pushed the gate so hard I thought I had knocked it off its hinges.

There to meet me at the door was Daisy. Her eyes were wet and red, and she was dabbing them with a hanky. "Oh, my sweet Angelfish, your sweet grandma is not here. Those funeral people took her body away, but her soul is home now with the good Lord."

"Daisy! Daisy!" I thrust the photo at her. "Who is this? Can't you see?" I cried out.

Taking the photo from me, she peered at it. There was a question mark on her face. "Can't say I know this precious little thing. Who is she?"

"It's Amanda, Daisy! It's our Amanda!" I insisted.

"Who?" was all Daisy could give me.

"No, no, not you too, Daisy. If anyone remembered her it would be you, because she was here almost as much as I was. Amanda, the girl who helped them, read to them, and fed them! How could you not remember her?"

"I'm sorry to upset you, Angelfish. You have been the only girl I've seen in this house. Children don't do so well around these folks," she explained.

Frustrated beyond despair, I flopped down into a chair.

In a calmer, quieter voice I pleaded with Daisy. "Remember when we made the pizzelles around the holidays, all the fun we had—me, Nonna, and Amanda?"

"Yes, you and your grandma had a good old time. I remember you wiping white flour on her pink cheeks. It was a sweet thing to see," Daisy agreed, not necessarily to my satisfaction.

I got up and lumbered into the dining area. I raised my voice and begged, "Does anyone remember Amanda?"

Silence followed my plea, until an old woman with thin wisps of sparse gray hair stood up from her seat on the sofa and wobbled over to me. Putting a finger on my cheek, she struggled to form her words. Her words came out in a whisper. "She's here, you know."

That was it! My *wow* moment. It suddenly was clear who Amanda had been. I collapsed with a euphoric epiphany onto the soft sofa and cried, torrents of tears but this time they were tears of joy.

Wow! There it was.

All this time, Nonna *had* answered me. At that moment, the universe exploded open for me. There was an infinite spirit within us. There *was* more. Nonna was there for me. There was a universe one could see only with the heart! Our essence was eternal! Energy and love could never be destroyed! All the people we've ever loved—they're here, you know.

§ § §

That summer I hiked up Slide Mountain during the Perseid shower and sprinkled some of Nonna's ashes under the scrub pines and into the breeze. Before dawn on a June morning, Anthony, Mr. DeVita, and I—I had kept my promise and enlightened Mr. DeVita about Amanda—waded out into the surf at Spring Lake, New Jersey, and christened the morning waves with Nonna's essence.

Italy had to wait a bit. But when Anthony took me to Rome and Sorrento on our honeymoon, we took a side trip to Sala Consilina and placed the last of her ashes into the Fiume Tanagro, a river that flowed through southern Italy, where little "Amanda" used to hike as a girl. I'd always love that little girl, forever.

I know "forever" exists now. She's here, you know.

ALSO BY DIVERTIR PUBLISHING

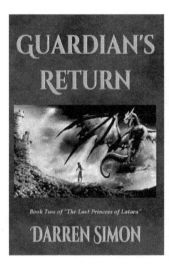

Guardian's Return
by Darren Simon

Theodora lives, and if Charlee's dreams of death and fields of spilled blood are true, her great aunt has avenged herself on that world across the dimensional divide. Charlee knows what she must do. Can Charlee defeat Theodora—for good—or will evil consume her? Can she even survive so far from home? Her only hope may rest in the Lord of the Dragons, but that beast turned his back on her grandfather long ago…

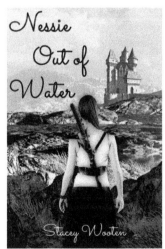

Nessie Out of Water
by Stacey Wooten

Awkward situations usually find Nessie, a post-college secretary at a portable toilet rental company, like the love-crazed stalkers of a pubescent boy-band sensation. She has dealt with unstable roommates and the ever-present toaster salesman, but this one takes the cake...

Darkest Hour
by Tony Russo

After the Great War, a terrifying new enemy conquers much of Europe before turning its sights on Britain. All that stands between the unstoppable Black Legion and invasion is Briley and a handful of brave pilots. With its historical twists, surprising romance and heartfelt tragedy, Darkest Hour is the first of a series of truly unique and epic adventures.